Only A Touch

Kasper Ridge, Book 4

Delancey Stewart

Contents

Chapter One
Sweet Dreams Are Not Made of This

TRAVIS

Night pressed down on me, the whirring of chopper blades stirring the air into a wild tempest, chaotic and confusing. Wind whipped and the screaming of hundreds—maybe thousands—of voices pulled at something inside me, bringing terror bubbling to a simmer just below the surface.

I stood ready to help, but I was blinded by the darkness, by the fierce slash of dust thrown at me by the helicopter. Who was I supposed to help?

Babies cried, women screamed. And in the background, shattering the persistent noise around me, explosions rocked the night.

My stomach roiled and sweat coated my skin beneath the heavy uniform I wore, under the Kevlar I knew was a paltry protection against what was likely to happen to me here.

A woman appeared in my field of vision, her head swathed

in a bright blue scarf that stood out vibrant and shocking against the smear of darkness closing in on us.

Her dark eyes met mine and the terrifying noise faded, my vision beginning to tunnel until I all saw was the desperation and fear in her fathomless gaze.

"Take him," she said, her voice coming as if down a chasm. "Save him." She pushed a bundle into my arms and vanished. I looked down to see what I held, what she'd given me, and the tiny pink face of a baby stared up at me.

The scream built low in my belly, spurred on by fear, by horror, by the knowledge I couldn't do anything against the force of this situation. I was one man, and even the scream I'd muster against the inevitability of death all around me would be impotent and futile.

When the sound ripped from my chest, it was more like a cry for help, a smothered, muffled gasp that had more to do with the pressure on my chest and my inability to breathe than the baby I held. I tried to suck in a lungful of air, but the pressure built, and then . . . rain?

Why was my face wet?

Why was my nose suddenly full of the stench of foul, musty heat?

Why . . . I pushed the heavy lump off my chest and sat up, sleep fading slowly as my vision cleared.

"Roscoe." My voice was gritty and harsh, as if I'd carried sand home from the nightmare inside my lungs.

Roscoe stood on the bed at my side, breathing his heavy dog breath into my face, and gave me one more sloppy lick for good measure, accompanied by a low whine.

"I'm fine. It was just the dream." Relief surged through me, along with the familiar feeling of failure, disappointment.

The dog seemed reassured by the fact I was now upright and

speaking—had I been screaming before?—and he settled again at my side, curling against my legs. Roscoe was good at his job, which was unofficially to keep me sane. When I'd gotten home, it had been clear to me I needed some kind of support, and a dog felt like the right solution. Roscoe was my best friend, and my lookout. I sank my hands into his thick fur as he laid his head down and closed his eyes.

I was glad one of us could get back to sleep. I already knew it would be pointless for me to try. That dream—more of a memory really—it was one I could never quite push aside when I wanted to. Whenever it appeared, I grit my teeth and lowered my head, recognizing that there was nothing for it but try to get through the discomfort. It was kind of like bumping into my mom's friend Lilac when I was back home. She'd talk your ear off for hours about goiter and backgammon, but you had to suffer through it or Mom'd teach you a lesson in manners when she heard you'd been rude.

Not that I'd been home in a while. Now I thought suffering through one of Lilac's hugs and monologues about the new recipe she was perfecting for mince pie might be a nice alternative to my reality.

Roscoe whined again at my side, dog language for "go back to sleep, moron," I figured.

"Can't, buddy. You get some sleep." I pushed off the twisted heap of covers and swung my legs over the side of the bed, letting out a sigh.

Ten minutes later, I was dressed and heading down the long hallway to the elevator. I'd hit the gym before most folks were even awake, and then head down into the kitchen to get the rolls baking.

Since the resort had lost our pastry chef, I'd discovered a knack for basic baking, and Ghost—the resort owner and an old friend who was tolerating me hanging out here—seemed to appreciate my willingness to get up to work hours no one else wanted to take on.

The resort fitness center was empty when I used my key to unlock the door. Not a real shock, since the guests here were mostly on vacation, and normal people didn't get up to work out at three in the morning when they were supposed to be relaxing.

As I pounded out a few miles on the treadmill, I pushed the last remnants of the dream from my mind, wishing I could somehow banish it permanently. That was the one that got me the most, that woman. The baby in my arms.

It hadn't really happened. It was an amalgam of things that had, or of stories I'd been told by the other people who'd served in that disastrous mess. I wanted to forget it all.

But that was the thing, wasn't it?

You didn't forget things like that.

If you were lucky, maybe you shoved them to the back of your mind so you could do your best to be a regular guy when you were around other people, and you didn't let anyone close enough to see what was really going on.

Only Roscoe really knew, and I was pretty sure he wouldn't tell anyone.

Chapter Two
Conception of Deception

CEECEE

"I was ninety-nine percent sure I was going to die this morning." The man in the passenger seat of the van, Vince from Columbus, laughed as he delivered this statement, and I grinned right back at him.

"You're not the first guy to think that when we hit the rapids on that first stretch," I told him, guiding the van around a smooth curve in the two-lane road heading back to the Kasper Ridge Resort. "But you handled it like a champion. You all did," I added, glancing back to where his wife sat with their four kids. "Did you have fun?"

"Is fun the right word?" Liz asked. She'd arrived in the lobby this morning after her husband had signed the family up for a rafting trip, and announced that she had no intention of going. But he'd cajoled her into my van, and through the training, and she'd finally strapped on her helmet and personal flotation device willingly.

I didn't blame her for having reservations. They had four

kids, ranging from eleven to seventeen. Moms worried. Dads did too, I knew, but I'd seen this exact scenario lots of times. Moms worried a little differently. And river rafting could be dangerous.

But I was good at my job.

"All of you did great," I assured her. "And if you want to come out for something a little less aggressive, we're doing stand-up paddle-boarding at the lake tomorrow afternoon."

"Dad, let's do it!" Seth, the oldest, piped up.

"Sure," Vince said.

"I think I might just spend the day with a book, or take a hike," Liz said. "No more adventure. No offense." She added that last part quickly, as if her desire for adventure was something I had a personal stake in.

"No worries," I told her. "It's your vacation. You should do things you want to do."

We pulled up in front of the resort, and the family piled out of the van onto the curb in front of the gracious timber and glass structure. The resort had been given new life in the last year, thanks to the unexpected arrival of Archie and Aubrey Kasper and their collection of friends, most of whom had flown with Archie when he was in the Navy.

I'd known the resort opening would be good for my adventure outfitter and guide business, but I hadn't realized just how good. At this point, I'd had to hire staff to help lead adventures, and I was doing quadruple the business I'd been doing before the resort came back to life.

But the best thing that had happened since the Kasper Ridge Resort had opened was the friendship I'd struck up with outdoor influencer Douggie Masters, who I was pretty sure was about to change my life.

I watched the family from Columbus head inside and parked the van in the employee lot, and then jogged inside.

"Hey you!" My best friend Lucy was seated at the end of the bar, and she rose as I entered, her dark mass of curly hair pulled into a sleek braid over one shoulder and her petite frame sporting an adorable sundress. Lucy and our mutual friend Bennie and I had been together since kindergarten.

"Look at you," I gushed, leaning in to give her a hug. "You're all dolled up and I smell like sweat and sunscreen."

"You always smell like sweat and sunscreen," she reminded me, retaking her stool. "And I hardly ever get out these days. It was worth a little time on hair and makeup." Lucy and her husband Will had a three-month old son, and Lucy had complained often that her entire life had changed before she'd really realized what she signed up for. But that didn't change the fact that my friend was happier than I'd ever seen her.

"You look great. Will and Teague doing okay?"

Lucy laughed. "Will is the most doting father I've ever seen. But I think he's desperate for Teague to grow past the sleeping and pooping phase and into the part where he puts on a glove and plays catch, or asks about being a pilot."

"I get it. He wants to do dad stuff," I said as Wiley, the bar manager, waved a hand at me, letting me know he'd be right down.

"Well, changing diapers and going to pick him up at three a.m. is all the dad stuff there is right now. The kid's not going to do tricks and stunts for a while." Lucy sighed.

I laughed, imagining Lucy's adorable son doing any kind of tricks or stunts.

After Wiley pulled a beer for me and set a glass of wine in front of Lucy, I turned to face my friend.

"So, I've got some news."

Her face lit up and she clapped her hands in front of her. "Oh good. Your news is bound to be more exciting than anything I've got going on at this point. Spill."

The giddiness I'd been fighting all day rocketed through me, sending my words out in a rush. "Remember when Douggie Masters from *Out and Outside* was here for the grand opening?"

Lucy nodded. The opening of the resort had been attended by several media outlets, but the biggest was Douggie, who had a crazy popular YouTube show that featured him on various outdoor adventures around the world, sometimes with his husband in tow. He'd kind of become my idol, seeing the world, experiencing everything there was to experience. I wanted that, and I'd told him so, many times.

"When he was here, he told me about this contest he was running with *Outdoor Adventures*, that show on Netfilms, where the winner gets featured on the show and wins fifty thousand dollars to go on the adventure of their dreams."

Lucy's jaw dropped open. "You won?"

"Not yet," I said, wiggling a bit in my seat. "But I'm one of the finalists! They're sending a crew out next week to film some of the lead-up segments that they'll piece together for the announcement show. Kind of a slice of life and kind of like a final audition." I felt ready to leap out of my seat, sharing this news. It was the best thing that had ever happened to me, and my chance to be like Douggie, see the world.

"So you're going to be on the show either way," she said, understanding making her eyes light up as she clapped her hands and then pulled me into a hug.

"Yep! And I'm hoping I win the whole thing. The trip would be a once-in-a-lifetime opportunity to see something outside of Kasper Ridge. Like, way outside."

"Where would you go?"

"I said Africa." Even the word held a certain mystique for me.

"Africa, huh? Big continent... any specific part?"

I grinned, furious glee bubbling up inside me as I told Lucy about the dream trip I'd planned in my head—the one winning this contest could turn into reality. "There are so many things I want to do, but the trip I sketched out for the network would include climbing Mt. Kilimanjaro, a guided tour through the Ugandan jungles to see gorillas, and finally a more touristy part to Luxor to see the temples and the Valley of the Kings."

"Oh, you already had to decide the details?"

I nodded, thinking about the application I'd spent hours working on, the video I'd submitted. And remembering the one thing I'd stretched the truth about forced a heavy sigh from my lungs. "That was all part of the final application. It's all set up. There's just one little thing."

"What? Why do you look like that? Like someone just stole your beer?"

I glanced at my beer, but it was still there, right where I'd left it on the bar top. That was a relief. But I still had a problem.

I wrapped my fingers around my glass for strength and dropped my eyes as I told Lucy the bad part of my news. "Before I put in my final package last year, Douggie told me they really wanted to feature a couple as the winners and that my odds would be much better if I submitted as part of a duo."

"Who's your duo? Wait, a duo like a boyfriend or some-thing? Or just..." Lucy's forehead wrinkled.

I gave a little shrug, hoping Lucy would skip the chastising and come up with a solution for my problem.

"They want a romantic duo. So I might have told a little fib..."

Lucy dropped her forehead into her hand. "Oh Ceese. You didn't."

"I did. I told them I run my tours with my boyfriend, and that he'd go on the trip too." Admitting this brought the reality of it crashing down. I didn't have a boyfriend—I didn't even have someone I could ask to be a date to a movie, let alone own a business with me. Desperation threatened to ruin the excitement I'd felt over being selected a finalist.

"Need I point out the obvious?" Lucy crossed her arms over her chest. "You don't have a boyfriend. Unless this baby stuff has caused me to miss more than I thought."

I shook my head miserably, taking a sip of my beer to console myself. "No. I don't have a boyfriend. Longest dry spell on earth continues."

"And the show people are coming next week? Won't they be expecting to meet this non-existent guy?"

"I tried to get Jensen to agree to pretend." I couldn't even look at Lucy as I admitted the depths of my desperation.

Lucy laughed. "Your brother is the least adventurous person I've ever met. Though driving that taxi is pretty adventurous, actually."

"He got new tires last month." Jensen was the only ride share driver in Kasper Ridge, and he'd been operating on a bit of a shoestring budget for a while.

"That's a relief." She ran a finger down the globe of her wine glass, collecting condensation on her fingertip. "No one would buy you guys as a couple, anyway. You look like twins and bicker like enemies." Her gaze turned soft, sympathetic. "So what will you do?"

It was hard talking to Lucy about this. She was the owner and operator of Dale Construction, the firm that had helped finish renovations on the resort. She was a badass, and I doubted she'd ever have gotten herself into this situation. My business was like a lemonade stand on the sidewalk next to Dale Construction, and I suddenly felt like a total hack.

"I have no idea." I took a long swallow of my beer and let my eyes wander the crowded bar as the situation I'd gotten myself into rolled through my mind like a pin-studded tennis ball. Ouch.

Then my gaze landed on a tall broad figure at the entrance of the resort bar, the man who'd just stepped into the space, his dog at his side.

I perked. "Actually," I told Lucy. "I might have one idea."

Chapter Three
Pretending to be pretending...

TRAVIS

It had been a long day, and part of me wanted to just go back up to my room and hide. The noise and constant movement of the common areas of the resort were exhausting, especially now that we were fully booked most of the time.

But when I had days like this, days where the past tried to creep forward and cast its shadow across the present, those were the days I knew I needed company. And if the Navy had given me anything, it was good friends.

Sometimes the original crew hung out behind the resort, lighting the fire and letting the night cast its cool fingers around us. But I'd wandered out there first, and there was no one at the fire pit tonight. So the bar it would be.

The long, wood-paneled space of the bar was busy tonight, people seated on most of the stools and crowded around the high-tops and tables at the back. I liked it in here, even with the crowd. The space had an old Hollywood kind of appeal, and just walking in felt a bit like taking a step into the past, into someplace glamorous. Not that I'd really know much about glamour, but it seemed that way to me.

Roscoe stayed tight at my side as I took a deep breath and pushed myself forward. I was big enough that people kind of instinctually moved out of my way, which was a blessing. If I'd been smaller, I might never gather the courage to leave my room.

I didn't see any of the guys, though Antonio had said he'd probably stop through before bed. Wiley and Aubrey were moving behind the bar with a coordinated grace that probably came from the fact that they were much more than co-workers. They'd been together a couple years now, having met when Aubrey's brother—my Navy buddy Ghost—first hatched the plan to open this place again.

"Sass!" A familiar voice broke across the din of the crowd, and I spun to see Lucy and CeeCee at the bar. I felt the same little pulse of excitement I always did when CeeCee was around. She was hot in an outdoor girl kind of way, which I didn't know was totally my thing until I'd met her. I crossed the space and pressed myself into a little gap between stools just behind Lucy.

"Ladies." If was honest, CeeCee made me a little nervous, and before I could stop it, my hand did some kind of fancy little wave, like an overpaid butler to the royal family, minus the bow that probably should have gone with it. I could feel even Roscoe giving me a judgmental look. What the hell was wrong with me?

"Hey Sass," Lucy said, swiveling to look up at me with a warm smile on her face.

I had a soft spot for Lucy. She had a commanding presence and just being near her made me feel assured that all was well in hand. But I liked her mostly because she kept Fake Tom in line. Another of my Navy pals, Fake Tom—or Will, as Lucy called him—could be a little full of himself.

"How are you?" CeeCee asked me, and my heart accelerated against my will at the sound of her voice. I swallowed hard and took a deep breath.

"Yeah," I managed. Very articulate. "Good."

She grinned, and I tried to steel myself against the effect the expression had on me.

There was something about CeeCee. I'd had it bad for her since the first time she strode in here at Lucy's side, the local girl who seemed to have the whole world in the palm of her hand. She was tall and athletic, with a silky curtain of strawberry blond hair that was usually pulled back into a braid or a ponytail. She was usually wearing some kind of khakis or shorts, and often with a ball cap on her head that said "Kasper Gear and Guides," and not a lick of makeup. And damn if she wasn't the most beautiful woman I'd ever seen.

"Drink, man?" Wiley was across the bar from me, and I turned, hoping my face hadn't changed color as I struggled for the millionth time with my attraction to CeeCee.

"Yeah, thanks. Jameson, neat."

"I will get you your Irish whiskey," Wiley said, shaking his head at me. "But I'm still waiting for the day you convert like the rest of us."

"You make good whiskey, Wiley Coyote. I just prefer the Jameson." Wiley's family made Half Cat Whiskey back in Maryland, and it was the resort's preferred whiskey. Pretty much everyone drank that exclusively at this point.

But I'd never been very good at doing what I was expected to do.

Wiley put the glass in front of me, and I took a healthy sip, letting the smooth fire work through me.

"So," CeeCee said, loud enough that I knew she was aiming the words at me, not at Lucy. I took another quick sip and turned to face her.

"So," I replied, meeting her soft blue eyes and wishing that the world was a little bit different than it was. That my life was a little different.

"Can I ask you something?" CeeCee looked the tiniest bit uncertain, something I hadn't witnessed before. She was always confident, sure of herself. What was making her look unsure? Whatever it was, I wanted to pound it into the ground.

"Always," I told her. Over the past months, she and I had become friends. We couldn't be more than that, and even though it was sometimes torture to be around her knowing it was true, I'd let myself get close to her. And I cared about her. A lot.

"You're not gonna like it," Lucy warned, her eyes dancing as she looked up at me.

I looked between the ladies, trying to read the situation better. "Let's find out," I said. "What do you need, Ceese?"

She took a swallow of her beer and I watched her throat move, a simple motion that caused an unwanted chain reaction inside my body. She was so damned beautiful.

"Just a little favor," she started, and I tried to keep my mind in the present so it didn't start running any scenarios involving favors that I might be able to think of. She probably didn't need someone to come home with her and help her scrub her back in the tub. I cleared my throat, and Roscoe leaned into my leg as if he could feel my body chemistry changing, preparing for the unexpected.

"I told you about Douggie and the contest, right?" She watched me for a reaction, that nervous glint still in her eyes.

"At length," I reminded her. We'd talked on multiple occasions about her hopes for landing a spot on some adventure reality show, about how it would put her business on the map, but how it would also take her far away from Kasper Ridge, something I was not super excited about. She'd become so busy since the resort opened officially though, that I wondered how much more business her little adventure shop could actually handle.

"Yeah, so I'm a finalist." She met my eyes, and though her smile spread, there was something wrong—her eyes were still wary.

"That's amazing. Congratulations. Shouldn't we be celebrating?" I turned to flag down Wiley again to get some champagne or something. Lucy sat between us, but her stool was positioned back far enough for CeeCee to drop her hand on the arm I was leaning against, and the warmth of CeeCee's palm sent fire licking through my veins.

"Don't celebrate yet," Lucy suggested, her voice holding a hint of humor.

I glanced between the ladies.

"There's just one thing," CeeCee said. "And this is the favor part."

"Hit me," I said, trying to keep my voice neutral even while her soft skin pressed into mine.

"Douggie says they're looking to feature a couple on the final."

"A couple."

"Yeah, and so when I applied, I kind of told a tiny little lie."

"About being a couple?"

She dropped my gaze for a second, which was good, it gave my brain a second to catch up. Was CeeCee telling me she had a boyfriend? No, that didn't make sense. Why was her hand on my arm? What was this about?

"Yeah, I told them I run the adventure shop with my boyfriend. But that was almost a year ago. I figured I had time, that maybe by now I'd actually be part of a couple. I mean, Lucy and Will got friggin' married and had a kid in that amount of time."

Lucy held up her wine glass, toasting CeeCee's words, and took a sip.

"Right," I managed.

"So I wondered . . ." CeeCee paused and looked at Lucy, as if for support. "I hoped maybe since we're friends," she started again. "I hoped you would maybe pretend to be my boyfriend. When the cameras are here."

"One sec." I did my best to control my reaction, turning back to the bar and slipping my arm gently from beneath CeeCee's slim, soft fingers. I lifted my glass, finished what was inside, and stared hard at Wiley until he returned, Jameson in hand. "Double," I said, my voice softer than I'd intended it to be.

He poured, I drank, and then I swiveled back to the ladies.

I didn't want to pretend to be CeeCee's man. I wanted to *actually* be her man. But that would be impossible, given my circumstances, so I'd never tried. Could I handle pretending?

"What would this entail, exactly?" I asked, stuffing down the riot of energy her words had unleashed inside my gut.

She smiled, tucking a long strand of silky hair behind her ear, clearly having no idea how sexy that simple movement was. I glanced around the bar, checking to see what other guys had noticed, but everyone else seemed engaged in their own conversations. It surprised me, because any time CeeCee was in the same room I was in, I knew every move she made. She was like my own personal lighthouse beacon.

"Well," she said. "I guess you'd hang out at the shop, probably guide a few hikes or rafting trips with me to make it look like we're in it together. We'd just have to make the cameras believe that we're a couple." She blushed, and I nearly fell to my knees right there as the pink spread across her cheeks and the smooth skin of her chest, exposed in the simple V-neck T-shirt she wore. "Maybe some, like, kissing? Holding hands?"

I pretended that the idea of kissing CeeCee didn't affect me at all. "How long are they here?"

"A week, I guess."

"When?"

"They come Monday." She dropped my gaze at this statement, and I sensed that she knew this was a lot to ask, that my preference would be to say no. Being that close to CeeCee for a week, touching her, but reminding myself it was all pretend? A wise man would definitely say no. I'd never been especially wise.

"Okay." The word flew out more in reaction to seeing her look defeated than as a result of careful consideration. I waited a second, expecting to feel regret or worry, but I didn't. Instead, the prospect of spending time with CeeCee, pretending to be her man, sounded a lot like the perfect solution. After all, pretending was the only way I could ever be with her. Maybe it would be enough.

"You're serious?" Lucy finally spoke, looking between us. "You guys, this is crazy."

"We're already good friends though," CeeCee said. "So it'll be easy, right, Sasquatch?"

Lucy speared me with her gaze and I tried to manage a reassuring smile. This would not be easy.

"Do you even know his real name?" Lucy asked CeeCee, pointing at me.

CeeCee frowned. We had spent a lot of time together, and I knew a lot about her. But I didn't actually think I'd told her my name. Most people seemed to think that "Sasquatch" fit pretty well and left it at that. I wondered if Ghost even knew my given name.

"Of course," CeeCee said, her eyes catching mine and widening in a silent plea.

"Everyone knows my name is Travis," I supplied.

CeeCee's lips pressed together and her eyebrows shot up. She had definitely not known that.

"Right," Lucy said, not buying a bit of it. "Well, Travis, I guess you know then, that CeeCee is crazy. I can't believe you guys are going to do this. It's almost a certainty that you'll get caught, and then what, Cee? Wouldn't it make more sense to just come clean and hope for the best?"

CeeCee traced a circle on the bar with her finger, making me wish we were alone, that that finger was tracing the circle across my flesh, that I could touch her.

"No," she said, dropping her hand and raising her chin. "This will work. It has to. Winning this competition would give me a chance I'll never get otherwise, to see some of the world, to experience something besides a tiny little mountain town."

"You love it here," Lucy pointed out.

"Right, and I'll always come back home. But I think I'll appreciate home even more if I'm not constantly wondering what else there is. Plus, winning this would set up the shop perfectly. I could expand into other locations—Aspen, Boulder, Durango." A sad smile crossed her face before she banished it with a grin. "I'm not going to get the guy and the family like you, Lucy. So I'm gonna do everything to get this."

Discomfort swamped my stomach. CeeCee deserved every-thing she wanted, even if the guy she got in the end wasn't me. I opened my mouth to say something, though I didn't know what, but CeeCee spoke again.

"I've got Travis here to help me. And Roscoe, of course." She smiled down at Roscoe and his tail thumped a couple times on the wood floor of the bar.

"Let's do this," I said, swallowing the last of my whiskey.

It was a terrible idea, and I already knew I'd regret every second of it. Being closer to CeeCee? Pretending that when the cameras were off and the lights were low I would be the one pulling her close, pressing my mouth to hers, letting my fingers slide over her skin? It might possibly kill me.

But I knew it would hurt more to see someone else doing it.

It was only a week. I could do anything for a week. Life had already taught me that much. Though who knew what kind of man I'd be, coming out the other side?

Chapter Four
Lying Eyes. (And mouths).

CEECEE

Sasquatch's name was Travis?

I had to think on that a bit as I drove back home from the resort that night.

It was odd to think that I'd known the man at least six months now, and I'd never stopped to ask his real name. I knew he'd grown up on a ranch in Texas, and that he'd known he would have to make his own way since he had three older brothers who already had plans to take over when their dad retired.

He'd told me he was a mistake, that coming six years after his youngest brother was not something his parents had intended. But he also described a pretty idyllic childhood—the baby under the wings of three older brothers, parents who adored all four of them, miles of wide-open spaces.

The things he didn't tell me about were far more recent. For instance, I didn't know why he'd quit flying, only that he'd joined the Navy, been selected for jets, been dubbed "Sasquatch" because he was huge, met Ghost and Brainiac and the rest of the guys, and then somewhere along the line . . . quit flying. It didn't sound like he'd stopped for the reasons Ghost had—no mishaps, no lawsuits—not that anyone would do more than whisper a word or two about what really happened to Ghost.

I turned into my driveway and parked next to my brother's car. We shared the house we'd grown up in and took care of my mom together.

Just as I was gathering my backpack and switching off the engine, my phone vibrated, mirrored on the smartwatch I wore. I looked down at my wrist.

Douggie Masters.

Excitement bubbled up in me. I still couldn't believe this was happening.

"Hey," I answered, practically singing into the phone I'd dug from the front pocket of my bag.

"Hey yourself, finalist. You ready for this?"

I let out a breath. "I think so. I mean, in some ways, I've been ready for this my whole life, dying for a big chance. And in other ways, I'm pretty terrified about the whole thing." I put my backpack aside and leaned back into the driver's seat, staring out the window into the dark trees bordering our property. The moon cast a layer of white frosting over the tips of the pine boughs, making them sparkle.

"What parts are you worried about? I've seen a lot of adventure operations in my work, CeeCee, and your place is top notch."

"It's not the work part so much . . ."

"What else is there? You worried about the cameras?"

"Kind of that, yeah."

Douggie blew out a little laugh across the phone. "Girl, don't be ridiculous. The camera will love you."

"No, it's more that thing you told me about how the

network wants a couple." I hadn't come clean with Douggie, but I felt like I owed it to him. He'd gotten me this far. I didn't want to disappoint him by letting him find out about my lie later.

"They picked you as a finalist, didn't they? So maybe I was wrong."

The tiniest lump of guilt lodged in my throat, and I tried to clear it before speaking again. "You weren't wrong, Douggie. They picked me, but maybe only because I told the tiniest white lie."

Douggie was silent too long and worry joined the guilt inside me in a frenetic game of tag that was making me feel nauseous.

"What white lie?" he asked, serious now.

"About being part of a couple. Nothing about the business, or about me, really."

"So the cameras will get there Monday and find out that you're not part of a couple?" Douggie asked, a note of chastening in his voice I didn't like, but knew I deserved.

"No, they'll find a couple. I've got it all set up." I tried to sound confident in hopes Douggie wouldn't point out the obvious—that this was a terrible idea.

"I'm confused. Are you part of a couple or not?"

"As far as they know, I run the adventure shop with my boyfriend, Travis."

"Travis. I've been talking to you since the resort opened, and I find this out only now? You've never mentioned him."

"I have, only I probably called him Sasquatch."

"The giant? The guy with the dog?" Douggie's voice held a note of disbelief.

"Yeah." Douggie hadn't met Sasquatch because he hadn't been there when the soft opening of the resort had occurred. But I'd told him about my friend.

"So you're dating now, and you never thought to mention it?"

It would have been easy to say yes, but I didn't want to compound one lie with another. "No, we're not. Not really. But he agreed to help me. With . . . this."

"Help you with the lie you told the network about running the shop with your boyfriend."

"It sounds so wrong when you put it like that," I said.

Douggie was quiet and worry sprouted inside me.

"Douggie? Are you going to tell them?"

He sighed loudly. "No, of course not. But you guys better be really freaking convincing. The crew has probably seen plenty of bad acting in their time. They'll find you out a mile away if you don't do a good job pretending."

"Very reassuring, thanks."

"Maybe you and this guy should just . . . actually date. You always seem to have nice things to say about him."

I thought about that. Sass was a nice guy, if a little unpredictable, and somewhat unmoored. I had yet to figure out what he really wanted out of life, not that it was my job to know that about my friends. "I don't think we're the right fit. But he's a good guy. This will work."

That last part didn't sound reassuring, even to me.

"Good luck then. You'll need it," Douggie said. "Call me Monday when the crew is all set up."

"I will. Thanks for everything."

"You got it. Go slay, CeeCee."

"I'll do my best." I ended the call and stared out into the moonlit sky for a few minutes more.

Could I really pull this off?

Inside, I took off my boots and set them on the mat by the door, the sounds of the television coming to me from the living room where Jensen and my mother sat in side-by-side recliners, watching some kind of action movie with a lot of swearing, shooting, and explosions. The noise stopped when I stepped into the room, and they both turned to look at me, the raised remote in Jensen's hand.

"Hey, honey," Mama said. "How was your day?"

"Good," I said, taking a seat in the corner of the couch and curling my legs under me. "Everything is all set for Monday."

Jensen grinned. "You're gonna make sure to plug my business, right? For the cameras?"

"If I can work in something about getting a ride, you're definitely getting pimped, Jen."

"Don't say 'pimped,'" Mama said, wrinkling her nose.

"Turn the movie back on," I suggested to my brother, snuggling back into my familiar spot on the couch. This was where I'd always sat when my family hung out in the living room. Jensen used to sit on the other end of the old plaid fabric couch, and Dad's recliner had sat empty for years. But somewhere along the way, it had become Jensen's spot. That made more sense than leaving it vacant, and Mama hadn't said anything about it.

As the movie blared into the room in front of me, I thought about how little my life had changed. This room had been the backdrop for so much of it. And this, coming home at the end of the day and watching TV with my family, this had been the way I'd spent too much of that life.

But this opportunity could change everything. I hadn't mentioned it to my mom, or to Jensen, but I hoped that some of the money I'd make if I won could help me get my own place. But my first priority was getting some experience, some perspective, seeing some of the world. I knew it would make me appreciate everything I had here in Kasper Ridge even more.

For now, though, this was comfortable and familiar. And while it wasn't everything I wanted, it was a lot.

Chapter Five
Rising Dough Will Lift All Bread

TRAVIS

On Monday morning, I was up early again, pounding out dough in the kitchen for the day's offerings. It was quiet in the austere steel-filled space, and there was a rhythm to kneading dough and running the mixers that I found soothing.

Roscoe wasn't allowed in the kitchen, which was fine with him. He got to stay up in the room, curled up on the bed.

CeeCee had asked me to be at her shop at eight, though she didn't expect the crew to arrive until the afternoon. We'd review the way the place operated and plan the week, finding a few things for me to be involved with, but not plugging me in so much that it might become obvious I didn't work there all the time.

I was trying to work out how I felt about the whole scenario as I turned and pressed the dough for what would become cinnamon rolls.

On the one hand, I didn't like the pretense of it. Lying wasn't my style and I'd spent enough time stretching truths to know when I was close to that edge. And this was way over the edge. We were going to tell these camera people something that just wasn't true—that CeeCee and I were romantically involved.

The thing was, I could see that stretch. It wasn't like telling these guys I was dating some movie star or something. For one thing, that would be hard to buy since I didn't think there were many movie stars here in Kasper Ridge. But the other thing was that it was something I'd absolutely thought about—CeeCee and me. It was something I thought about a lot.

I flipped the dough into a greased bowl and set it aside to rise, scrubbing my hands in hot soapy water and doing my best to press down the feelings I'd had for CeeCee for as long as I'd known her. I steered my mind away from the way her red-blond hair framed her heart-shaped face. From the way her big blue eyes widened when she smiled. From the way my heart squeezed tighter inside my chest when she was around, like something about being close to her made it work harder to get my attention to remind me it was in there.

What my heart needed to understand, however, was that I was done listening to it. I'd done that before, and had the scars to show it was a bad idea. That and the other scars I carried were enough to remind me that getting anyone else involved in my shit was a recipe for failure.

An alarm beeped at the far side of the kitchen, a reminder to pull the loaves of brown bread out to cool. It also brought me back to reality. I was here to help out Ghost. Or maybe he was helping me out, depending on how you looked at it. Either way, what I'd agreed on with CeeCee was nothing more than that. Helping out a friend.

* * *

"Hey Sass." Ghost strode across the lobby, catching me just as Roscoe and I were about to head out to CeeCee's place.

"Yeah brother, what's up?"

Ghost stopped in front of me, squinting his eyes in that worried way he had, rubbing one hand through the dark red hair on his head. I hoped he didn't have bad news. I didn't like seeing Ghost worry.

"Thanks for taking over things in the kitchen on the early shift. That's been working out surprisingly well." He grimaced and I got his meaning. He hadn't expected it to work at all.

"Yeah, well, I don't sleep anyway, there's no one else in there to bother me, and baking is basically just following rules. I've been doing that most of my life."

He nodded, dropping my gaze. "You okay in there though? You like it?"

I lifted a shoulder. "I guess so," I told him. "I don't know if I still have the ability to actually like things. Pretty sure I don't hate it, though. It's quiet. Kinda therapeutic, I guess."

"Better than hanging out with Brainiac on the mountain?"

"Ghost," I said, making a point of catching my friend's gaze and holding it. "I'm here to help you. Doesn't really matter what jobs you throw at me. I'll do what I can. If you need me to spend more time with that condescending asshole, I can do it." Harrison, aka Brainiac, was not my favorite person, though he'd definitely mellowed now that Penny was around and he was a daddy.

"Yeah. Okay. Well, I've got one more ask for you."

"Does it have anything to do with booty? I particularly like booty-related jobs." I winked at Ghost, waiting for him to take the bait about the insane treasure hunt he was obsessed with. His uncle, who left him the resort, also left him a wild goose chase, and Ghost and his sister Aubrey were convinced there were riches at the end of the very long winding trail they were following.

"No booty," Ghost confirmed, his voice low and potentially annoyed.

I grinned. "That's too bad."

"It's a wedding, actually."

"Been there, done that. No thanks."

"Not your wedding, moron." Ghost sounded irked enough to get Roscoe's attention, and my dog immediately rose to all fours, his amber eyes intent on my friend.

"Stand down, boy," I told him. Roscoe dropped his tail end back down next to my left boot.

"He's actually a decent dog, huh?"

"I don't know why you sound surprised." No one believed I could train Roscoe myself, but it wasn't like I was pulling methodology out of my ass. You could learn anything on the internet these days. And when you don't sleep much, you get back a lot of time.

"It just seemed a little crazy when you first got him is all."

"Adjustment takes time. Roscoe had been through some things before we met."

Ghost met my eye again, searched my face for a long minute. "Yeah, anyway. This wedding is in a couple weeks, and we're supplying the cake."

I considered, feeling a little put out, but wanting to make Ghost's life easier if I could. Still, fuck. A wedding cake? "I'm good with bread and rolls, muffins. Not towering cakes. And I don't decorate."

"Monroe's got someone to decorate. Can you just bake the layers?"

"Maybe?" I felt a bit of pressure mounting in my brain. No one cared if I screwed up a batch of rolls or muffins. But I was willing to bet there was a chick in a white dress who'd be pretty put out if I didn't succeed in baking my first-ever wedding cake.

"Needs to feed one-fifty."

I looked down at my dog, who met my eyes as if he thought maybe he could weigh in on this idea.

"Sure, I guess," I said, having no idea how to make a cake that big. "Flavors?"

"Up to us," Ghost said. "No peanuts."

"No one puts peanuts in a wedding cake," I said, my mind flashing back to the cake tasting I'd attended once. That bakery had given us some kind of weird peanut butter cake to try, and it had led to a full on blow out. I'd ended up with a wedding cake I did not enjoy in the least. Maybe it had been a sign. Mom liked it though, so I guess that was a win.

Ghost gave me another evaluative look. "Saturday September fifteenth," he said.

I nodded. "Gives me time." I'd be watching a lot more YouTube, I guessed. "What about the dinner? Rolls? Breakfast morning after? Pastries?" I needed to understand exactly how many ways there were for me to fail around this particular event.

"I'll have Monroe get you the plan," he told me, relief smoothing his features. "There probably is some of that stuff, yeah. It was the cake I was most worried about."

"Hey," I said. "You just run this place. You delegate the worry." He'd had enough worry in his life.

"Thanks." He frowned at me, taking a step back and looking me up and down as if he'd only just noticed that I was heading out. "You going somewhere?"

"Yeah. I'll be over at the adventure shop a lot this week. CeeCee needs some help with a few things." It felt shitty telling Ghost anything but the whole truth. Still, I didn't necessarily feel like it was my lie to spill. Was I nuts to think maybe I could pretend to be CeeCee's boyfriend without anyone finding out? There was one thing Navy buddies were good for—giving each other shit. And I didn't really want to hear it.

"Okay," he said, drawing the word out.

"Kitchen's all set, turned over to the chef for breakfast."

"Yeah, I wasn't worried, man."

"You always are."

He nodded, acknowledging the truth of it. It had been years since I'd seen Ghost smile in a way that didn't look haunted.

"I'll start researching wedding cakes," I told him. "Maybe whip up a sample or two in the process."

"Sounds good. Thanks. Appreciate you jumping in wherever you're needed."

I shrugged. I was a human patch, filling holes and covering gaps. It suited everyone involved. I didn't get in too deep, didn't make any serious commitments, and I was available to pitch in where I was useful.

"See ya," I told him, turning back to the doors.

It was time to go patch another hole for CeeCee. This one felt bigger and a bit more unwieldy, but I told myself it'd be fine. CeeCee needed me, so I'd be there. The tricky part would be keeping my stupid heart under control.

Chapter Six
No Touching the Giant

CEECEE

I didn't sleep.

The camera crew was coming sometime this afternoon, and as the darkness of the previous night surrounded on me, it had brought with it all kinds of worst-case scenarios about what might go wrong with my plan.

What if the crew figured out I'd lied about being part of a couple? Sasquatch—I'd have to get used to calling him Travis—was a good guy, but he was a little bit of a wild card. I'd known him long enough to have heard plenty of stories about his antics back in the Navy. Word was, he enjoyed being a joker but didn't always think about consequences. And then there were the parts of his service no one seemed willing to talk about. Could he pull this off?

Could I?

I hoped so.

But if something went sideways, it could ruin me,

depending on how the television people decided to deal with it. What if they sniffed an even better story in the scandal of our deception and told that story on the show? Exposed me as a fraud on national television? Losing my chance to experience the world was one thing, but the shame that kind of scandal would bring to our little town was something else. What would my mother think? She'd hear about it from everyone if something like that was on television, and she wasn't the kind of woman who could laugh things off. Mama was proper and straight laced, and she'd brought us up to be the same.

Not to mention what the scandal might do to the business. Would people come in just to gape at me, or would the shop down the road get all the business if something like that happened?

I shook my head, trying to escape the thoughts of what would happen if we failed. It would be bad. Very bad.

I moved through the front of the shop as sunshine streamed in through the high windows overhead, and flipped the sign on the front door to Open, just as Travis's truck pulled into the lot. I stepped outside to greet him. The driver side door swung open and Roscoe leapt out, turning in one quick circle in the gravel lot before spotting me and charging.

"Hey boy," I laughed, bending my knees and bracing in case he didn't get the brakes on in time. Roscoe was pretty well trained, but he was still a puppy. And even though he was totally loyal to Travis, and seemed to provide whatever support the big guy needed, he wasn't a proper service dog—Travis had trained him himself, so there were certain bits of etiquette that Roscoe hadn't picked up on.

The dog skidded to a stop in front of me, his tongue hanging out one side of his mouth as his big brown eyes caught mine.

"Hey buddy," I crooned, burying my hands into the scruff of his coat. "Who's a good boy?"

"Hope you're talking about me," Travis quipped, slamming his car door and striding toward me. "Cuz I'm the one doing you a favor, remember?"

I looked up as he stopped a couple feet away, the sun catching strands of gold in his sandy brown hair. He wore it cut close, and had a scruff of darker hair over the skin of his square jaw, giving him a rugged look. With his aviator shades on, dressed in a fitted T-shirt that hugged every muscle in his impressive chest—not to mention the biceps bulging from the sleeves—he looked the part of an adventure guide, at least.

He also looked delicious. It would not be hard to feign attraction to him. I wouldn't actually be pretending, after all. We were friends first, but I'd have to have been blind not to notice that Travis had an easy smile that perfectly complemented the muscular physique that caught the attention of women any time he was at the resort. Mine too.

I swallowed hard. Pretending. We were pretending.

"I remember. Thanks again." I stood and we headed inside together, Roscoe at Travis's side. "You ready?" I asked him, nerves flinging themselves around inside my stomach. I couldn't figure out if the nerves were one hundred percent related to our lie and the problems we'd encounter if we were found out, or if some of them had to do with being alone with Travis.

"Totally ready. Watch this," he said holding up a hand for me to stop just inside the front door.

Travis strode around a circular rack of men's pants, a wide smile on his handsome face as he came near me. "Hi there, welcome to Kasper Gear and Guides. What kind of adventure are you in the mood for today?" His exuberance was over the top, and a laugh bubbled out of me at the way his dark eyes danced with amusement.

"Too much," I told him.

"Take two," he suggested, doing another lap of the rack.

"What's up man? You like, wanna do some adventuring?" This time, his delivery was leisurely and drawling, and just a little slurry.

"You sound drunk. Or high. No one wants to trust their life to a guy who spent the morning smoking."

He laughed. "Maybe I shouldn't hang out by the door then. I'll handle the tactical side of things." He crossed his arms in front of his chest, standing tall and clearly waiting for me to laugh.

I obliged.

"Or," I said, turning toward the back of the shop and lifting a finger for him to follow, "I can tell you what's on the schedule this week and explain a bit about what goes on in here each day. And then you can just help me with that."

"I mean, yeah. That could work." Travis shrugged and followed me around the long glass counter in the back of the shop. "I could be your knife guy," he told me, gazing down at the variety of blades under the glass.

I chuckled, "Okay, you be the knife guy. But I need help with some other stuff too."

Roscoe sniffed his way around the counter into the little back office and settled next to where Travis stood, and I went through the bookings we had for the week. Travis sat close by my side, his thick arm pressed against my elbow as I tried to focus on the screen we were looking at. It was hard though, and it felt like the heat generated by his touch was zinging through my body. Part of me wanted to lean into it, and part of me wanted to step away, back to safety.

We sat there, tightly squeezed into the small space, as something occurred to me. "Should we, ah . . . like come up with a story?"

Travis turned to face me, his knee pressing into mine.

The contact was distracting, but so was his deep, thoughtful gaze.

"A story about us?"

"To tell people. I mean, there are a lot of people in town who could give us away. Maybe we need to have something ready to explain this?"

Travis's eyes held mine and a warm thrill rushed through me. It was just the two of us, alone here in this intimate space. It was the closest I'd ever been to him. The only time I'd been alone with him. I wanted to lean in to his warmth, his size. I wanted to see what would happen if I did.

"Right," he said, pulling his gaze from mine and breaking the spell. "So we say that you came into the kitchen at the resort, drawn by the yeasty smell of my baking bread . . ."

"I'm thinking a 'how we got together' story should not involve the word yeast."

"Sure. Okay." He chuckled, a low rolling sound that comforted me and stirred me up all at once.

"How about, we've been friends for a while, and recently it's just evolved into something more?" I caught his eyes again as I finished my suggestion. The dark centers of his gaze expanded, his eyelids hooding slightly.

"Yeah," he said. "I mean, that's realistic." He said it as if it wasn't just realistic, but was real.

"It is," I agreed, my voice dropping without me intending it to.

"Hey, yo!" A voice called through the shop as Travis and I sat side by side in the back office, staring at one another. We pulled apart, each of us redirecting our gazes to the computer screen, and I did my best to show him how I reviewed the reservations for this afternoon's rock climbing outing.

"Hey Cole!" My employee Cole was a local kid I'd known a long time. He was in college, trying to figure out what he wanted to do next. He was a good worker, and great with customers, if not always the most motivated to do the less glamorous jobs.

He stepped into the back office, his phone in his hand as he tapped at the screen. Our HR system was totally online, and I heard the ping of him clocking in on the desktop in front of me. "Are they here yet?" he asked, glancing around as if he expected to find a camera crew squeezed into the tiny back office with me and Travis.

"Not until two," I told him.

"Ah, cool." Cole stood there, staring at Travis with open interest, and I realized that we would need to let him in on the plan. Kind of.

"So, Cole," I said, pushing the rolling chair back to stand. "This is Sass—er, Travis." I swallowed hard, glancing at my friend and then back at my employee as I felt the lie form on my tongue, bitter and foreign. "My boyfriend."

Cole looked like he was holding back a laugh, and I felt Travis stiffen at my side. Still, Travis shot out a big hand and Cole shook it, looking a little mystified. "I didn't know you were, uh . . . I mean, Jensen didn't say anything about, uh." He shook Travis's hand, still mumbling, and finally concluded with, "Cool."

"I put some boxes to the side of the floor out there," I told Cole. "Should be the first of the snow gear for the winter season. You'll need to move some stuff around to get another rack situated, and we can shift some of the summer gear to the discount racks. Not the fancy stuff, but those cotton shorts and T-shirts. Cool?"

I was trying to rush Cole out of the back office, hoping if I redirected him, there'd be no room for questions, no need for explanations. He didn't seem to pick up on anything odd, and I was relieved.

"You're the boss," he said, heading back out the door. I tried to keep him out on the floor if possible, so I could do what needed doing in the back or head out to guide. We had one other part-time employee, Adelaide, an older woman who didn't know a lot about the kinds of things we did here, but who loved people and was more than willing to upsell sunscreen, Chap-Stick, and whatever else she could press on those who came in. She wasn't on the schedule much this week, but I didn't look forward to lying to her about Travis. It'd be like lying to someone's grandmother.

I turned to move back to the chair in front of the desk, only to bump right into Travis's immovable form in the tiny space. "Oof, sorry." I jumped back quickly, but his hands moved to grasp my upper arms, keeping me near.

"Hey," he said, looking down into my face with a warm intensity that stirred me up even more. "If we're supposed to be together, we probably shouldn't jump away from each other if we accidentally touch."

He had a point, but I wasn't sure that part of our lie would be so easy to fake. His warm hands on my shoulders offered something more than just comfort, and if I was being honest, having his big rough palms on the skin of my arms was doing something to my stomach too.

"Right," I said, meeting his eyes and shivering as my stomach shimmied again. "You're right."

"And," he went on, releasing me, but sticking close. "This camera crew might be expecting to witness a few signs of . . ." A blush crept up my friend's jaw and cheeks, and he dropped my eyes, running a hand over the top of his close cut hair. "I mean . . ."

"PDA?" I asked, realizing it was true. I'd said it in the bar when we talked about this, but I hadn't thought about it in real terms until now, with the heat of his body pressing in on me, making my insides all squirmy.

He blew out a sigh, and stepped back, gazing around the space as if he was sorry he'd mentioned it.

"Yes," I said. We couldn't pull this off if they didn't think we were a couple. And couples were comfortable together. Physically. They held hands. They hugged. They . . . did other things. Heat flooded my body as I thought about Travis touching me in other places, other ways.

Travis had stopped talking and I was a little worried he'd stopped breathing. He looked so uncomfortable I wasn't sure what to do. Was it that repellent to him to realize he would have to touch me?

But no, that would have been obvious before. Like a moment ago when we'd been sitting side by side, pressed together in the office. I was sure I wasn't the only one who'd felt the sparks there.

"I mean, not all couples are super touchy," I said.

He didn't speak right away, but seemed to gather his thoughts, then those dark eyes found mine and something burned deep in the obsidian depths that I didn't recognize. "If any guy was lucky enough to be with you for real," he said, his voice an almost inaudible rumble, "he'd want to touch you all the time."

My stomach flipped again as I stared up into his serious gaze, the air around us seeming to vibrate as I leaned in closer to the heat radiating from Travis.

"Boss?" Cole's voice came from the floor of the shop, and it broke whatever strange atmosphere had so suddenly appeared in the office. Disappointment replaced the anticipation that had been growing inside me. What had I expected to happen?

I cleared my throat, shot Travis a smile I was pretty sure didn't look especially cheerful, and headed out to see what Cole needed.

Chapter Seven
Pretending is Fun

TRAVIS

CeeCee headed back out into the shop, and my shoulders relaxed even as other parts of my anatomy remained uncomfortably hard. I blew out a breath and adjusted myself, shaking my head slightly.

"We're pretending," I muttered. "Just pretend."

Roscoe cocked his head at my reminder, and followed me out into the space behind the long glass counter at the back of the shop.

CeeCee was with Cole toward the front, and for a moment I watched her as she helped him put together a long metal rack, bending and moving with as much grace as I imagined a dancer might have. She flowed, really, like something born of elements —water, air, fire. CeeCee was a force of nature, and so beautiful that it almost hurt to look at her.

The thing was, it wouldn't be hard to act like I was in love with CeeCee. The hard part would be going back to normal at the end, when the crew left. It was very likely that this week would kill me. And if it didn't, I hoped maybe I'd win some kind of acting award.

But if it would make her happy, if it got her what she wanted most in the world, then I'd do it. I'd do just about anything for her, I realized.

Feeling things getting way too deep inside my head, I strode around the shop and selected a few items I thought I might need for the rock climbing outing this afternoon.

Once I'd donned the trucker hat reading "Kasper Ridge: We do it at altitude" and slipped on an obscenely tight pair of leggings over my cargo pants, I rosined up my hands and approached CeeCee and Cole. "Ready for our rock climbing, boss," I told her.

Cole looked at me first, his eyes bugging out before laughter spewed out of him.

CeeCee turned, and had the exact same reaction, only her eyes caught just a moment longer on the bulge at the top of my tight leggings and a pink tinge colored her skin as she dragged her eyes back to my face and laughed.

Pleasure replaced the awkward tension I'd felt between us before—being the clown was a role I took on comfortably.

"That's probably not going to be the right gear," she said, shaking her head. "But we should maybe get a photo or two just in case."

I modeled as CeeCee pulled her phone out and took a few shots. I was more than used to prostrating myself on the shrine of silliness in order to lighten the mood. I'd been doing it for years now, and it was a very effective way to keep people— including me—from dwelling on the more serious side of things when you didn't want them to.

"Oh crap," CeeCee said, still holding her phone.

"What's up?" I asked, worry replacing my jovial mood.

"I have an email from the camera crew," she said. "They're going to be arriving early."

Even as she spoke the words, a bit of a commotion sounded up front, and the front door chime rang, the high tone echoing through the shop.

A man with a scraggly beard and a notebook came striding in, looking around with an evaluative gaze. His eyes found CeeCee and stopped. "You CeeCee Moore?"

CeeCee nodded, striding forward confidently. "I am. Are you Ned?"

"Guilty," the guy confirmed, a half grin lifting one side of the scraggly beard. "Great place here," he told her. "The guys are setting up out front, getting a few shots of the shop while the light is good. Sorry about the schedule change. The airport was a lot more efficient than we figured it would be."

"Yeah, Denver can take forever or it can surprise you," she said.

Ned's eyes scanned the interior again, skittering past me and then snagging, coming back to rest on my face and then dropping down to take in my outfit. A slow smile spread across his face, and his eyes crinkled. "Hey man, nice pants."

CeeCee's face was turning bright red, but I didn't bother with embarrassment. I had a job to do here. I took two steps forward, stretched out my hand to shake Ned's, and then slapped an arm around CeeCee's shoulders.

"Thanks," I said. "I'm Travis. CeeCee's partner. And fiancé."

"Woah," Ned said, looking between us with a happy expression. "Things have advanced since you applied. Engaged? Awesome. Congratulations, guys."

Oops. I'd pushed a bit too far. I had no idea why I'd suddenly advanced our relationship to the next level. We could barely look at each other without one of us blushing furiously.

No one would buy an engagement. But it was out there now, and I couldn't back down.

"You're engaged now?" Cole asked from where he was hanging a neon yellow parka.

"Yep!" CeeCee piped up in a strangely shrill voice, lifting her left hand and then quickly tucking it behind her. "I'm not really into jewelry. Too much trouble when you're climbing or out on the river."

Oh crap. A ring. I hadn't thought of that. Did I need to buy a ring now? Shit, what had I done?

"Totally get it," Ned said. "Well, that's awesome. You're a lucky man, Travis." Ned's gaze caught on my outfit again, his brow wrinkling slightly. "So, network says we're doing a rock climbing outing today? Somewhere pretty close?"

"Yes," CeeCee said, stepping away from me. "I can show you on the map. It's not until three. It's a group staying over at the resort, and it's really more of a bouldering session. First timers, some kids. They just want to get out and do something a little adventurous, so I suggested this. There's a spot not far from here with great views and some challenging rocks."

"Cool," Ned said. "I'm gonna head back out and help the crew get what they need out there. I'll get you guys all set up with the microphones, then we'll just be flies on the wall in here until it's time to go."

CeeCee had explained the bouldering outing to me already, and I wasn't worried about that. But I was worried about this fly on the wall situation. If they were really unobtrusive, there was a chance I'd forget they were here. That would not help CeeCee.

"Great," CeeCee said.

"Great," I agreed. The leggings I wore were starting to become pretty uncomfortable. "I'm just gonna change, I think I'm losing circulation in my junk."

CeeCee whacked me hard in the chest as I turned and headed to the far side of the shop where some dressing rooms stood. I didn't need privacy, but I kind of wanted to get away from Ned for a moment and try to get my head on straight. I couldn't screw this up. Especially now that I'd ratcheted things up a notch for no apparent reason.

I peeled the leggings from my body, realizing I was going to have to pay for them now since they were stretched out beyond recognition, and sat for a moment on the little stool in the dressing room. I could see Roscoe's paws beneath the dressing room door, standing guard outside.

He was a good boy. Doing his best to take care of me, save me from myself.

What he couldn't know—what no one really understood—was that it was impossible. I'd already screwed everything up for myself. I could only hope to survive this week with my heart and my friendship with CeeCee intact. The rest of my life was already unrecoverable.

Chapter Eight
Roscoe and Rocks

CEECEE

Once Travis returned from the dressing room, the ruined leggings in his hand and a sheepish look on his face, we settled into kind of a rhythm. It wasn't like a regular day at the shop, except that plenty of people came and went, tourists and locals alike. It was more like an odd play we were putting on, where no one was sure of their lines but there was some acting award at stake.

Ned and his camera crew set up in a far corner, and one guy followed me pretty much everywhere I went, a little camera held in front of him and his voice constantly suggesting I just "act natural" and "do what I normally do."

The issue was that none of this felt normal at all, and in the rush of excitement and confusion storming around inside me, I could barely remember what I did on a regular day at work.

As time to head out for the rock climbing adventure approached, it occurred to me that Travis and I had moved around each other all day, but hadn't really given the crew any together time to catch on film. Beyond the awkward half hug he'd given me when he announced our sudden engagement, my "fiancé" hadn't touched me all day. I really had no idea why we were suddenly engaged—it was going to be hard enough to act like a couple, let alone one headed for the altar. But it was out there, and I knew that somehow, Travis was probably just trying to help.

I moved to where he was finishing up helping a man at the glass counter. He actually was great with the knives, and I watched as he closed the sale on a Karambit I'd ordered in on a whim. He had a natural ease with people, making them comfortable and engaging them in conversation easily. But as he moved to the tablet to ring in the sale, I realized I hadn't shown him how to use the system, and I didn't want his confusion to tip off the crew in any way.

"You need a hand ringing that up?" I asked, smiling at the man as Travis put the knife back into the little felt pouch before sliding it into its box.

"That'd be great." Travis gazed over my head for a second and then looked back down at me, adding, "babe."

Warm pleasure filled me at the nickname, even though it was for show. A quick glance over my shoulder confirmed that the camera guy was right there, catching this all on film. The man at the counter looked slightly uncomfortable being on camera, but every customer who came in this week while the crew was here got briefed on the situation and signed a release.

I rang up the man's knife and processed his card. "Thanks," the customer said, and with a quick glance at the hovering cameraman, he turned and fled the shop.

I needed to make this seem real, to give the network what they came for, so I took a deep breath and turned to face Travis, who was standing stock still, as if he knew something was coming.

"Hey," I said, trying for a sexy familiarity despite the painful awkwardness I actually felt.

Travis raised an eyebrow and looked down at me, but something in my face must've signaled my plans to him. He grinned and reached for me, his hands brushing my hips and then circling to my back, tugging me closer.

It was strange at first—Travis had never touched me this way. But once I moved past the initial urge to step back, to stay out of another person's personal space, I realized how very much I wanted him to touch me. I stepped into the radiating warmth of his body, my own arms going around his waist as I looked up into his face.

Unfamiliar and not totally unwelcome shivers were radiating through me, and something about the simple nearness of my very big, very masculine friend had all my lady parts switching on. One of Travis's hands was stroking up and down my back, and I pressed into him, laying my cheek on his chest. It wasn't sexy—I'd actually thought maybe I'd try for some light banter or even a quick kiss—but it was intimate. And the stranger thing was that it wasn't awkward at all. I melted into the strength of his body, my hands sliding up the planes of muscle on his back. And when I sensed, more than felt, Travis's lips land on the top of my head and drop a little kiss there, whatever tension had been coiled inside me unspooled just a bit.

"Thanks for helping out," I whispered, turning my face to look up at him again. His big brown eyes were soft, unfocused, as he returned the look.

"I'd do anything for you," he said. He dropped another kiss on the top of my head, and then stiffened, stepping back and breaking the contact between us. "Sorry, phone," he said, reaching for his back pocket and turning away.

My head was buzzing a bit, and I busied myself organizing stock behind the counter in an effort to catch up mentally to whatever had just happened. It was only a hug, right? And we were acting. But it had felt like a lot more.

I straightened up, bringing a box of sunscreen with me to replenish the basket at the end of the counter, and took a few steps down to where the basket sat. Travis was just to my left, and though I wasn't eavesdropping on purpose, I heard a few words.

"You don't mean that," he said, sounding exasperated. "It's really okay. I'm fine with everything." I tried not to focus in on the sad undercurrent in his voice. "Daphne," he said, drawing the name out into a plea. "I made a promise." Then, "I'm just trying to do the right thing here. For once." He sighed, and I glanced at him again, comforted slightly by the fact that Roscoe also seemed to have heard the notes of distress in his voice. The dog was pressed against Travis's leg, while Travis had a hand wrapped around the back of his neck, the other holding his phone pressed to his ear while "Daphne" said whatever it was that was upsetting him so much.

"Okay. We'll talk later," he said finally, and stuffed his phone back into his pocket.

Suddenly, I felt like an intruder, and I quickly dumped the rest of the sunscreen and practically dashed to the other end of the counter, finding the trail maps we kept there very interesting suddenly. I glanced around to see if any of the camera crew had gotten that on film, but they were talking in a huddle at the front of the shop.

Travis wandered the floor of the shop for the next twenty minutes or so, helping the occasional customer until it was time for us to turn things over to Cole and head out in the big van I used for adventures. Despite the tone of his call, Travis seemed to have sprung right back into his usual upbeat demeanor, but I couldn't help wondering who Daphne was.

As we packed up, I hoped we could pull this off. The camera crew had explained that we'd be mic'd on the hike, and that would eliminate any possibility of me giving Travis quiet instructions. He said he'd been rock climbing before. I was just going to have to trust him.

"This everything?" Travis looked over the huge duffel I'd packed up with climbing shoes, harnesses, and other gear. I had two day packs that we'd divide it into. I'd do a rappel demonstration, but we didn't really need all the usual climbing gear since we were just bouldering freestyle. Still, I liked people to wear the harnesses and learn a little about roping in, in case they decided to come back.

"It is," I told him. "You ready?"

He wiggled his eyebrows and grinned. "You know me, babe. I'm always ready."

Ned chuckled over my shoulder, having caught that little gem evidently, then he stepped near as we closed the back of the van up and I moved to the driver's side. "What's the plan?"

"We'll go pick up the group at the resort," I told him. "Then we'll be heading to the spot I showed you on the map. There's a trailhead there that's well marked. Just a quick half mile hike or so to the spot where we'll be climbing."

"Gotcha. We'll just stay behind you here then, but if we get lost, we'll head to the trailhead."

"Sounds good."

Ned strode over to the man and woman who made up his crew, and they all got into the little sedan they'd brought, and followed us out of the parking lot.

"You be good, boy," Travis told Roscoe, who looked a little miffed that he wasn't invited on the hike. "Stay with Cole."

Cole looked a little uncertain about the arrangement too. "He doesn't bite, right?"

"Only if you're trying to hurt me," Travis told him.

A surprised laugh burst from Cole. "Yeah, right. You'd kill me with one hand, man."

"Then you'll be fine. He'll just sleep till I get back," Travis said, seeming to enjoy the recognition of his size and strength.

Travis was quiet on the car ride over, and I wondered if he was thinking about his phone call with Daphne. I wondered a lot of other things too, things that would have been considered none of my business. Like who the hell was Daphne? Why did he seem so distraught as he spoke to her? Was she a sister? A cousin? It couldn't be his mother, he would call her Mom, wouldn't he?

Before I realized I was speaking, words were tumbling out of my mouth. "What do you call your mom?"

"Um." Travis turned to face me, and I used the curving mountain road as an excuse not to meet his gaze. "Mom. Why?"

"Just curious. I call mine Mama." What the hell was wrong with me? Thank god we weren't mic'd up yet.

"But you're not from the Deep South or Texas."

"True. But that's just what I've always called her."

He was quiet a second, and then said, "Glad we got that out in the open. Ned's definitely going to quiz us on that later."

I freed a hand from the wheel long enough to whack Travis on the shoulder.

We pulled into the roundabout in front of the resort, and I let Daphne slip from my mind as I leapt down from the van and headed inside to meet the group.

Aubrey and Archie Kasper were both at the massive wooden desk in the lobby when I stepped inside, and I gave them a happy wave. Travis followed me to one side of the wide space to where a group lingered on the low couches scattered near a little wooden table.

The group was made up of both kids and adults, and they were all buzzing with an air of excitement. I loved this part of my job—meeting different people, introducing them to things that were new to them.

Ned and his crew set up cameras and lights in a flash, and I waited only a few seconds longer than I normally would to greet the group, which had already been briefed by the resort staff about the filming.

"Hi there," I said, addressing the men, women, and kids who smiled back at me. "I'm CeeCee and this is Travis. We're here from Kasper Gear and Guides to take you guys bouldering this afternoon. Are you ready?"

The group smiled and nodded, a few words were uttered, but they seemed nervous. That was normal, and it was my job to put their minds at ease.

"Can we do a quick intro?" I asked.

"I'm Toby Wright," one man said. "This is my wife Deanna, and our daughters Beth and Adrian." The girls were probably ten and eight—perfect ages for this adventure, and both bouncing at the edges of the low couch, smiling tentatively.

"And we're the Hallstens," the other woman said, indicating a second family. "From Arizona. I'm Sandy, and this is Todd, and our three kids, Eric, Sam, and Conner." These kids were tweens, I thought, though Eric might've been fifteen or so. The older kids had a slightly bored air about them, but I'd guided enough teens to know it wasn't personal, and that it would shift as soon as the activity caught their interest. I loved teenagers—they were just on the brink of independence, and they shifted easily back and forth between an unbridled little-kid excitement and this faux adult ennui. My goal was always to get the little kids back for a bit, and the Rocky Mountains usually helped me do it. It was just so gorgeous and overwhelmingly awesome up here.

"Perfect," I said. "Well, I've got all the gear we need in the van, and we'll go over some basics once we reach the site. Until then, it's mostly just a gorgeous walk up an easy trail. How does that sound?"

"Sounds great," Travis said. I shot him a look to see if he'd forgotten he was actually supposed to be in charge, but his sentiments were echoed by the family, and no one seemed to think anything of his enthusiasm.

"Terrific," I said. "Just to do a quick check, does everyone have water, sunscreen, a hat, and some ChapStick? The sun is pretty fierce up here, and I'd hate for anyone to miss out enjoying themselves because of sunburn or dehydration."

Toby looked distressed suddenly. "I don't think we remembered about the water. We didn't bring bottles." He looked around like his wife might suddenly produce four water bottles from her tiny fanny pack. She returned the look, her eyebrows climbing as she shrugged.

"No worries. They've got a great gear shop here at the resort." I made a point of pushing business back there, since Archie and Aubrey had done so much to help support my business. "Travis, could you run Toby in to grab some water bottles? I've got the cooler full in the van, and you can fill up out there."

"You got it, hon." He and Toby headed through the lobby toward the resort shop. A weird little thrill shot through me at the familiar nickname. I'd dated before, but I'd never gotten close enough with anyone for them to use terms of endearment like that. "Ceese" was the closest anyone ever got, and there was something comforting about the way Travis had said the simple word. Something that made me feel like we shared things, like we were in it together. Which, for the week at least, we were.

I made small talk with the remaining guests, reassuring

them about the ease of today's climb, and the fact it was perfect for newbies. My eyes flicked to the camera crew repeatedly, and I was conscious that they could hear every word I spoke through the tiny microphone they'd clipped to my shirt. I had a little battery pack in my pocket that Ned had said I could switch off if I needed to say anything that shouldn't be caught on film.

My eyes were pulled to the side of the lobby as Travis and Toby emerged from the shop, bottles in hand. Travis walked beside the smaller man, and it was impossible not to appreciate his sheer physical presence. He was bigger than any guy I'd ever dated, and he had a confident and easygoing air that followed him wherever he went. He looked intimidating and sexy all at once, somewhat at odds with the goofy guy I knew him to be.

"Your boyfriend is pretty handsome," Toby's wife said at my side, watching them approach.

"He is," I agreed. I didn't have to act to make that sound genuine. "And we're actually engaged." That was harder to get out, but I knew the crew would wonder.

"Congratulations!"

When they'd returned, four Kasper Ridge Resort water bottles in hand, we headed outside and loaded up. Soon, we were on our way to the trailhead.

It felt different, though. This is what I did almost every day, but most of the time I did it myself or with one of the contract guides I used up here in the mountains to help with the more aggressive adventures. Today, having Travis at my side felt nice, like I suddenly wasn't in it alone. Like someone had my back. I wasn't used to relying on anyone else—even my brother was pretty flaky at the best of times.

It would be hard to go back to doing everything alone. But since I'd be on an incredible adventure, I figured I'd manage.

Chapter Nine
Smolder Boulder

TRAVIS

CeeCee was a total professional, getting those two families geared up and hydrated in the parking lot before we set out. It reminded me a little bit of prepping for missions back in the military, but the gorgeous day and the fresh air made it easy to keep bad memories at bay.

"It's a quick hike up to the bouldering area," she explained. "And if you'll carry your own shoes, we've got chalk and the crash pad and everything else we're going to need up there.

"Bouldering is a lot of fun, and it's a great way to enjoy the incredible scenery here in Colorado. It's pretty safe, obviously depending on how aggressive you decide to be with it, but there are a few technique items we'll cover once we get up there."

She grinned around at the group, her smile bright beneath the brim of her hat. She looked every bit the adventure guide in her cargo pants and tank top, her slim athletic build reassuring in itself. She also looked gorgeous—confident and sure. It was sexy as hell, and I found myself pulled toward her even more than usual.

She made me feel safe. I knew it didn't really make sense since I was twice her size, but CeeCee seemed to have the world on a string, and if I was next to her, I did too. It was part of why we'd become friends in the first place—I was drawn to her.

But if I was honest, the way her small firm breasts filled out her tank top and her long tanned limbs didn't hurt a bit, either.

We headed up the trail, me shouldering a pack with one of the pads inside and CeeCee carrying the other.

As we hiked a gentle grade toward the bouldering area, I tried not to think about the call I'd taken back in the shop.

Daphne was part of the past, part of my failures, part of what I was trying to escape up here among these soaring mountains and shadowing trees. And I'd been doing my best to put the whole situation behind me. But now she wanted to discuss it, reconsider it. In my mind, we'd done what we'd done, and I would move on from there. I'd never thought it would be something we would need to think about again.

I'd been wrong, clearly. But I didn't want to think about it today.

It took less than thirty minutes to reach the area CeeCee had in mind, and as the group put down their packs and changed their hiking shoes for flexible climbing shoes, CeeCee gave us all a quick introduction to rock climbing. She stood at the base of a big rock, explaining the way difficulty was measured, using something called the Font scale, and talking about how rock climbing like this built strength and mental fortitude, how figuring out a bouldering problem often helped her figure out how to handle other problems in her life.

Maybe bouldering was exactly what I needed.

CeeCee dipped her hands into the bag of white powder she'd brought, showing the group how she shook it off and rubbed her hands together, leaving a thin coating just on her palms and fingers for grip. Then she turned and faced the rock, and climbed it slowly, explaining her next move to the group as she located the footholds and hand grips that let her climb to the top.

Her body moved with ease and grace, and I was struck again at how capable and strong she was. It was funny, actually. I was huge and muscled and people assumed that meant I could handle anything and that I was tough. But CeeCee had me beat, up, down, and sideways. And dammit if she didn't look sexy as hell doing it.

"You don't need to climb all the way up," she called down from fifteen feet over our heads, the sun making a bright crown of her light hair now that she'd pulled off her hat. "You go as high as you feel comfortable. It is a bit harder climbing down. And if you need to just let go, well, that's what the pads are for. Just remember what I taught you about falling safely."

The group was shifting their feet and murmuring with anticipation, and once CeeCee had descended, she split the two families up, sending Toby's with me to a nearby boulder. His kids were younger, and our boulder was smaller. My job, she'd said in the van, was just to eyeball them as they climbed, helping them spot the next hold and assisting them down if needed. I was fine being responsible for their safety—even the kids. Something inside me had always been drawn to the idea of helping people. Maybe it was my size, or my strength. I wanted to use it to ensure the well-being of other people, to look out for them if I could. Looking out for this family felt second nature to me, even if bouldering wasn't something I'd done much of before.

We were near enough to the other group to hear them and see them, but not so close that it was hard to focus on the face of the rock in front of us.

"Who's going first?" I asked them. I'd eyeballed our boulder and had a good sense of where they'd want to begin.

"Dad!" Toby's kids volunteered him, and he made quick work of scaling the rock to the top.

"Show off," his wife laughed. "He's done this before," she told me.

I grinned at her, feeling a lightness in my chest I wasn't accustomed to. Something about the clear, fresh air, the wide blue sky overhead, and the confidence I felt in helping this family have a great day all worked together to relieve some of the ache I usually carried around.

"Me next!" Beth piped up. She was the younger of the two daughters, and something about her sheer excitement had me grinning as Toby finished his descent.

"Great. Let's get you all ready," I said, pointing at the little rosin bag. Beth plunged her hands inside, sending little puffs of white dust up around her, and came out with her hands completely coated.

"That ought to be plenty," I laughed, helping her brush off the excess over the bag. "Rub 'em together a bit to get it between your fingers there," I suggested.

Beth, it seemed, did everything with great enthusiasm. She practically flung herself at the rock, finding her first two hand-holds easily. She couldn't use the same holds her dad had used, and it was a little tougher finding low holds that could accommodate her shorter wing span. I loved her determination and zest, and found myself grinning as she spread out over the face of the rock, her little limbs stretched. Her head turned to me, looking for help, and I stepped up close to her.

"There you go," I told her, pointing at a grip just above her left hand. She was spread-eagled on the rock, only about three feet over the pad on the ground. "Just need to move your left foot up a notch to this bump here so you can grab it."

Beth didn't move immediately, and when I caught her eye again, there was uncertainty growing there. "I can't." Her voice had decreased in both volume and excitement. My heart squeezed. I knew that feeling.

"Sure you can, honey!" her mom called from behind us.

I shot Deanna a reassuring smile and stepped a bit closer to Beth as Toby and her sister watched in silence. Beth's little face was even with mine as I leaned down next to her.

"You've got this, little buddy," I told her. "Just pretend you're a monkey."

She gave me a half smile at that. "I like monkeys."

"Well, they're pretty good climbers, right?"

She nodded.

"So all you need to do is just move your back paw"—I tapped her left calf—"up a teeny tiny bit, and you'll be able to move your front paw here." I showed her the next hold, about four inches over where her little hand gripped.

She took a shuddering breath. "Okay," she said. "You stay right there, okay?"

I nodded seriously, every protective instinct I had firing at once. "I'm not going anywhere, monkey."

Beth slid her foot up the rock and found the bump I'd shown her, and then, without a pause, she moved her left hand up to grab the next hold. I wanted to jump and yell and cheer her on, but I stood quietly by, ready to help if she needed it.

"There you go!" Toby called from behind us.

After her initial hesitation, she seemed to gain confidence, and soon my little monkey pal was scaling the rock like she was born to it.

"Not too high, Beth," her mom called. "You've got to come down, remember."

"I'm a monkey!" Beth called back. And she was, she scrambled up and back down without a second wasted. A warm satisfaction spread inside me and I let it soothe the parts of me that didn't feel so confident, the parts that knew life wasn't always this good.

"Hey," Toby said, stepping close to my side once Beth was back on the ground. "Thanks for that. Must be nice to know you're really good at your job, huh?"

I chuckled, feeling the praise work itself through me. I'd never been especially great at any job, so it was a strange compliment, but one I accepted happily. I was just glad I hadn't screwed anything up, especially with the cameras on. So far, I was doing a good job acting like a confident rock-climbing guide.

My group finished up a bit before CeeCee's, and we moved over to watch them wrap up. It was enlightening watching how CeeCee encouraged and assisted the family. She had such a reassuring nature, like if you were with her, everything would be fine. And when she was explaining something or helping someone, her eyes shone with genuine care and her voice held both her love of her job and of the people she worked with. She was so entirely in her element, it was hard not to be completely taken in.

I wanted that. If I couldn't have it myself, I wanted to be closer to whatever it was in her.

"You really love her, huh man?" Ned was suddenly at my side, and I realized I'd probably been staring at CeeCee with something like open adoration. I hadn't meant to be so unguarded, but at least it would play well on camera.

It didn't feel like a lie when I responded. "I do." I felt the truth of it in the way my heart squeezed with the words, the way my skin warmed. I tore my eyes from her and looked at Ned, who smiled back at me. "Yeah man, I really do."

"That's awesome. You guys are a great couple. I really hope you win this thing."

For a second, it felt like he'd punched me or someone had

sucked all the sunshine out of the day. I'd just about forgotten that there was an end goal to this, and that winning meant CeeCee leaving. "Me too," I told him, knowing what it would mean to CeeCee to win.

"Where will you go? With the trip money?"

CeeCee had told me that part of the prize was money for an adventure trip, but I hadn't pressed to find out to where. I didn't like thinking about Kasper Ridge without the possibility of bumping into CeeCee. And even if it was just a trip and she would eventually return, I hated the idea of her leaving at all.

"I don't know," I admitted. "I guess we didn't want to jinx ourselves by planning too far in advance."

"Cool. I hear you, though. About planning too far ahead." Ned nodded and then headed over to talk to the woman who had a camera on a tripod, trained on CeeCee as she set up a system of ropes while the families looked on.

CeeCee demonstrated the way climbers would use ropes on bigger climbs, hooking into anchors that had already been placed in the rock. As she finished, I belayed her back to the ground, feeling strangely aware of my own body as I carefully lowered her down. It felt like the most important thing I'd done in a while—ensuring her safety. The enormity of that idea worked its way into my mind while we packed up and hiked back down to the vans, and by the time I we were in the van, taking the families back to the resort, my head was spinning.

What had I gotten into?

Chapter Ten
Ruh-Roh, Daphne!

TRAVIS

We dropped the families back at the resort, and then rode back to the shop together, the big van suddenly quiet without the excited voices of our adventurers. I held a fifty dollar bill that Toby had palmed me when he'd said goodbye, thanking me. It felt strange to me, being paid like that. As if it cheapened the whole thing.

"Nah," CeeCee said when I showed it to her. "I make all my fun money in tips. Most people are really generous on vacation, especially if they spend their day feeling like they're actually facing a fear or challenging nature. You earned it."

"It should be yours. It's your business."

"You're helping. And I appreciate it."

I shrugged. Fifty dollars was nothing to shake a stick at, so I shoved it into my pocket. I wasn't hurting for cash, but I definitely appreciated the value of a dollar. I'd find a way to give it back to CeeCee later.

At the shop, Roscoe bounded toward me as I came in, and Cole reported that he'd stayed in the back all afternoon, curled up asleep.

"Like he was just waiting for you to get back."

"Good boy," I told my dog, lavishing him with love. I'd thought of Roscoe as we'd hiked—mostly about how much he'd love sniffing along the trail and the rocks—but I hadn't felt unmoored without him at my side. Roscoe was usually my anchor, but maybe CeeCee had played that role today. Or maybe I'd managed to do it myself.

CeeCee checked in with Cole and then let him go for the evening and turned to me soon after. "You can head out too, Sass."

The camera crew had gone back to their house rental for the night, and no one was around. It felt strange to hear CeeCee use my callsign after she'd called me Travis all day.

"I think I like you calling me Travis better," I said.

She stopped moving around behind the glass counter and turned to face me, her bright eyes glowing as she smiled up at me. "Okay," she said. "Thanks for all the help today. See you tomorrow morning?"

"I'll be here," I told her. "What's on the agenda?"

"River rafting bright and early. Eight o'clock pickup at the resort."

I'd be done baking long before then anyway. "Meet you there?" I asked.

CeeCee's eyes clouded, and she drew her bottom lip between her teeth. "Well, I guess. But if Ned is with us, don't you think he'll find it weird that you're staying at the resort?"

I let out a quick breath, realizing she was right. "Yep, sorry. Forgot about that."

CeeCee dropped my gaze, one hand touching her freckled

cheek softly. "I'm sorry about all this, Travis, I feel crappy for pulling you into my lie and disrupting your schedule and—"

"Hey," I dropped a hand on her shoulder, letting my fingers feel the soft skin there, and trying to ignore the thoughts racing through my mind at the touch. "I'm here because I want to be."

She didn't say anything for a second, just stared up into my face in a way that was causing a series of tiny explosions to chase one another up my spine at the contact and the warmth in her eyes. "Okay," she finally breathed.

"Just gonna go grab something," I said, forcing myself to step away from her and heading into the back. I needed to put a little space between us before I forgot this was all pretend. I tucked the fifty-dollar bill into the side of CeeCee's bag with her car keys, and then headed back out. "Let's go, Roscoe!"

My dog trotted to my side, and we headed out the front door of the shop and to the SUV, my heart feeling strangled and tight inside my chest as I considered how natural it would have felt to lean down and kiss CeeCee in that moment back in the shop. I'd wanted to. A lot.

* * *

The resort was busy when I arrived, and I dodged through the lobby with Roscoe, heading upstairs to my room without bumping into anyone I needed to stop and chat with, which was a relief. I had a lot on my mind, and needed a long shower.

I needed to figure out how to handle Daphne. I wasn't sure she really knew what she was asking for, or if maybe she was just asking out of some misplaced belief that it would be better for me if I did what she wanted. Or if she was feeling guilty somehow. I owed her a call back, but wanted to see if I could understand her motives by replaying the conversation in my head a few times first. We'd had an agreement, and I didn't back away from things like that easily.

The hot water sluiced down my body as I did my best to push away the anxiety that threatened to overtake me as I considered. I turned away from the beating stream, bowing my head and letting it pummel my back as I breathed deeply, exhaling some of the stress and uncertainty.

I knew I needed to try to put my feelings for CeeCee back into their box. We were only pretending, and while there were moments when she looked at me in a way that made me feel like this was anything but pretend, I had to keep myself in check.

I finished up in the shower, working hard to remind myself what this was. And what it wasn't.

When that was done, I felt a little bit better, though my mind was still a jumble. I needed a distraction, so I went to the little desk at the side of my room and sat down at the computer there.

For the better part of an hour, I searched photos and recipes for wedding cakes, feeling more and more certain I would be able to deliver on the promise I'd made Ghost. I'd have to see if we had all the ingredients in the kitchen later, and would need to put in a quick order to the restaurant supply if not.

My search for cake photos morphed into looking at wedding photos before too long, and soon I found myself staring at pictures of smiling people, towering cakes in the background or not there at all. The styled photos—the ones that were clearly from magazines or wedding sites—were glossy and perfect, smiling people posing for the camera in a way that made me wonder if they were married in real life, or if it was all just an act. But in the candid shots I found, there was a lot more to see.

Some of the grooms looked terrified or angry. Some of the brides looked scared too, and some looked beautiful, of course. I flipped to a folder of photos I kept on my desktop. The bride in these looked gorgeous and happy, even though her dress was simple and these were snapshots from the courthouse in our little Texas town. And the groom? He looked terrified and unsteady, half-drunk, and like a complete idiot. I hated that guy. His family looked proud, though. They had been proud. What would they think if they knew the truth?

I slammed the laptop lid down, startling Roscoe to his feet.

"Sorry, buddy," I told him.

I rose, rubbing my hands through my hair and over my face, taking deep breaths and trying to force my mind to focus ahead, not behind. There were so many things I couldn't change, but what I did right now? I could affect that.

Roscoe followed me to the big plate glass window that overlooked the front of the resort. It was dark out, and I figured the crew would probably be out back by the fire.

"Let's go," I told Roscoe, and we headed out to sit with the others under the dark Colorado sky.

Sure enough, I could see a flicker of flames through the canopy of trees, at the fire pit in the center of the yurts out back. Aubrey had envisioned a glamping experience when the place had first opened, but it had never taken off. Now the yurts were staff housing, and the central fire pit back there was the place we usually gravitated at the end of a long day when the resort was full of guests. We used to spend a lot of time in the bar, but that was before the Kasper Ridge Resort had become a real destination, a place that was booked up almost a year in advance.

"There he is," Ghost called as I stepped into the flickering light of the fire pit.

"Hey man," Antonio said, slapping the arm of the big Adirondack chair at his side. "Saved you a seat."

"How was the adventuring today?" Monroe asked. She shared a chair with Mateo, wrapped in his arms and looking gorgeous and happy.

I grabbed a beer from the cooler by one of the yurts and sat down. These guys knew I was helping CeeCee. They didn't know the extent of the help though. As in, they had no idea we were pretending to be a couple. I wanted to tell them. There'd been enough missteps in my past that I was certain creating complication was never a recipe for success, but this wasn't my secret to tell.

"Yeah, it was good," I told them. "Did some bouldering with a couple families. They seemed to enjoy themselves."

"More adventures tomorrow?" Aubrey asked. She sat across the circle, and the flickering light caught the highlights in her dark mass of long hair. She too shared a chair, and the long lanky arm wrapped around her waist belonged to Wiley, who looked relaxed and content.

"Rafting," I said, taking a long swallow of my beer. I was a little bit worried about the rafting trip. I'd never been rafting, but I knew it could be serious, even dangerous. I wasn't worried about me, more about whether my lack of experience would allow me to be the help I'd need to be for Ceese, and for the families who were trusting us. The last thing I wanted was to let anyone down.

Soon enough, the conversation went back to whatever it had been about when I'd arrived, and I was able to sit quietly and just absorb the reassurance that came with being an accepted part of a group. These guys knew me as well as anyone, the guys I'd served with at least. And then there was Antonio, who knew me better than anyone since I'd been out. I caught him watching me a couple times, a question in his gaze, and I gave him a quick nod to let him know I was okay. He was a good guy. A little too worried about me. But maybe he had reasons to be.

Eventually the talk around the fire ended up in the same place it almost always did if Ghost was present, and I grinned.

"I just don't understand it," he was saying. "Uncle Marvin wanted us to figure out that he wrote a bunch of movies? We already knew that."

"Yeah, but he pointed us to movies he didn't write," Aubrey said.

"No," Wiley said. "You said earlier they were movies he might have written."

She blew out a frustrated breath. "I miss the days when we were running all over the mountain following an actual map."

"Searching for booty," I added. Ghost shot me a look.

"That was fun," Fake Tom agreed. "But this part of the hunt, where we have to actually figure something out, something real—it feels more authentic."

"Except we haven't figured anything out," Ghost said. "Marvin and Rudy were friends and partners. And then they weren't. And then they were enemies. Rudy opened Mountaintop Studios, Uncle Marvin came up here. End of story?"

Aubrey nodded. "And don't forget that Rudy and Uncle Marvin both loved Aunt Lola."

Lola, we'd discovered, was the rising star Annie Lowe, who had starred in a number of old Hollywood films and had been engaged to Rudy at one point. The crazy treasure hunt Uncle Marvin had left his niece and nephew had led us all over the place, and finally to an actual treasure chest in a tunnel below the resort. But the chest had been filled with costume jewelry and a photo album that contained a bunch of old photos of Marvin, his wife Lola, and other people who'd been captured in the midst of their lives in the pages of the book. The last page had held a list of movie titles. It was a puzzle I was intrigued by, though I doubted I'd be much help solving it.

"You get a daddy pass tonight?" I asked Fake Tom.

"Something like that," he said, raising his beer. "Tomorrow night Lucy's hanging with the ladies, so I got tonight. I'll be on wakeup duty later though."

There were murmurs of understanding around the circle, particularly from Penny and Brainiac, who sat to Antonio's side, Brainiac wearing a baby strapped to his chest.

"I don't think I got to compliment you on your accessories when I arrived," I said now, leaning toward him.

It was meant to be a lighthearted jab—Brainiac historically could not handle much real taunting without becoming angry—but he just smiled and patted the back of the tiny baby he held.

"You like it?" he said, grinning. "She's my favorite thing in the world." He glanced at Penny then, his eyes darkening. "Maybe my second favorite, actually."

Penny and Brainiac had welcomed their daughter, Maggie, the same night Lucy and Fake Tom got married. She was a tiny little red-headed thing whose full name was Magnolia, and my heart squeezed every time I stared down into her tiny perfect face. I couldn't wait until she called me Uncle Sass and I could teach her all kinds of things that would drive Brainiac absolutely crazy.

It was actually a bit much, all the love around the fire. I'd come out here so I didn't feel alone, but for some reason being in the middle of all these happy couples made me feel lonelier than ever. "Got an early morning on the river," I told the group, rising. "Gonna call it a night."

I went back to the resort, but I didn't manage to get much sleep. As usual, my mind didn't seem to want to relax. I did research a full history of Mountaintop Studios, however, and Annie Lowe's full catalog of films. I'd also baked three different sponges, trying to figure out which would be sturdiest for layers but still moist and delicious.

Only A Touch

By the time Roscoe and I were heading to CeeCee's place, I was almost tired enough not to feel confused about every choice I'd ever made in my life.

What better time to risk one's life on a roaring river?

Chapter Eleven
Bump! Or Not...

CEECEE

I was at the store early the next morning, and as the sun began to lighten the trees outside, promising another gorgeous blue-sky day, Travis pulled into the parking lot. I watched as he stepped out of the big SUV, Roscoe on his heels.

There wasn't enough light yet to see his face clearly, but I'd seen enough of it the day before that my mind could fill in every detail. The scruff of a beard covering the square jaw, the dark soulful eyes that so often danced with laughter, the wide full mouth so quick with a joke.

I didn't want to jinx anything, but the previous day had gone well—better than I could have expected. Travis had been great with the guests, and that part was no surprise. He was warm and generous, and people naturally liked him. But he'd been great with me too, managing to work as my back up, my partner even, as if we'd been working together for years.

My stomach turned a little flip as he stepped inside the

shop, that smile appearing as soon as he caught me watching him from behind the counter.

"Hey," he offered, sounding almost uncertain.

"Hey," I said back. "Sorry to drag you out of bed so early today."

His smile flickered a bit and he shook his head. "Not a problem. I'm usually up anyway."

I wasn't sure exactly what that meant, but assumed he was saying he was a morning person. I knew he baked for the resort and that had to happen at ungodly hours, so figured that must be it. I pointed to the coffee pot on the far side of the store where I kept a pot full for customers most mornings, and he headed toward it.

Roscoe sat down facing the counter and stared up at me with his big amber eyes, as if waiting to be properly greeted.

"Hi Roscoe," I said. I moved around the long counter to kneel down in front of the dog, who sniffed at my neck as I pushed my hands down his back and rubbed his furry chest. "I've got something for you today too," I told him, standing back up and moving toward the counter.

Roscoe seemed to understand this was an invitation, and he followed me curiously to find the spot where I'd put down a mat and a big water dish. I kept a dish outside for visiting dogs—as most places in Colorado did—but Roscoe was the only inside dog, so I figured he deserved his own dish.

Travis watched Roscoe drink greedily as he sipped from a coffee mug. "That was nice of you."

"He's a good dog," I said. "And I actually always wanted to get a store dog."

"Oh yeah?" Travis smiled down at his dog, like he was considering this new title for him.

"Totally," I said. "But since I live with my mom and my brother, it's not really my decision."

"You didn't have a dog growing up?"

I watched Travis sip his coffee, his biceps bulging in the black T-shirt he wore as he lifted the cup to his full lips.

I had to tear my eyes away. *Drinking coffee is not sexy. Drinking coffee is not sexy.*

Except . . . I was coming to realize that pretty much everything Travis did was sexy, especially when you threw in the genuine interest and concern that had accompanied his question.

"No dog," I answered, forcing my eyes to Roscoe again. "When Dad was around, he and Mama both worked a lot. It probably wouldn't have been fair to the dog. You had a dog growing up?"

Travis grinned. "A couple, yeah. The first one was Buck. He was supposed to be a working dog, sleeping in the barn and all that. Domesticated but not coddled."

"I sense a 'but' coming."

Travis laughed. "Yep. Since I was the youngest, I'd get left behind a lot when my brothers rode out to help Dad, and if Buck didn't have to work, he and I had adventures."

I laughed. "Adventures?"

The huge man in front of me nodded, putting his cup on the counter. "I took him inside and read books to him sometimes, and other times we just explored out behind the property line where there was a river flowing. He became my companion, and eventually he slept in my bed with me."

"Your parents must have loved you a lot to have given in to that one."

"They didn't know for a few months. I'd sneak him in at night. But one time I was sick, and Mom came in to check on me, and Buck was there."

"Was she mad?" I asked, trying hard to picture Travis little and mostly failing.

"Nah, she's my mama. She's got a soft spot for her sons," he said. "Long story short, Dad got a new working dog, and when Buck died, I brought that one in too. And then the next."

I laughed. "Oh my god, that's hilarious."

Travis beamed at Roscoe, who returned the adoring look.

It was quiet in the store this early, no music playing over the system and no hum of customers shopping. Usually I enjoyed the quiet, but with Travis's enormous form on the other side of the counter, I felt unusually self-conscious.

"I, uh, we should get ready and do a gear check," I told him. "The boats are down at the outpost, and I've got a contracted guide meeting us there. We just need to bring the PFDs and paddles, first aid kit, and my gear."

"You have special gear?" Travis raised an eyebrow.

"There are certain things I'm required to carry as a certified guide and some things I bring because I might need them." I retrieved my raft bag from the back and brought it to the counter, pulling out the items I'd carry with me. "The pulleys and prussic loops, rope and carabineers probably aren't necessary on this trip, but I like to be extra careful."

"You use those to design fancy dumbwaiters in case you see tasty treats up high in the trees?" Travis joked.

"Or to allow me to lift hundreds of pounds of water in the super unlikely event of a raft getting pinned under the river."

"Or that," Travis nodded, crossing his arms and watching me gather my things with interest.

I wrapped my flip line around my waist, fastening it with another carabineer, and met Travis's eyes, waiting for the question.

"The height of river fashion," he quipped.

"The flip line," I told him. "I can use it to right a flipped raft and help get everyone back in." I pulled the bag open wide for him to see the rope coiled inside. "And we'll bring the rest of this in the bag. If someone goes for an unexpected swim, this is our first rescue tool."

"Gotcha." Travis rubbed his neck, something I was beginning to see was a sign of discomfort. "Hey, CeeCee, do you think I'm going to get in your way here? I've never done this before."

I shook my head, but it took me a second to respond. Seeing Travis less than certain was new. The sudden vulnerability made him even more attractive and I thought again of the little boy, adopting the work dog because his brothers left him behind. "You'll be with me, and the contracted guide at the outpost will take the second raft. It's all good. The only thing we'll need to account for is your size in the boat. Hopefully one of the guests will be big enough to balance you."

A buzz of excitement was beginning in my veins. I loved rafting, and there was a part of me that couldn't wait to share it with Travis. Knowing he'd never been made me giddy to experience it with him, but also a teensy bit worried, realizing he would have to pretend like he knew what he was doing.

Adelaide arrived just as I was finishing outfitting Travis and making sure he had sunscreen on.

"Good morning, Adelaide."

The older woman stopped in the center of the store, looking between me and Travis, her head finally swiveling to Roscoe, who sat at Travis's feet. "Hello," she said, her tone curious.

"This is Travis," I told her. "My, er. Um, he's my . . . fiancé."

"Good morning, ma'am." Travis reached out a hand for her to shake, but I could already see the wheels turning furiously beneath the short gray hair.

Adelaide looked Travis up and down, shaking his hand lightly. "Pleased to meet you," she said, and then fixed her gaze on me. "Care to explain anything?"

Oh crap. I should have told her earlier about all this, maybe even let her in on the plan. Adelaide had known me my whole life and was friends with my mother. I was certain she was wondering why she hadn't known about this before. But on second thought, I couldn't let her in on the plan—she was the worst gossip in town.

"It happened kind of suddenly," I said, knowing she wasn't going to be satisfied with that. "We can tell you the whole story when we get back from rafting," I said, forcing laughter into my voice. "It's pretty funny actually."

Travis elbowed me in the back. "Funny?" His voice was amused.

"Is this animal going to remain here while you raft?" she asked, watching Roscoe uncertainly as Travis and I gathered gear together.

"He's a good companion, ma'am. But I can take him back to the resort if you'd rather."

Adelaide looked at Roscoe again, and then over at me. I gave her a little shrug and a smile, letting her know it was up to her. She would only be here an hour or so, just until Cole came in to take over, but I didn't want her to be uncomfortable.

She put a hand out, and Roscoe, as if sensing that he should be gentle and calm, rose and padded toward her, putting his big head into her hand like he needed her to hold the weight of it for a moment. I chuckled as he just stood there, waiting for her to pet him.

"Oh, you're a lover, aren't you?" she asked the big dog, rubbing the top of his head with her other hand. Relief wound its way through me, both at Adelaide's acceptance of her morning companion and at her willingness to drop the questions about my new fiancé. Soon, Roscoe had laid down and rolled to his back, and Adelaide was busily rubbing his belly. "I think we'll be fine," she laughed. "In fact, I might not give him back."

"Roscoe will keep you company," Travis said, "But I'll definitely want him back if I survive this crazy river trip."

"CeeCee will take good care of you," Adelaide said, straightening up. "Congratulations, by the way. I am a little surprised to learn y'all are engaged, I have to say. Darling girl, I didn't even know you had a boyfriend." She sniffed as if this omission offended her slightly.

"Thanks," I said. "I'm sorry I didn't mention it."

I exchanged a worried look with Travis, and then I told them both, "We'd better run or we'll be late."

* * *

An hour and a half later, we were standing to one side of the wide rumbling river, nine Kasper Ridge guests decked out in helmets and PFDs, smeared with extra sunscreen, listening to me explain the way we'd work together to move down the river. The camera crew was off to one side, also wearing gear. They'd be splitting between the rafts for the actual trip down river. The extra guide I'd contracted, Allie, was at my side, piping up with additional tips here and there, and Travis had even managed to sound official as he reminded guests about the altitude and need for extra sun protection.

"The chances of anyone going swimming today are slim," I assured them. "It's late in the season, and the river's not too high. In the spring, there are some class four spots in here, but we're not going to see anything faster than a three today. Should be a nice, leisurely ride for the most part, with one fun little chute at the end."

We went over everyone's roles, I talked about paddle holds and some of the commands the guides would use depending on the situation. Soon enough we were loading up and launching into the gently rolling water, the crowning points of pine trees spearing the brilliant sky on either side.

Travis was at my left side as I sat in the back of the boat to act as a rudder and get the best view of what was coming. I was a little worried about Travis having never done this before, but he seemed comfortable, and even authoritative as he took his spot next to me. Arthur, the biggest guy from the guest group, was on my right. The rest of the crew from the resort was teenagers and adults, half of whom were in the other guide's raft just behind us. There were no kids, which was a relief. Sometimes having those light little bodies in the raft made me nervous, since they were often the most likely to end up in the water if things got rough.

My group was doing great with their paddles, keeping us facing forward and helping steer away from rocks. We paddled down the river for just over an hour, enjoying the scenery and the beautiful day.

I found myself relaxing as we went, enjoying the sound of the water, the laughter of the group, and the nearness of Travis's reassuring form at my side. He'd proven to be a fast learner, and his thoughtful presence put the rest of the group at ease. Every now and then, his leg would press against my bare thigh, sending a rash of shivers through me that had little to do with the icy water through which we paddled.

I'd always liked Travis, had found him to be good-natured and easygoing. And maybe it was the pretense that had started me entertaining thoughts of what it would be like to be with him —to *be* with him—but I was finding myself wishing we could spend time together without the cameras. What would it be like to go out on a real date with Travis? And did he think about me that way at all, or was he just being the nice guy he was, doing me the favor I'd asked for?

The raft behind us was a good distance back, and overall

there was a sense of calm enjoyment among the rafters. The total trip was just two hours long, which was plenty if you were actually having to work to keep the boat upright. Late summer rafting was much more leisurely than early season, that was for sure.

As we approached the speedy section toward the end of the route, I gave them a few reminders. Everything so far had gone so well, I wasn't worried. I found Travis's eyes on me, a thoughtful look on his face as I reminded the rafters what they'd need to do to navigate the faster water. I liked his attention. Maybe more than I should have.

"If you hear me yell 'high side,' we need to move weight to the highest part of the boat to help keep it from flipping."

"But that won't happen, right?" the woman named Trina asked from her spot toward the front.

"The flipping part, probably not. At least not if we all do what we need to do!" I gave her a grin, trying to be sympathetic to her fear. People tended to forget that this was actually a pretty dangerous sport, depending on the time of year. I was definitely prepared to save people if I had to, but so many problems on the river could be avoided if people just paid attention to the instructions and followed directions. Most people, I found, were pretty good at doing what was needed when the tension was high, and groups like this tended to look out for one another.

The river was picking up some speed, and I caught Travis's eyes as we bumped along toward the turn that would shoot us through the rapids and back into calm water below. "Having fun?" I asked him.

"Hell yeah," he grinned.

I loved his excitement, his aptitude and his willingness to throw himself into things. If I did have a boyfriend, I'd want him to be like Travis in that way.

Ned was in our raft, hovering in the middle so he could film. It wasn't my favorite situation, but I understood that it would be nearly impossible for him to paddle and film. We'd come out without our mics on for today since they weren't waterproof and he was close enough to catch our conversations on camera.

"Oh no," someone at the front of the boat called, clearly having spotted the roiling whitewater of the little rapids ahead.

"It's not as bad as it looks," I assured them. "Just a little bumpy and quick. Let's paddle on the left here!" We maneuvered the raft around a rock, the right side of the boat leveraging by holding paddles into the water as Travis and Arthur actually paddled backward, exactly as instructed. This was going perfectly.

"Great!" I called out. "Bump!" The group reacted appropriately, dropping their paddle ends to the bottom of the boat and moving inward. At least everyone but Trina did. When I called bump, she shot me a panicked look, like she'd forgotten what the command meant.

I began reminding her, but there wasn't enough time. "Center of the boat!" I called.

The raft collided on the right side with the big boulder we'd sweep around, but Trina was half standing, moving into bump position too late. When the raft shuddered, it sent her backward, and she flew over the side into an open pool swirling with white water.

Adrenaline surged as the boat righted itself and I scanned for my ousted passenger. She hadn't hit a rock on the way out, but I didn't see her.

"Crap!" I called, grabbing for the throw bag. "Back to positions!"

Trina's head popped up about six feet from the boat, her paddle about three feet from her. Relief calmed me slightly. She was bobbing in the water, clearly having ignored every bit of instruction I'd offered about what to do if you ended up in the water. There were plenty of hidden rocks under the surface and the water was moving fast enough to create the force needed to break a bone if she smashed against one—or worse, to pull her down if she got caught.

"On your back, head up!" I yelled.

Trina's teenaged son was leaning out toward her, extending his paddle for her to grab, but it was at least three feet away. "You!" I commanded, "Back in the boat, paddle in the water."

Travis was calm and collected at my side, I heard his authoritative voice calling commands to the other paddlers as we approached the final chute. I was on my knees in the back of the boat, readying the rope and keeping my eyes on Trina, who'd finally assumed the position that would keep her safest—feet downstream, head up and arms out.

I threw the rope, calling out to her as I did so, "Rope coming. Over your shoulder when you've got it."

Trina missed the rope the first two throws, and I was beginning to worry. We were seconds away from entering the final chute, and I wanted her on the rope before we went in or I was likely to lose sight of her. If she had the rope, she'd follow the raft's path and hopefully make it unharmed to the calmer water below where we could easily pull her back to the boat, but every second that passed upped the possibility of injury.

Trina managed to miss the third throw as well, despite the rope practically landing in her face. She was wailing, loud enough to hear over the rush of the water.

I had to get her in the boat, but there wasn't time for another try or I risked being ejected myself as we flew through the narrow passage between rocks.

"Got her!" Allie in the boat behind us shouted to me. They'd fallen far enough behind that I couldn't see them for a while, but now they were beginning the descent through the rapids. It would be safer to get Trina into their boat if she could, before they took the chute. I called back.

"Okay! See you at the bottom!" I hoped Allie would have more luck than I did.

"Mom!" The boy in the front of my boat screamed, his voice laced with panic.

"Focus," I called to him. "They'll get her in. We need to paddle." We rounded one side of the chute, and seconds later were thrust between the steep walls of two enormous rocks, a swift and sudden descent accompanied by screams from several of those in my boat. Normally, I enjoyed the excitement this part of the route always brought, but right on the heels of a passenger being ejected, these cries held a lot more authentic fear than I liked.

And then, suddenly, the chute was behind us, and we floated almost lazily into a broad pool of wide, open water, the gentle riverbanks sloping away on either side. As the rest of the rafters relaxed, I double checked that everyone was accounted for and safe. The teenaged boy had a worried expression, his eyes fixed on the chute we'd just come through.

"Allie will get her," I assured him, hoping it was true.

I guided the raft to one side of the pool, anchoring us on the bank until we could ensure that Trina was safe. This was usually the spot where I invited guests to get in the water, but it seemed a little inappropriate at this point.

I stared at the chute behind us, waiting for the second raft. Adrenaline shot through me, giving me a familiar but uncomfortable sense of utter calm in the face of chaos. As I squinted up toward the bottom of the rapids, I felt a big hand cover mine on the side of the raft, and I turned to look at Travis.

His eyes met mine, communicating more than I would have thought possible in that simple look. "It's okay," he seemed to say. "We've got this. I've got you." A cooler kind of calm washed through me, and I took a deep breath, pulling comfort from his touch and his reassuring presence.

"Where's my mom?" The boy at the front was asking now, sounding on the edge of panic.

"Allie's an experienced guide," I assured him. "Your mom will either be in her boat or on a rope just behind."

"She can't go through there on a rope," the boy said, his voice cracking.

"She can. She'll be okay," I said, my voice much calmer than I felt. She could come through on a rope, but the odds of injury would be increased. I hoped she was in the raft.

Just then, the second raft appeared, bouncing through the chute and spearing its way out and down into the entrance of the big pool where we waited. Trina was in the center of the boat with the cameraman from Ned's crew, looking shaken, but unhurt.

Travis's hand tightened around mine as I exhaled, all the fear and worry whooshing out of me with that released breath. I looked up at his face, and found him looking at me with concern. "You okay?" he mouthed.

I nodded, smiling at him, wishing we could talk freely. "Thanks for taking over back there."

"Sure thing," he said in a gentle voice, giving my hand one more squeeze.

It was an odd sensation, to feel like I had a real partner, like someone else had my back. I wasn't used to it, but I realized that when the pretense was over, I'd miss it. A lot.

Allie guided her raft to the bank next to mine. She shook her head slightly, telling me that it hadn't been simple. The way Trina shook and shuddered as she huddled in the center of the raft told me that her trip was done.

"Mom!" The boy leapt out of the raft and splashed over to

the other boat, helping his mother to dry land, where he hugged her fiercely. "Are you okay?"

I was prepared for Trina to break down. Everything I'd seen from her so far indicated that her fear would definitely get the best of her, though she'd apparently kept it together well enough to help Allie get her back into the boat.

Trina let go of her son and turned to us all with a grin. "Water's a little cold," she said. "But very refreshing. You should all hop in for a swim! Maybe down here though. It's a little rough up that way." She pointed back to where she'd been in the water, and the group let out a relieved chuckle.

"You did great," I told her, stepping out of the raft to check her over for bumps and bruises. Despite the unplanned adventure, Trina seemed to be fully intact and unhurt.

"Thanks," she said quietly, glancing at her son again. "I've probably had enough swimming for a while, though."

I put a reassuring hand on her shoulder. "It's a lazy river from this point to the pickup spot. You can even just sit in the middle if you don't want to paddle. You earned it."

"I lost my paddle," she said, looking back up the chute.

"We'll find it later. I've got extras."

We spent a little time at the pool, a few of the other guests getting wet. The sun was hot overhead, but the water was runoff, and still held the chill of snowpack, so no one stayed in long.

I sat with Travis on the bank, the two of us companionably side by side as if we did this all the time, and the same comforting calm flowed through me at his reassuring presence. There was something else there too, that now-familiar tension building in the space between our bare arms. It was like a form of magnetism, laced with an electric buzz. Something instinctual told me that if I leaned into it, which every cell in my body pushed me to do, I might be hurt. But I suspected it was would be worth the danger.

"Hey guys," Ned said, strolling up and seating himself beside Travis.

"Hi," I said. "Everything going okay?" I wondered how many of these adventures Ned had been on now, and if he was enjoying the process or ready for it to be done.

"Definitely," he said. "Got some great footage back there. Very exciting."

"Are you tired of adventuring?" I asked him.

He shook his head lightly and smiled. "I'd rather be holding a paddle than a camera sometimes," he said, "but it's usually pretty fun. Plus, I had faith in the two of you. It's clear you know what you're doing."

Travis bumped my shoulder, sending chills over my skin at the warm familiar contact.

"How long have you two been guiding together?" Ned asked.

"Not long," I said at the same time as Travis answered, "forever."

Worry blared a siren inside me as Ned chuckled. "I know how that is."

Travis and I exchanged a look. We needed to get our story straight.

Soon, we were floating back toward the pickup spot and loading gear into the vans that waited for us there.

When we'd said goodbye to the guests, thanked Allie, and returned our gear to the shop, I sagged against the counter, watching the camera crew load up outside.

"That was quite an adventure," Travis said, crossing his arms over his broad chest and grinning at me.

"Don't call it an adventure outfit for nothing," I said. It was early afternoon, but I'd had enough. I might have been an adventure guide, but most of my days were pretty benign. Real danger took it out of me.

"Wanna go grab a drink?" he asked softly, seeming to understand that I needed a break.

I nodded. After today, I could use one. "Cole, you got the shop for the afternoon?"

Cole shot me a thumbs up, and anticipation at being alone with Travis trickled through me.

"Ride with me," Travis suggested, and moments later, Roscoe and I were in his big SUV, headed for the Surly Fox.

Chapter Twelve
The Happiest of Happy Hours

TRAVIS

By the time CeeCee and I were seated side by side at the bar of the Surly Fox, it was almost happy hour. Not that I had qualms about drinking before happy hour, actually. But since the two of us were supposed to be running a business, I figured this was the kind of thing responsible business owners would think about.

CeeCee had been quiet on the ride over, and I had the sense she needed a little time in her head, a little time without me making jokes or asking questions or generally intruding. But at the same time, I had an urge to try to soothe whatever worry she might be feeling, push away any issues.

Of course, there was the chance that the issue was me. It was a pretty good chance, actually, since my biggest issue had definitely become her. Though my struggles with my attraction to CeeCee were definitely my own. I worried more that today had demonstrated how poorly suited I was to be a partner to her. At work, or in any other way. Though I hoped that wasn't what was making her quiet.

We ordered our drinks, and then I turned to CeeCee.

"You were pretty amazing today," I said. I meant it. My admiration for her had only grown in the past days, and that was something I would have said was impossible previously. CeeCee was an incredible person. I'd known she was kind and generous, smart and confident. I hadn't realized what a badass she was.

"Thanks. It's never fun when someone gets launched, but it does happen pretty regularly." She grimaced and took a long swallow of the beer she'd ordered. I stared at the way her graceful neck moved as she drank, having flashes of putting my mouth against it, sinking my hands into all the wavy strawberry hair she'd pulled loose from the braid she'd worn all day.

She put down her glass and met my eyes, surprising me with a gaze full of warmth. "You were actually a huge help. I'm really glad you were there."

Happiness swept through my chest, and I felt my lips lift in a little smile. I'd always been a sucker for praise. "Thanks. I hope I wasn't just dead weight in the boat."

She shook her head.

"You know I would have jumped in to save Trina if I needed to," I told her. I'd considered it at the time, but that definitely hadn't been part of the emergency protocol CeeCee had outlined. This was her show, and I was following orders, something I was used to.

"Then we would have had to worry about getting you back in the boat too, and you're a hell of a lot bigger than Trina is." CeeCee smiled and moved a fraction closer to me as I agreed.

"But I could probably handle myself." My mind wasn't on the river, it was back in the service, at the very end of my time overseas. Chaos and emergencies had been par for the course, and even though I hadn't been in charge back then any more than I was here, I'd had to make plenty of split-second, life-or-death decisions. It wasn't a pleasant memory.

"Your face just went dark," CeeCee said softly.

Roscoe whined and sat up, pressing his head against my knee. I didn't train my dog to know when my moods shifted—that was all him, but I was grateful for it.

"Sorry," I muttered, taking a long drink of whiskey.

"What were you thinking about?" CeeCee's voice was gentle, kind.

"Nothing worth talking about," I said, putting the glass down a little too hard and forcing a smile.

CeeCee watched me for a moment, and I had an urge to hide my face, or worse, get up and walk away. I looked around the crowded bar, my mind beginning to judder like it did when my anxiety got hold and wouldn't let go. I wasn't going to run, not from CeeCee. I took a deep breath instead, surprised when she asked, "Why did you quit flying, Travis?"

It wasn't the question I expected, and my eyes jumped to meet hers. There was open concern in her gaze, and real interest. Something about the way she leaned into me as she waited for me to answer calmed me, soothed the frustration that had arisen inside me.

"I'm huge. The cockpit was tiny. Every year I had to get a waiver because I was over the size requirements for the plane, and I basically had to sign a form that said that if anything happened, the ejection seat would probably not work, and I'd most likely end up dead. And oh by the way, I wasn't allowed to sue the Navy if I lived but things didn't go quite right." It was as good a reason as any, and it was true.

"You must've been told all that when you started flying." CeeCee's voice was calm, conversational. She tilted her head to one side, keeping her eyes locked with mine and making my omission of details feel a lot closer to a lie.

"Yeah, I knew."

"So why?" She seemed to realize she was pressing a bit and she leaned back, breaking a little of the tension that had begun to ping between us. "I mean, you don't have to tell me. I'm just curious. About you."

Something about the way she added that last part made me want to tell her things, tell her something, at least. "It just wasn't quite what I thought it would be," I admitted.

"In what way?"

"It was fucking terrifying, for one thing."

She barked out a single laugh, her eyes dancing. God, I wanted to touch her, fit my palm to the side of her face, trace the line of her lip. "That seems like something you would have known."

"Smart people could guess at it." I gave her a half grin. I'd never pretended to be smart.

"Lucy told me that most of you guys graduated with engineering degrees before joining the Navy." CeeCee frowned at me.

I nodded. "Just because I've got the degree doesn't mean I'm some kind of genius though. Not like Brainiac."

She made a face that made it clear she knew what I meant about my less-than-humble colleague. "Go on."

"It felt . . ." How could I explain why flying didn't feel like real service? "It felt wrong. We flew around training most of the time, and when we did anything important, it was usually some kind of exercise with another country. It just didn't feel like what I'd joined the Navy for." I wasn't sure I'd ever voiced my reasons in quite that way. It felt good to be honest with her.

"What did you join for?" CeeCee had leaned in slightly, and if I leaned in too, I could almost kiss her. The thought of it was distracting, tempting. I felt my stomach tighten as my cock grew harder. I blew out a breath, working to focus on her question and not the way her body radiated heat at my side.

So close.

I scrubbed a hand down my face. "To do something meaningful, I guess."

"Lots of people want to make a difference in the world. Most don't join the Navy," she pointed out.

I sighed. How could I explain it all? "Where I grew up . . ." I started, realizing that wasn't quite right. "I was an accident," I told her. I was pretty sure I'd given her the family rundown once before, but this was a different context. "So I was six years younger than my youngest brother. And with three of them above me, I was destined to be the baby forever, never mind that I'm bigger than the three of those assholes put together." I grinned as I said it, thinking about my brothers. They weren't little guys, but it was fun to poke at them about it, even when they weren't here to defend themselves.

"So I never got to do anything growing up. They did it all for me, always looked out for me, took care of me."

"That sounds pretty good, Travis."

"Yeah, it was. But I knew I couldn't stay on the ranch forever, and if I did, I'd never experience a damn thing on my own."

"I get that," CeeCee said, and I paused, wondering what she meant. I was about to ask her, but she urged me on, nodding gently and leaning in. "Everything was foam padded for me. It was like I was getting the 'lite' version of life because my family was so busy protecting me."

"Okay.. . . ." CeeCee said. She took another swallow of her drink and I nearly wrapped my hand around the back of her neck and pulled her to me. She was so damned sexy.

"I wanted something real. And it seemed like protecting my

country, serving in some kind of real and potentially dangerous way, would scratch that itch. But my parents insisted on college, so I joined ROTC as soon as I got to school and started working on a deal with the recruiters to get to flight school. That seemed like the most 'real' service I could imagine."

"What did your parents think?"

I leaned back, remembering how my mother had cried when I told her, how my dad had nodded silently and then clapped me on the back. "I think they were proud."

"You think?"

"They were." It was always harder for me to acknowledge things I'd done right than it was for me to shrug and blow off what felt like another failure. "Yeah, they were. And I was sure that was going to be the thing that set me apart from my brothers, gave me a place to make a mark."

"But it wasn't?"

"Once I was there, it felt like cheating."

She shook her head, a half-exasperated smile on her pretty pink lips. "What?"

"There were guys still on the ground in Afghanistan, and things were a mess over there as we tried to get out. Jets hadn't seen real combat since the early two thousands, and all the practicing just felt a lot like pretending to me. So I turned in my wings and requested to help with the shutdown in Afghanistan." It sounded so simple when I said it, the words revealing none of the complex emotions I'd had at the time, leaving the squadron, practically begging to be allowed to go.

"I didn't know things worked that way."

I shook my head. "They don't really. Turning in your wings usually ends your career, but they didn't have a lot of people begging to join the shitshow, either. Fake Tom's—er, Will's—dad helped me make a deal to get attached to a general over there who needed someone to project manage the closure."

"And did you get the 'real' experience you were looking for?"

I took a deep breath, realizing this was far more than I'd even told my family. My regular nightmares flashed through my mind as I wrapped a hand around the back of my neck and leaned on the bar. Shit, I was tired. I hadn't even really realized it until that moment. "Yeah."

CeeCee watched me for a long moment, something passing through her eyes that I couldn't identify. It wasn't sympathy or pity, thank god. I couldn't stand that shit—it was part of why I generally provided comic relief. If people were laughing at me, they didn't ask too many questions, and they didn't pity me just because I didn't sleep much.

We sat like that for a few minutes, the silence between us full, pulsing with unspoken words and feelings that didn't seem completely platonic. If I hadn't been so fucking exhausted, I would have found a way to lighten the mood, said something to see that gorgeous smile light up her beautiful face. But I was beat, and I felt myself seconds away from telling CeeCee everything. About Antonio, about Daphne. I felt the words forming in the back of my mind, but either of the bombshells I held could ruin everything—if there was actually anything here. I swallowed the words and held her gaze, everything in me wanting her more with every passing second.

There was a low buzz in the air, or maybe it was just in my mind, and I would have sworn CeeCee was leaning in, her lips parting slightly, looking exactly like I imagined she would if she was going to kiss me.

A bit of a commotion at the entrance to the bar broke the spell, and CeeCee turned at the same time I looked to see what was going on. I fell back down to earth. Hard.

Ned and his coworkers had stepped inside, clearly having the same idea we did after the day's events. They spotted us and made their way across the space to talk. I did my best to put back on my fiancé veneer.

"Hey guys," Ned said. "Good to see you on dry land."

"Glad we could give you guys some real adventure today though," CeeCee laughed. She pushed back her hair, smoothed her napkin on the bar, like she was nervous. Had CeeCee been about to kiss me for real? The gentle blush on her cheeks made me think I was right, and the thought sent excitement rushing through me.

The other two members of the crew—I'd learned their names were Simone and Paul—both chuckled. "Yeah, I'd be fine with not actually participating in the rest of the adventures you have planned," Simone said. "Next time someone suggests rafting, I'll be the shore crew."

"Do you have a lot of other outfits to film?" CeeCee asked.

"Had two before we got here, and a few more after you guys," Paul confirmed. "One out in Tahoe, a couple on the East Coast, and one in Florida."

"Cool," I said, for lack of anything else to add. In reality, I didn't care who else they were looking at. CeeCee was the only contestant in my mind. I'd help her win if I could, even if it meant she'd leave Kasper Ridge. She deserved anything she wanted.

"Hey, didn't mean to intrude," Ned said. "Great footage today though. I'm rooting for you guys. Got some good Insta posts out of it too." He gave us a thumbs up and the trio moved off to a table a little ways away.

"Insta?"

"Do you live in a cave?" CeeCee laughed. "They post on their socials while they film, the lead-up to the show is a whole promotional thing for the network."

"Insta . . .?"

"Instagram, Travis."

"Right." I didn't do social media. Maybe I should.

CeeCee didn't ask more questions about my past, and I was relieved for it. Before the crew had stopped by, I'd been seconds away from telling her everything, including the details of the arrangement with Daphne. I hadn't really told anyone about that—none of the guys knew. I just needed to handle it, and then I could go on doing my best to forget the last ten years or so of my life.

"It's hard to imagine you as the baby," CeeCee was saying as our second round was delivered.

"Oh yeah? Why's that?" I asked, pretending I had no idea I was a six-foot-four, two-hundred-and-forty pound giant. I batted my eyes at her.

"Seriously?" She laughed and poked my chest, and before I could think better of it, I'd captured her hand, holding it there against my body.

She sucked in a quick breath, but her eyes held mine, widening slightly and then seeming to darken as her pupils grew.

Time shuddered and stilled, and I pulled a bit on the soft smooth wrist under my fingers, leaning in the tiniest bit and inhaling the scent of coconut and fresh air that always clung to CeeCee.

She didn't drop my gaze, and her lips parted slightly.

That did it. I purposely forced my brain to stay checked out and let my body do the planning, raising my other hand to rub a thumb across that pouty bottom lip of hers gently, reverently.

CeeCee inhaled sharply again, her eyes dropping shut as I traced the perfect plumpness of her lip. The motion was slow, careful, but everything inside me was the complete opposite. My body tightened like a coil, my cock hardening painfully. I tried to memorize the feel of her soft lip beneath the pad of my thumb.

It wasn't enough. I cupped her jaw, dropping her hand at my chest and pushing my fingers into the soft full hair around the back of her neck, letting my fingertips trace the soft skin there and pulling her gently toward me.

When our lips met, I closed my eyes, and for the first time in as long as I could remember, my mind cleared. The noise and chaos that always hovered on the sidelines of my thoughts quieted, and all I knew for those few blissful seconds was the softness of CeeCee's lips on mine, the press of her taut athletic body to my chest, her hands slipping around my waist.

When her tongue teased at my lip, I shivered involuntarily, every cell in my body reaching for her, desperate for more. I tasted her lips with my tongue, and when she met me there, pushing into my mouth, I nearly lost it.

It was the single best kiss of my life, and it had the effect of making me forget everything. Everything I hated about myself, about my life, about my situation... but also the fact that we were in a bar, that I was on borrowed time, that this was just pretend.

As my body struggled to deepen the connection, my mind kicked back in. What was I doing? I wasn't the guy CeeCee should be kissing in the Fox. It didn't matter how much I already loved her or how cherished she'd be if we could somehow be together for real. It was all for show, and it had to stay that way.

After all, I was a married man.

Chapter Thirteen
Don't Poop in the Plane

CEECEE

I'd thought about kissing Travis before.

I'd thought about a lot more than that . . . After all, he was a big, strong, good-looking guy, and I wasn't dead. I'd wager half the women in Kasper Ridge had thought about what it would be like to be held within those strong muscled arms, what it would be like to press themselves against the firm steely planes of his chest.

It was good, by the way. Better than I thought it would be.

Because the sheer masculinity that Travis couldn't even control was coupled with a tenderness I never would have expected.

The way his thumb had rubbed languidly over my lip, the way his eyes burned before he leaned in to take my mouth . . . it was overwhelming.

And that was how I found myself essentially boneless in his

embrace, hoping for nothing more than that somehow he'd never stop kissing me. Ever.

But like all amazing experiences, this one had to end. And when Travis pulled back, I practically fell back onto my barstool, dazed and completely off balance.

I was breathing hard, and it took me a moment to recover, almost as if I'd hiked fourteener at a sprint. When I was capable, I looked into those deep eyes of his, hoping to find the connection I'd felt growing between us. But he was looking beyond me somehow. Our eyes met, but his expression was closed, focused inward.

What was that look? Was it regret?

"Hey," I said, wishing I could just say . . . I didn't even know. "Hey."

He grinned at me then, and I felt as much as saw, the old Sasquatch slip back into place. "Left you speechless, eh?" He chuckled.

I shook my head. I didn't want the jokester. Not now. "Travis . . ."

"Sorry, Ceese. Got carried away there. Must've been the near-death inner tube experience today."

"No," I said, still searching for words. "It was—"

"Good for the Insta," Travis grinned.

I turned to look at the table where Ned and the crew sat, and Ned flashed me a thumbs up. My heart deflated just a bit, and a heavy sensation settled within me as whatever lightness I'd felt in Travis's arms sifted out of me.

Travis had only kissed me because they were watching. It was all part of the role I'd asked him to play.

And I was getting in way too deep.

"Right," I managed, unwilling or unable to look back into his handsome face. I lifted my beer and drained it. "I suppose we'd better call it a day here. Just a half-day hike tomorrow, at the trailhead out behind the resort." Humiliation threatened to swamp me, taking the warm, buzzy happiness I'd experienced just seconds earlier and using it against me.

Why had I thought Travis was anything but a great actor? I was the one who'd asked him to pretend. And judging by the interested eyes I spotted looking our way all around the Surly Fox, he'd done a bang-up job. I just wished my heart didn't feel so banged up.

"So I'll come into the shop early? Help out there?" Travis sounded just as cheerful and upbeat as ever.

I risked a look up into his eyes, hating how much I hoped to see something there that would confirm that my growing feelings for my friend weren't one-sided. But Travis looked nonchalant as ever, giving me an easy smile and wiggling his eyebrows.

"No," I said, half on a sigh. "Why don't we just meet at the resort at noon?"

His face fell the tiniest bit, his expression dimming. "You don't want—?"

"It's fine, Travis. I know you have a life outside this. Take the time. I'll play it off at the store." I needed the distance. Needed to remember what this was, and what it wasn't.

"If you're sure . . ." he sounded the tiniest bit doubtful as I slid off my stool and picked up my phone.

"Yep. Just a lift back to the shop?" I wanted to call Jensen for a ride, but that would undoubtedly deepen the frown lines appearing around Travis's eyes. I needed to play it off. If he could do it, I could too.

"Oh, right." Travis and Roscoe stood, Travis paid the bill quickly, and then we all headed to the door, pausing at the crew's table.

"Half day hike at Kasper Ridge Resort tomorrow. We'll gather out back around noon," I told them. I wanted some time alone in the shop, some time to push myself back in line. A bit of normal.

"Probably hang out in the store a bit first then," Ned responded.

I sighed, realizing that as long as the cameras were around, as long as my fake fiancé was here, nothing would be normal.

Simone and Paul offered a wave, and I headed outside, not waiting for Travis to push the door open for me.

I felt angry and confused, but couldn't explain to myself exactly why. I was getting what I wanted, wasn't I? Exactly what I'd asked for. A convincing portrayal of a doting boyfriend who helped me run my adventure guide business. If anything, the kiss had just pushed me one step closer to the finish line.

"Hey," Travis said softly after a silent ride back to the parking lot in front of my shop. "You okay?"

I cleared my throat, pushing down the stupid threat of tears. What was wrong with me?

"Yeah, just fatigue," I tried. "Today was a lot."

"Uh huh." The skepticism in his voice made me ashamed of myself. Since when did I tell lies or cover up how I really felt about things? It had been the key factor in all my interpersonal relationships—and the most likely reason why none of the romantic ones had ever gone anywhere. With me, what you saw was what you got.

"See you tomorrow," I told him, opening the door. "We'll just tell the crew you had an appointment to take care of or something to explain why you're not there. It won't be a stretch for them to imagine you have an actual life that doesn't revolve around me." I stepped back and closed the door. I heard the hum of the electric window lowering.

"Ceese, hey." Travis's voice followed me out, but I kept moving, digging out my keys as I walked to my own car across the gravel lot. I didn't want to talk about the kiss. I wanted to go home.

* * *

My mood did not improve back at home.

"So, Sis," Jensen said the minute I walked in the door, my mom in her matching recliner at his side. "Anything you'd like to share?"

I stared at them as they both shot me hard looks. "No?"

"CeeCee," Mama said, using the quiet hurt voice she'd used when I was little and needed to apologize for something. "I overheard Adelaide at the grocery store talking about your fiancé." She waited, and whatever she saw on my face told her what she wanted to know. "Why didn't we know anything about this?"

"Sis," Jensen said, his face turning serious. "You in trouble? I need to take care of this guy for you? He knock you up?"

"Jensen!" Mama threw a shocked look at my brother.

"No, guys, look. It's complicated." I stumbled to the sofa and took my old familiar seat, my mind working through scenarios. I didn't want to lie to my family. But Jensen was not good at secrets, and Mama would never understand. She'd most likely march me over to Ned's rental house and insist that I come clean immediately, followed by a trip to apologize to Travis. I didn't have it in me tonight. Besides, the only thing going for me at the moment was the fact that Travis's stellar kiss performance just upped my chances of actually winning.

"Explain," Mama suggested, crossing her arms.

"Yes," Jensen said. "Explain."

I sucked in a deep breath, and threw caution to the wind. Caution, actually, had probably drown in the river earlier today. "I'm in love. Travis and I are engaged. I'm sorry I didn't tell you, but it happened so fast. We were friends first. I've known him for almost a year." Mama's face didn't soften and her mouth dropped open. "He's from Texas," I added for no known reason.

"Texas," Jensen repeated, as if this last bit of information was the most critical.

"When will he be coming over to meet the family?" Mama asked.

"Soon?" I tried. The last thing I wanted was to play act some version of the very thing I'd always imagined might happen someday, were I to meet someone for real. I didn't want to deepen this lie. "He's super busy."

Mama frowned. "The boy who wants to marry my daughter is too busy to meet her mama?"

"No, no. That's not what I meant. I'll ask him." I pulled my phone out, happy for a distraction.

"You do that," Jensen said, aiming the remote at the television and bringing *Magnum P.I.* back to life.

I sat in my familiar spot on the couch, texting with Lucy and our other best friend, Bennie, while pretending to be texting Travis. They'd sent a text as I left the shop, inviting me to hang out, but I just didn't have it in me. Instead Bennie and Lucy were together at Bennie's place, and I stayed here, the familiar backdrop of my entire life both comforting and distressing at once.

Bennie: How's your big lie going?
Me: Let's not call it that, ok?
Lucy: Charade? Falsehood? Pretend romance? Aren't you guys engaged now?
Bennie: Wait, what?
Me: yeah, Travis threw that grenade the second

*we met the camera crew and now we have an extra
layer of shit to spread on.*

Lucy: You okay with all this, Cee?

Me: What choice do I have now? It's fine.

Bennie: Is he a good actor?

Me: Surprisingly, yes.

I tried not to think about the kiss. But I could think of nothing
else. My stomach churned and hot embarrassment flooded my
cheeks again. I'd thought it was real.

*Me: He kissed me tonight. Because the crew was the
at the Fox and they're posting on social as they film.*

Lucy: He kissed you for a post? Is it up?

*Me: I honestly haven't looked. But yes, it was
pretend.*

Bennie: Was it good?

Me: It was pretend.

Bennie: See above question.

Lucy: Tell us

Me: It was... yes.

Lucy: And...?

*Me: And nothing. It was all for show. He blew it
off like it was nothing. Because it was nothing.*

Bennie: So he's a better actor than you are.

Me: Maybe so.

Lucy: Wait, CeeCee. Do you like him?

Me: We're friends. That's all.

. . .

It felt like a lie. It was a lie. I knew it was.

Everything was confusing now. Asking Travis to help me fake this relationship had turned me inside out. What was real? What wasn't? I didn't even know.

Lucy: *Do you want to be friends with him? Or do you want more?*

Did the answer even matter? I'd fallen for my friend. A guy who was simply doing me a favor. Exhaustion waltzed with the embarrassment inside my mind.

Me: *Hey, ladies, I have to go.*
    Bennie: *Avoidance. Classic.*
    Me: *Good night.*

My phone dinged again, but I switched it to silent and put it on the floor at my feet. I could feel my mother's curious eyes flicking to me now and then, but I ignored the questions I felt there.

Jensen was unconcerned, snoring lightly in Dad's recliner.

* * *

I spent the morning puttering around in the store, my head still feeling like someone had gone in while I'd been away and moved everything around. I was bumping into things in there and having trouble finding things that I'd never had to search for before.

Things like my realistic and practical nature. My sense of humor. My frigging pride.

Customers came and went, thankfully, and when Cole came in at noon to relieve me, I had almost gotten my head back on straight. A morning without Travis's hulking presence helped, and Ned and the crew stayed in the periphery of my activities.

"You're internet famous, boss!" Cole hooted, practically skipping toward me.

"What?"

"Check it." He dropped his phone face up on the glass counter, and a series of video clips flitted by. There were images of me on the river, Travis at my side. Travis's hand on mine as we shared a look that even I thought was pretty hot. And finally, Travis pulling me into his arms at the Fox and kissing me like he meant it. The story was had hashtags like #heatingupthecompetition and #hotcoupleadventure, along with more helpful things like #voteforceecee and #kasper-ridgeadventure.

"Oh," I managed. The kiss looked even hotter from the outside. My stomach twisted up again.

"Yeah, they've posted a ton. You guys are giving them a lot to work with, I guess. You're everywhere on social."

"Oh good." I was glad I'd told my mother and brother already. There was no way this wasn't all over this small town by now.

"I think you're gonna win this thing, boss."

"They still have a bunch more guides to film," I told him, mostly to remind myself. But hearing him suggest it was good put me back in the right frame of mind. This all had a purpose. And if I won, my petty problems would all be put in perspective. I'd see the world and forget the silly tangle my heart had gotten into back here at home.

It wasn't about me and Travis. That was all a means to an end.

"You good here?" I asked Cole. "I have to do a hike out at the resort."

"All good," he confirmed.

I took a deep breath and headed out to pretend I wasn't in love with the man I was pretending to be in love with.

* * *

The resort was bustling when I arrived, and a quick chat with Aubrey at the front desk explained the uptick in activity. There was a wedding in a week, and some of the people rushing to and fro in the common areas were vendors checking out spaces and contractors building some custom arches and flower stands.

"They're going all out," Aubrey said. "And this woman is kinda crazy bridezilla, if you want the truth."

"That sounds fun," I laughed. If I ever got married, which I figured at this point was probably not going to happen, I'd want something small and intimate. I didn't understand the drive to make one day such a big deal.

"It's good for business." She shrugged.

"Is my tour group here?" I looked around the lobby but didn't see anyone dressed for hiking and ready to head out.

"I think Sass already grabbed them," she said. "They headed out back."

I frowned, feeling a little territorial. But then I realized that Travis exercising some leadership and ownership just helped the cause. Of course he'd be comfortable starting without me if this was his business too.

"Thanks." I headed out the glass doors at the back of the

resort, and found Travis standing at the far edge of the sweeping patio, surrounded by a half-circle of guests who seemed completely enraptured with whatever he was saying. Ned and the crew were just behind the guests, filming.

Travis was dressed in a pair of loose cargo pants with a tight black tee hugging his chest and arms. His muscular form looked more ripped than ever, and the way the sun caught the gold in his hair made him even more handsome. The rough scrub of hair along his jawline sent a shiver through me, and I fought to keep my emotions in check as I approached.

"And then Ghost was like, 'I'll never eat another boxed lunch before we fly.'" Travis chuckled.

"Oh my god, that's hilarious," one of the women said. "And disgusting!"

"He pooped in his plane!" One of the younger kids howled.

Travis caught my eye over the heads of the group, and shrugged apologetically. I had no idea what stories he was telling, but the group seemed in good spirits at least.

"And I guess that's enough with the poop stories," I said, moving around to join Travis at the front of the group. "Ready for a hike?"

The group was enthusiastic, and after checking for water bottles, footwear, and sunscreen, we headed out.

The trail behind the resort went all the way up to the back-country cabins—that was where Douggie had gone when he'd filmed an episode of his popular YouTube show *Out and Out There*, and also where Annalee and Mateo had gotten stranded in a freak summer snowstorm—but we weren't going that far. There was an offshoot from the trail that led to an incredible vista point, looking slightly north and west and offering a view of the Rockies that took my breath away every single time.

Travis brought up the rear of the group as we hiked up, and we didn't speak as we climbed the trail in the late summer sun.

Inside, a mass of emotions fought for precedence. Was I hurt? Angry? Worried about how the silence I was pushing between us was going to play on camera? I didn't even know. We really didn't interact at all until we reached the peak and everyone took some time to sit and enjoy the view.

"This is beautiful," Travis said at my side as I stared out over the mountains with their craggy peaks and sloping sides. There was snow lingering atop a few of the distant mountains, and something about it settled a melancholy deep in my chest.

I turned to look at him, only to find him staring right at me. I searched for something to say, but the best I could do was turn back to the view.

"You okay?" he asked.

"Fine," I said, conscious of the microphone I wore.

"You seem . . . different."

"I'm good." I was being short with him because it was easier than admitting I'd made a fool of myself.

"Hey," he said, taking my hand where it hung at my side. His warm fingers wrapped mine, and his touch twirled things up inside me even more. I didn't want to like him, I didn't want to want him. This was not supposed to happen. "Hey," he said again, tugging my hand gently to get me to look at him.

"I'm okay," I said, finally letting myself meet his gaze.

"You're not." He stated it like a fact.

I dropped my chin and looked at the ground, and then, with another little tug from him, leaned into him, pushing the top of my head against his broad chest, letting out the breath I'd been holding since the kiss.

When I sighed, his arms went around me, and he held me there as the laughter and conversation from the guests a few feet away filtered through the clear cool air around us. Roscoe had laid down with one of the boys who'd hiked up with us, and now was getting his belly rubbed as the boy lavished attention on him. I didn't know where Ned and the crew were, but had no doubt their cameras were on us. Still, the nearness of Travis and his arms around me had the effect of stealing all the frustration and anger I'd been feeling. I melted into him, finally turning my cheek to rest against his beating heart.

Shit. This was bad. I liked him. A lot.

"Tell me," he said softly.

I cringed. How could I tell him?

"It's okay," he suggested in a near whisper.

I shook my head against him. I couldn't tell him anything, not with the microphone on. "It's just . . . it's confusing."

"Us?" he asked. "This?"

I nodded against him. "It's getting all screwed up in my head. I know it's not . . . I mean, with the show and everything, the contest. It's hard to remember that we have real lives outside of this." I didn't want to voice our deception aloud and this was as close as I was willing to get.

"But, I mean," Travis's voice was thoughtful. "Maybe it's all real."

Talking in code was making my emotions even more confused. "What is?" I whispered.

"All of it."

I turned my head to meet his eyes, which were deep and soulful as they held mine.

"Maybe it has been for a while. For me, at least." He said this in a quiet voice, as if he was testing the waters for a reaction.

Did I dare to hope he meant what I thought he did? A quiet hope sprang up inside me. Did Travis feel the same way I did?

We were talking in code, but I didn't doubt I understood. Travis's warm embrace and the soft glow of his eyes confirmed it. "Me too."

A tiny smile lifted one side of his mouth.

His arms tightened around me, and the hug turned from

something warm and comforting to an embrace laced with possibility. Desire flashed to life inside me, and I suddenly wished we were alone.

Travis watched me, that smile staying in place, and then after a long moment, he lowered his head and took my mouth once again, nearly knocking my knees out from under me.

We kissed—not the intense passionate kiss of the night before, but something more reassuring, meant to confirm a mutual attraction that could be further explored, maybe. The tension in my chest unspooled, and I pulled a good measure of confidence from the kiss.

It wasn't just me.

It wasn't just for show.

But what now?

Chapter Fourteen
It's a Piece of Cake to Bake a Pretty Cake

TRAVIS

I took up the rear of the group as we hiked back to the resort, feeling like it was a natural spot for me to be. Something in my nature wanted to be there behind everyone, making sure they were all okay, that everyone got home safely. Roscoe seemed to feel the same way, veering from the trail here and there to sniff out a new scent, but quickly coming back to assure himself that all his charges were in place up ahead.

Being in the back also gave me a chance to keep an eye on CeeCee, who I spotted around curves and through the trees as she led the group down the sloping terrain. Every time I saw her, a jolt of desire shot through me, and there was something else—something that felt a lot like happiness.

I was glad to be in the back. It gave me time to think.

I had things to deal with, and I knew I couldn't put them off much longer. I owed Daphne some closure, and a good man wouldn't begin one thing without ending another completely—

not that there'd really ever been anything between Daphne and me. Besides the certificate stating that we were legally married, of course.

Back at the resort, I wished the guests well and watched them head off in various directions after thanking CeeCee. And then the two of us were alone on the back patio near the big fire pit, which was just being lit for the evening.

Ned and the crew lingered off to one side, and CeeCee stood beside me, both of us staring at the back of the massive resort.

"Um. So," I said. We probably needed to talk about what had been said up there, about that kiss. I definitely needed to tell her about the complications in my life, about my plans to deal with them.

"Right," she said, turning to face me. We were still wearing the microphones and CeeCee looked adorably uncertain, even as she took my hand, wrapping her cool fingers around mine.

"Should we talk?" I asked, feeling awkward suddenly, shoving my free hand into my pocket because it felt foreign, and I didn't know what to do with it.

"Well, yeah, but maybe we turn these in first." She pulled her microphone off and took the battery pack from her pocket, switching it off. I did the same, feeling anticipation building within me.

We walked to Ned, handing him the microphone units, and then CeeCee took my hand again. "See you tomorrow," she said.

"Got it," Ned mouthed, answering his phone as he turned away from us.

We walked toward the back door of the resort, Roscoe trotting along next to me as CeeCee took my hand again.

"Where do you want to go?" I asked her, hoping she'd say my room. But I knew we had things to discuss. And I wasn't about to take her to bed while I was still entangled in this thing with Daphne.

She looked at me uncertainly, then dropped my gaze. "I mean . . . I don't know. This is complicated."

"A little," I agreed. "Doesn't have to be." What was I even saying? She didn't know about half of the complications I was bringing into this, and I needed to tell her. "Wanna bake a cake?"

"Wait, what?" She laughed, and I loved the way her eyes crinkled at the corners.

"I have to make a wedding cake. For the wedding next weekend."

"Isn't it a little early then?"

"This is just a dry run. Practice. But I need to get the plan solid because I've got a bunch of other things to make too. Rolls, and muffins for the morning after. Things like that." I was worried about getting it all done, but I also figured if CeeCee helped me bake, we could talk while our hands were occupied with other things. Less chance mine would end up on her.

"Oh," she said, looking around, as if someone would tell her this was a bad idea. "Um. Okay, yeah. Let's bake."

The happiness that sprang to life in my chest wouldn't have been any bigger if she had suggested we go to my room. I was happy just to spend time with her. But I really needed to come clean. I'd do it over cake.

"Roscoe has to go upstairs," I told her. "He's not allowed in the kitchen."

CeeCee nodded, bending over to pet Roscoe gently. "See you tomorrow, Ross," she crooned, making me only a tiny bit jealous of my dog. "I'll wait for you here?" she said, looking around the lobby where we stood.

"Perfect. Be right back." I took Roscoe to the elevator and tried to calm the rush of my heart as the doors slid shut. The knowledge that I'd get to spend more time with CeeCee alone felt almost overwhelming, and I couldn't move fast enough to get Roscoe settled and get back downstairs.

CeeCee stood to one side of the lobby, and the smile she gave me when she saw me coming from the elevator made my heart swell and other parts of me try to follow suit.

"What kind of wedding cake is it?" CeeCee asked as I led her into the kitchen.

"Four layers," I told her. "The bottom is a vanilla sponge with a raspberry filling. The second layer is chocolate with ganache. Third will be pistachio sponge with a vanilla bean fill, and the top is red velvet with cream cheese."

CeeCee stopped next to one of the long steel counters and stared at me.

I faced her, waiting, but she didn't say a word. "What?"

"You're serious? That wasn't a joke?"

It didn't shock me that she was surprised I could bake. It didn't exactly fit my image, I guessed. "Not a joke. I never joke about cake."

"Wow," she laughed. "I guess I just expected you to say yellow cake or something."

"Would you want your wedding cake to be plain yellow cake?"

"Maybe," she sniffed.

"Then that's what you'll have. I'll even bake it myself," I joked, biting my tongue when I realized what I'd just implied.

CeeCee smiled up at me, making my heart thump, and asked, "Where do we begin? And do I have to call you chef?"

"I'd like that very much," I told her. "And we should probably wash our hands. Then, we'll get the pistachio layer going. It's the most complicated."

We were side by side at the sink washing our hands, and I was searching through my mind for the right words to explain to

CeeCee what I needed to say. "I'm glad we have a little time together alone," I started.

She smiled at me, a flush climbing her cheeks. "Me too."

I pulled a large metal bowl from the shelf over the counter and pointed at the jar of cake flour on the far counter, which CeeCee went to retrieve. "There's, uh, actually something I need to tell you. Maybe a couple things. But one especially."

"Oh?" CeeCee grinned at me, and I realized she thought I was flirting. I was just about to try again to let her know this was a serious conversation when her phone piped out a jaunty tune from her pocket. "Hang on, that's Jensen," she said, pulling it out and stepping away from me to talk to her brother.

I used the moment to gather my thoughts. The situation wasn't complicated, not really. But I knew it sounded bad on the surface. How did I tell CeeCee I was married without her getting all the wrong ideas?

"I'm really sorry, Travis," she said, coming back to where I was measuring flour.

I stopped moving, our eyes met.

"I have to go rescue Jensen. His car won't start and he's all the way down in Floyd's Mill."

I had no idea where that was, but I definitely heard the part about CeeCee leaving, and while relief was my first reaction, it was followed swiftly by disappointment. I needed to talk to her, get things out in the open. And once that was done, I hoped we'd have a clear path to move forward. Together.

"Oh," I managed. "Okay, well . . . Should I come to the shop in the morning? What's on the docket?"

She stepped close again. "Weekends are usually pretty busy. This weekend it's mostly hikes. Half day tomorrow afternoon and then a full-day loop Sunday."

I nodded. I was seeing more of Colorado this week than I'd seen in the months since arriving here.

"Don't worry about tomorrow. It sounds like you have a lot to do here to get ready for the wedding," she said, and my heart shriveled a bit in disappointment, though she was right. "But I could use you Sunday if you're up for it."

"Okay. You sure? What will you tell the crew?"

"You've got responsibilities here too. You and Archie are friends. They'll understand that."

My mind meandered through wedding cake plans and vague ideas I'd had about Ghost's treasure hunt. I did have a lot to do, but nothing seemed as interesting as spending the day with her. "Yeah, okay."

* * *

That night I had a drink out at the fire pit with most of the crew. Antonio and Wiley sat on one side of the fire, and I sat between Brainiac, Fake Tom, and Ghost on the other. Monroe and Aubrey had opted to watch tonight's movie with the guests, and it sounded like Penny and Lucy were combining kid-watching forces over at Lucy's place with a bottle of wine.

"This wedding just might kill me," Ghost was saying.

"A lot of demands?" Antonio asked.

"Over the top," Ghost confirmed. "Things like filtering the light through the windows just so with some kind of gauze and making sure that no one walks down the pathway behind the ceremony during certain times." Ghost shook his head and sipped from the rocks glass in his hand.

"I'll make sure there are no complaints on the cake front," I told him. I'd finished two of the layers this afternoon after CeeCee left, and wasn't worried about the other two. I'd just need to leave plenty of time to bake the real thing. "And Aubrey left me a list of the other stuff I'll need to bake. I can get a few things made ahead this weekend."

"Thanks, man."

"You doing okay?" Antonio asked me. "Helping CeeCee and the baking? It's a lot."

"It would be a lot if I needed sleep," I reminded him.

"Everyone needs sleep, man."

I didn't want to talk about me. So I diverted attention. I was good at that.

"How's the mountain bike operation going?" Antonio had suggested they add mountain biking down the main run in the summers, and it appeared to be a hit.

"It's been great," Antonio confirmed. "And gave the shop a whole new line of gear to sell between helmets and gloves and actual bikes."

"Great idea, man," Ghost told him, nodding.

"So you gonna stick around for a while?" I asked Antonio, lowering my voice just a bit.

"Maybe," he said. "You?"

"Maybe," I said, my mind roving to CeeCee. Would I want to stay here if she was gone? Off on some wild adventure trip to see the world?

The rest of the group had continued talking about the bike operation, and Antonio gave me a frank look. "How are things with CeeCee?"

"Confusing as shit," I told him. "I like her, man. And I'm pretty sure it's mutual. But . . ."

"Daphne."

"Yeah." Guilt washed through me at the mention of her name. "I need to call her tomorrow and sort everything out." I'd told Antonio about her call a couple days before, but none of the rest of the guys knew about my situation.

"I think you're making it complicated for no reason. Give her what she asked for. You don't want to be with her any more than she wants to be with you."

"I'm just surprised," I told him. "I mean . . . I figured that was just a forever deal. The idea of ending it just feels so much like failure. Like another failure." A dark weight lodged inside me imagining my mom's reaction if I gave Daphne what she'd asked for.

My friend shook his head. "This was never a marriage, Travis. And success and failure are just two ways of looking at one thing. We've talked about this."

I stared into the flames for a long beat, and I was certain we both knew exactly what I was thinking about. I struggled with the words, but knew I needed to acknowledge the painful past that had brought us together. "Your brother . . . that was failure."

Antonio didn't say anything for a moment, no doubt thinking about the way we'd met, the thing I'd had to track him down to tell him. "No. That wasn't your failure, either. That was circumstance. And that was his choice."

"It should have been me." Guilt and darkness swirled inside me, the way they always did when I thought about what had happened to Antonio's brother, a Marine I'd served with overseas at the end of my time there.

"We can't change the past, Sass. Things happened the way they happened. And now you and me? We're friends because of it." His face was clear as he spoke. Antonio was better at processing than I could ever hope to be. When I'd gone to find him, doing my best to honor his brother's wishes, I found a guy who mourned his brother emotionally, and who then picked himself up and moved forward. I hoped to be as strong and flexible as my friend someday.

"I'm still sorry."

"And you have nothing to be sorry for." Antonio touched my glass with the edge of his. "To the future," he said.

"To the future," I agreed, knowing there'd be little sleep

tonight now that thoughts of the past had been invited in again. "Speaking of which, I'd better get back to the baking."

He gave me a half smile as I rose and excused myself from the group, Roscoe at my side. I'd brought him down to enjoy some time outdoors, but it was late. Unlike me, he enjoyed a good nine or ten hours. "Time for bed, boy," I told him. As I switched off the main light in my room and pulled the door shut again, a tired sigh worked its way out of me. Was CeeCee in bed? I wondered if she was asleep. If she'd thought of me at all before drifting off.

I headed down to the kitchen, taking comfort in the silence around me, the long empty counters, the serenity of the space.

The quiet and stillness gave me the equivalent in my mind, and I slid my phone from my pocket. There was something I needed to do, and putting it off wouldn't help anyone at this point. Daphne didn't love me. I didn't love her. She'd asked for a divorce. Even though we'd never lived together, never consummated the marriage, it still surprised me that she wanted out. She was taken care of, provided for. That was what I'd intended. Of course, I'd never intended to return from Afghanistan, and definitely hadn't considered what would happen if I ended up in love with someone else.

I dialed the familiar number, and it rang four times before I thought to check the time.

Shit. It was past midnight back home. But just as I was about to hang up, Daphne's voicemail picked up, and her familiar voice was in my ear, suggesting I leave her a message. For the briefest second, the sound sent a rolling homesickness through me. Daphne wasn't a wife in the way most people thought of that relationship. But she was a friend, and had been practically my whole life. Hearing her voice made me wish briefly to have succeeded in all the places I'd failed.

"Hey Daph," I said, leaning back against the long steel prep counter and closing my eyes. "You surprised me the other day, but I just want to make sure this is what you want. I made a promise, and ending this feels like I'm letting you down." I paused.

"Anyway. Yeah. Whatever you want. Send me the papers, okay? I'm at the Kasper Ridge Resort. Mom has the address, or you can just look online.

"So . . . yeah. Okay. Sorry. Hope you're good." I cut myself off and hung up, knowing I'd just left what was potentially the most pathetic voicemail ever. But it didn't matter. The only thing she wanted was for me to agree to sign the papers and end our sham of a marriage. And now? I wanted the same thing.

For a few hours, I lost myself in baking. The prep for the regular needs of the resort and the practice versions of the enormous rounds of the wedding cake I'd be assembling for the following weekend.

By the time I got back to my room, my mind had settled slightly, but I knew sleep was still not going to be possible. My body was tired, though, so I hauled my laptop onto the couch and dug into the other thing I'd been thinking about.

If Ghost's uncle was walking around quoting movie lines and saying he'd written them, there had to be some record of it. But as I checked everything I could find about the long list of titles we'd discovered in the back of the old photo album Marvin had left behind, I found more questions. Every one of the films listed had been produced by Mountaintop Studios, a place Marvin Kasper had never been linked to by name. The only real link was his former friend, Rudy, who ran the place.

There was a possibility that Marvin was just obsessed with his old writing partner, or following his career closely once Marvin and Lola had left Hollywood for Kasper Ridge. But that didn't feel quite right. And there'd be no point sending his relatives on a hunt just to uncover some lingering obsession.

There was something else. Something about these movies in particular. If he said he wrote them, it seemed like he probably did. And if he and Rudy had ended up enemies, was there a chance Rudy produced Marvin's films without giving him credit for them? Was this whole hunt about seeking compensation for work that was stolen from Marvin Kasper?

It felt like an answer of sorts, but not one that helped anyone. We'd need to find some proof that Marvin had written those movies. I just wasn't quite sure how we'd do it.

As the clock turned from three to four in the morning, I finally felt calm and quiet enough to try to sleep. I pushed the laptop aside and went to bed, where images of CeeCee lulled me finally to sleep.

The next day, I found Ghost in his room, which he used as his office. He'd claimed the first of the rooms in what we now thought of as the staff wing, one side of the hotel that was slowly being renovated for guests. The entirety of the other wing was finished, and that was where guests stayed now. Eventually— and probably sooner than later—demand would require that we finish this wing too and book these rooms for guests. But for now, we had our side and they had theirs. And ours was slightly out of date and a little run down, but hey, it was home.

Ghost's room was a suite, complete with a huge dining room table, which we still used for staff meetings. He had a desk to one side of the room, and that was where he sat now, having called for me to come in after I'd knocked.

"Hey Sass," he said, turning as Roscoe and I headed into the enormous room. "What's good?"

Ghost looked tired—he often did. I knew I wasn't the only one who didn't sleep much around here. Despite that, he smiled as he faced me, and when Roscoe trotted over to him, the dog got a friendly rub of the scruff as I seated myself on the long couch.

"Couple things," I said.

"Aren't you helping CeeCee this weekend?" Ghost asked, as if suddenly realizing I wasn't where he thought I should be.

"Yeah," I said. "But she didn't need me this morning, I guess. Full day hike tomorrow."

He nodded, and I could see another question forming as his mouth dropped open to speak again. "And you're, uh...you guys are dating?"

Shit, nothing stayed quiet around here. "Not really."

"Kind of dating?"

"Not dating. Just pretending to date."

Ghost just stared at me.

"For the cameras. For this contest. Like, a show." Guilt bubbled inside me at what felt like a lie of omission.

Ghost opened his mouth and then closed it again.

"I'm pretending to be her fiancé so she can win this adventure show where they told her they wanted to feature couples running guide shops together. If she wins, she'll get some big adventure trip and a bunch of money for the shop, I guess." And then she'll leave. I didn't add this last part because I wasn't sure I could say it without giving everything away.

"That's . . . nice of you." Ghost's face gave almost no hint of what he was thinking. He just looked at me, knowing the blank expression he was showing me would drive me to keep babbling.

"Right, just helping a friend. Same way I'm up here helping you."

"I haven't asked you to pretend to want to marry me though."

"Well she didn't ask that, that just kind of happened. We were just supposed to be dating." I still cursed myself for the way the word "engaged" had slipped from my lips the first day the crew had been with us.

"Sass, do I even want to know?" Ghost looked even more exhausted by my explanation.

I shrugged. "Like I said. Helping."

"And there's really nothing else between you? It's all pretend?"

"There wasn't supposed to be. There might be, actually." My heart bumped around inside me as I said this, like it was trying to get my attention.

Ghost just watched me struggle as emotions flung themselves against the confines of my mind.

"You look exhausted."

"Back at you."

"Is this all too much? The baking and the cake and this adventure stuff?"

"Course not." A thread of irrational fear joined the other emotions warring for center stage inside me. If Ghost cut something out, I'd have too much free time. Free time wasn't traditionally something I did real well with.

"Even you have a limit."

"Haven't hit it yet."

"All else good? Don't get mad, but I worry about you sometimes."

Outwardly my knee-jerk reaction would be anger. No one should be worrying about me—I worried about other people. But internally, it was nice to hear. "I'm good, man."

Ghost leaned back in his chair and rubbed his hands through the mop of dark auburn hair on his head.

Like a yawn, the action proved contagious, and I found myself stretching too.

"Did you, uh . . . need anything, Sasquatch, or is this just a social call?"

I grinned, pulling on the personality I usually wore around my old squadron buddies. "It's not what I need, Ghost. It's what you need."

"I'm too tired for riddles."

"Then you're definitely in the wrong line of work, because your uncle seemed like a pretty big fan."

"Uncle Marvin," Ghost practically moaned it. "We're totally stuck. I think the whole thing was just some kind of ruse to keep me busy. He was always worried about me after . . . everything."

We did not talk about the everything to which Ghost referred, and if anyone should be worrying about anyone, it was me about him. Ghost had a lot to unpack, but now was probably not the time. "Right. Well. I have news on that front. Kind of."

Ghost's eyes widened and he sat forward.

"Do you think it's possible that this whole thing is meant to get us to dig into a bunch of films he wrote but never got credit for?"

Ghost shrugged, his face falling a bit.

"I've been looking into the movies on that list we found. Marvin told you he wrote some of them, right?"

"I mean, not in so many words, but yeah, certain lines and stuff he would talk about a lot."

"But he's not listed in the credits of any of those movies. And they were all produced by Rudy Fusterberg's studio, Mountaintop."

"Okay, yeah." Ghost's face told me this was nothing new to him.

"So I have a hypothesis."

"Hit me."

"Marvin is trying to get you to dig into those movies, to prove that he actually wrote them but never got credit. And if that's true, then he's owed decades of royalties or some kind of compensation."

"Do screenwriters get royalties?" Ghost asked. "I don't know how that works."

"Google knows. I can't remember what I figured out last night." I pulled out my phone and did a bit of searching to remind myself what I'd discovered the night before. "So maybe not royalties, exactly. But he'd be owed something."

"How do we know he never got anything for them?"

That was a good question. "I guess we don't, really. Except if he was paid, wouldn't he be named as the writer in the credits?"

"Maybe."

"We need to find two things. The original scripts and the books for Mountaintop for the years around the time those movies came out."

Ghost slumped in his chair. "That's not an easy ask. The scripts, maybe. Those might be here somewhere." The other parts of the hunt had all be on the premises.

"If we find the scripts, we can get a lawyer to demand the records. Maybe. I mean, I don't know how lawyer shit works, but that seems right." I wanted to be right about this. Considering the mess I'd made of most other things in my life, I felt like I needed a win, and helping Ghost would be a double success.

Ghost stared at his hands for a moment, turning them over in his lap. "You think it's even worth it?"

"I think it's what your uncle wanted us to do," I told him. "But I don't know where to start looking for the scripts. Do you?"

"It's not like they're on a hard drive anywhere," Ghost said. "They'd probably be typed out if he kept copies. And that'd be a lot of paper, right?"

It was my turn to shrug.

Ghost shook his head. "We've renovated most of the original resort at this point," he said. "It's possible they've already been tossed. Maybe some of the guys found them and didn't know what they were."

"You gave pretty stern orders than anything unusual got brought straight to you."

"That's true. And Lucy's crew knew what was going on..."

"So somewhere around here is a big pile of paper that can prove Marvin wrote movies he never got credit for. And Mountaintop owes his estate whatever he was due, plus interest." I grinned.

"It's a stretch."

"Let's find them anyway."

Ghost finally smiled, and just like that, the hunt was back on.

Chapter Fifteen
Distance is Overrated

CEECEE

I opened the shop the next morning, a kind of lightness I hadn't known before filling me every time I thought about Travis. I helped customers, and then Cole and I led a half-day hike through Dunsten Meadows, a beautiful trail that offered a sweeping view of the landscape south of here and often included wildlife along the way. Today we'd seen a herd of elk on a far slope, and found plenty of bear tracks, which were enough for the city kids I was guiding.

Every turn in the trail, every new discovery had me thinking about Travis, wishing he was with us. I loved showing him the parts of Colorado I loved, the places that felt most like home to me. We hadn't spent much time pretending to be together, but I'd known him long enough that my attraction to him had always been there, in the background. And now that I'd let it rise to the surface? I couldn't seem to forget what it had felt like to have Travis's hands on my waist, his dark eyes fixed on mine —or what it felt like when he'd kissed me. My body reacted even to the memory as if it was happening all over again, and I had to shake myself to stay focused on the hike. Why had I told him not to come to the shop this morning?

I knew why—the man had a lot on his plate. It was clear he'd taken on more than any man should between the help he was giving me and the things he'd easily accepted for the Kaspers and the wedding at the resort. I was trying to give him time, but my heart wished I hadn't been quite so generous.

Back at the shop late in the afternoon, it got quiet, and I took care of all the little things that needed doing while my mind continued to fixate on Travis, on whatever was happening between us. On whatever he'd needed to tell me but hadn't gotten a chance to, thanks to Jensen's car trouble the night before.

"Hey, great stuff today," Ned told me as his crew headed out for the evening. "Final day of filming tomorrow and then we'll be off."

"Okay," I said. I had mixed feelings about the end of filming. It would take off a hell of a lot of pressure, and hopefully move me a step closer to the adventure I'd been longing for. But it also meant the end of my time with Travis bound to my side. Maybe we didn't need the pretense now, but I wasn't sure what that would look like—would we really be a couple? And what would happen if I won the trip? Would he want to come with me? "Thanks for everything, Ned. You guys have been great. I barely knew you were there most of the time!"

"You and Travis are a great couple. I'm not supposed to say this, but I'm kind of rooting for you." He grinned at me.

He'd actually said that before, which made me wonder if he said that to every guide he'd worked with. "Thanks." Something uncertain swirled in my gut, making me uneasy. "We'll meet here at eight tomorrow morning. The hike package came with some gear, so we'll go pick the group up and then come here to get outfitted."

"Sounds good," Ned said. "See ya!"

I watched the crew load up their sedan and leave the parking lot, and then let myself sag against the counter.

My mind returned to the kiss at the Fox. The way Travis's thumb had gently swept over my lip, the depth of his gaze pulling me deeper and deeper before the actual kiss had sent my mind shivering and shuddering to a full stop. And then the quiet conversation we'd had on the mountain.

I wanted more. I wanted to find out what it would feel like to really be with him, to lie down beneath him and let that huge powerful body dominate me. The sheer size and strength of the man, combined with the tender way he touched me, looked at me—I knew it would be an incredible combination in the bedroom. My cheeks warmed just imagining the way he'd look down at me beneath him, the way it would feel to be pressed against him.

I had definitely not asked him to pretend to be my boyfriend with this outcome in mind, but now that I had a few minutes to think it over in the quiet of my shop, I was beginning to wonder if there could be something real, something long-term between Travis and me. Sure, I planned to leave Kasper Ridge at some point, to see more of the world. And relationships traditionally didn't work out well for me. But nothing about this was planned. It was just happening, sweeping over me like a rogue wave I hadn't seen and could definitely not control.

I picked up my phone.

* * *

"I'm really glad you called," Travis said, leaning closer as we sat side by side at the fire pit between the yurts. It was still early, and the sun hadn't sunk completely below the trees yet, but most of the staff was still engaged with guests, so it was just us.

Travis had lit the fire, and the stutter and stretch of the morphing flames gave us something to look at, which made it easier to talk.

"Want?" I offered him a slice of the pizza I'd brought.

"Definitely." He accepted, also taking a beer from the cooler between us. I'd texted, suggesting we grab an early dinner if he was up for it, and his response had been immediate.

We ate without talking much, the cooling breeze lifting the branches of the trees around us and making the fire dance as the sky smeared itself wide in dark shades of blue and orange.

The silence between us did nothing to dim the feelings I was more and more aware of, feelings I knew would need to be addressed at some point.

"Ceese," Travis said after a while, turning his big body in the wooden chair to face me. "I don't know if maybe I made you uncomfortable yesterday, if things kind of just went too far—"

"No." I'd meant to say more, to explain a bit about how I was feeling, but the word slipped from my lips like it just didn't want to hear another syllable from him about the time we'd spent so far being wrong in any way. "No, you didn't make me uncomfortable. I just"—I glanced up into his eyes, hoping something there would make me bolder—"I didn't expect to develop real feelings for you. And when I realized I had, it just kind of took me by surprise."

A slow smile lifted one side of his full lips. "You have feelings for me, Ceese?" His tone was low, teasing.

"I think you know that."

The smile turned a little smug, then slipped as he dropped my gaze. "That makes me really happy," he said, his eyes coming back up to meet mine after the words were out.

My stomach flipped, and for a second I wanted to leap from the seat and let the sudden energy his confession created take me on a victory lap of the fire or something. But I forced myself to stay still.

"So," I breathed. "What does this mean?"

He smiled, leaning back in his chair and turning his gaze to the fire. "I don't really know."

Now that it was out, and we'd both admitted how we felt, it seemed like something should happen. My skin burned with a desire for his touch, and the space between us felt wide and treacherous. I wanted to cross it, but wasn't sure how.

"So . . ." I tried, discomfort seeping back into my bones.

Travis turned back to me with a sigh, and then he gathered the food we'd forgotten and zipped up the little cooler. He stood, and reached out a hand to me.

Pushing down my uncertainty, I took his hand, standing to face him. We stood there for a moment, only our fingers touching and the fire dancing to one side, casting shadows across Travis's handsome face. And then he let out a long breath.

"I've been trying to keep a distance, Ceese," he said, his voice low and rough. "But I don't know if I can do it anymore."

I held his gaze, willing him to give it up. Mentally pressing him to touch me, to pull me to him.

One of his big hands lifted, and he gently pushed the hair back from the side of my face, cupping my cheek in the same motion. I leaned into the touch instinctively, letting out a breath and feeling my eyes drop shut.

And then he moved closer, his other hand finding my hip, resting there, his fingers wrapping my waist as I sensed the warmth of his chest just centimeters from mine. I opened my eyes to see him leaning in, down, until his lips brushed mine gently, sending a delicious thrill through me.

The hand on my hip slid around my low back, dipped, cupped my ass and pressed me into him. At the same moment, his mouth took mine, no longer soft, gentle, but more demanding now.

I let out a moan as I felt the evidence of his desire between us, and I slid my arms around him, increasingly desperate to get closer, to feel more. My hips were pressed hard against him, and I could feel the steely length of him as his mouth did things that had rational thought hopping a train headed far, far away.

His tongue teased the seam of my lips and then swept my own, the push and pull of the kiss mirroring press of our bodies.

Roscoe let out a whine from his place on the ground, and it shattered the moment. I pulled back, feeling like I'd just run some kind of footrace.

"Um . . ." I didn't know why I was trying speak. I had no idea what to say.

"Do you want to go inside?" Travis asked quietly, his eyes burning like fiery obsidian as they met mine.

I nodded.

Without another word, we picked up the food and cooler, doused the fire, and headed back into the lodge, Roscoe on our tail.

The lobby was packed. It was Saturday night, so that wasn't a real surprise. Guests lingered near the front doors—Jensen had told me he made more on a Saturday night driving people back and forth from the resort to the Surly Fox and Toothy Moose than he did the whole rest of the week.

Music and laughter spilled from the bar's wide doorway to the side of the front doors, and I could imagine the space inside, packed with guests and visitors as Wiley and the other bartenders moved behind the long wooden counter, serving drinks and conversation. I liked the resort bar with its wood paneling and movie star photos on the walls. But right now, I wouldn't have gone in if someone had offered to pay me. Right now, I was slipping into the elevator behind Travis, my entire body shivering with anticipation.

We stepped into the small wood-paneled space, and as soon as the doors slid shut on the lobby, he turned, caging me in the corner between his muscular arms. Those dark eyes met mine and pinned me in place, stealing the breath from my lungs, as he leaned in and kissed me softly, carefully. The second the elevator chime sounded, signaling our arrival at the sixth floor of the staff wing, he stepped back, putting space between us again.

The hallway, however, was empty. Probably because Travis had said he was the only staff member living on this floor. The air around us was still and quiet, and for a brief moment I thought about how it might freak me out to be alone as he was, the only resident on an entire hotel floor.

He took my hand when it was clear no one was around, and practically pulled me to his door, where he made quick work of the old fashioned lock with the key from his pocket.

I stepped inside when he gestured for me to do so, an uneasy awkwardness mixing now with the anticipation I'd felt before.

The room was a suite, a living space with a couch and coffee table made up most of the room we'd stepped into, and I could see the bedroom through the open door. The sight of the huge bed, rumpled with a white comforter atop it, caused my nerves to rise. I wanted to be here, wanted Travis to lay me down, to touch me—but the bed made it all seem so real. After a quick sniff of the room's perimeter, Roscoe went to curl up on a cushion beneath the window. There was a desk with a laptop against one wall in the living area, and a makeshift kitchenette set up along the long buffet on the other wall, a mini fridge plugged in next to the wooden cabinet.

"This is home," Travis said, shooting me a smile that suggested he felt the sudden uncertainty in the air too.

"It's nice," I said, the sweeping glass wall of the far side of the room catching my eyes. "Great view." His room looked out at the front of the resort, but he was high enough to be able to see just over the trees that filled the land on either side of the parking lot and entrance drive. Right now the view held a sky filled with stars, but during the day I'd bet he could see the mountains in the distance.

"It is," he said, and I turned to see him looking right at me. It was a line, and it should have felt cheesy. Instead it sent a shiver through me, warming my skin and flipping my tummy.

He crossed to where I stood in front of the window, a question in his smoldering eyes—one I must have answered with my own return gaze because he lifted a hand and pushed it into the hair at one side of my face, cupping my cheek again.

I lifted my chin to look up at him, loving the rough heat of his palm against my skin, the gentle way he held my head in his big hand.

He leaned in then, barely touching my lips with his own and sending fire streaming through my veins. I lifted a hand, landing it on his solid chest, relishing the feel of the muscle there, hard and unyielding under the softness of his shirt.

As if my touch unleashed something within him, Travis stepped closer still, his other arm looping my body and pulling me into him, his mouth turning demanding, hungry. He kissed me then like a man seeking his own survival, like a man who thought I held the keys to the future. And I returned the kiss, giving him what I could, losing myself in the passion of the connection.

Travis's hands found the hem of my shirt, lifting it and then exploring the flesh of my back, my stomach. One hand pulled me closer still as the other rose to cup my breast. I gasped, wanting more, needing more. My own hands were sliding beneath the fabric of his soft T-shirt, smoothing miles of flesh stretched over the steely muscle of his back.

The kiss went on as our hands explored, and then Travis's mouth dropped lower, teasing and nipping the skin of my jaw, my throat. My head fell back and I pushed myself into him harder, wanting more. Wanting...everything.

"Every time I sit close to you, I struggle with my desire to touch you here," he whispered, worshiping the skin of my throat.

"And here," he said, one hand sliding up my torso, cupping the other breast.

A needy moan escaped me at his words, my hands dropping lower to pull his ass toward me as I pressed my hips to him.

And then he released me, his eyes never leaving my face as he stepped back, putting space between us.

Each of us was breathing hard, our chests rising and falling in time.

"I just . . ." that hand went up to rub the back of his neck. "There's something I should tell you," he said.

This was not the time. Everything inside me was reaching for him and certain parts of me were becoming extremely impatient. "Maybe you can tell me later," I suggested, stepping close and putting my hand back against his hot chest.

"I just want to do the right thing," he said.

"I don't care about the right thing right now," I told him, pressing onto my toes to kiss him again. Maybe I should have listened, but my brain wasn't making the rules.

"Ceese," he said pulling his mouth from mine but staying close. "There's just—"

I kissed him again. There was nothing he could tell me that would stop this from happening. I was too invested now. We'd been friends for long enough for me to know what I needed to know about this man. He was gentle and caring, he was loyal and devoted. He was a good man, and while I had no idea what kind of future we might have, if any, I wanted tonight.

Travis let out a groan, and his arms swept around me, one looping beneath my knees and lifting me from my feet.

I cried out in surprise, but Travis stole the sound, capturing my mouth with his as he carried me to the bedroom. Evidently Roscoe had followed us in because Travis broke the kiss long enough to order the dog out of the room, and then he deposited me gently on the bed and went to close the door.

I looked around, taking in the wide expanse of the bed, the window offering the same view as the one in the other room, and the general tidiness of Travis's room. Before I could comment on anything, he returned, his massive presence wiping everything from my mind but desire for more. For him.

"Just promise this won't change things between us," he whispered, his hand lifting the hem of my shirt and skating up my side as his mouth found my throat.

"It won't," I sighed, losing myself in the feel of his body on mine, his mouth nipping and licking the tender flesh of my throat, my collarbone, while his fingers caressed the skin of my torso.

My own hands were busy, seeking the feel of his skin, and I pulled the back of his shirt up, letting my hands move slowly across the hot skin of his body, my nails trailing up his back.

We stayed like that for a while, relishing the heat, the building tension between us. We were both fully clothed, but there was something about the intimacy between us that made me feel more vulnerable than I had during any of the few sexual encounters I'd ever had. Those had been rushed scrambles in the dark, clumsy explorations. This? This was something else, something reverent and worthy of patience, though mine was waning as Travis palmed my breast through my bra.

I pulled his shirt up, hoping to signal that I was ready to lose some of the layers between us. He lifted his head, shot me a grin, and then reached behind himself, pulling the shirt off in one motion that was sexy as anything I'd ever seen.

And then I was lost. Despite his size, Travis moved gracefully, carefully, and he seemed to know exactly how to coax my body out of my control and into his. I'd never really felt comfortable letting myself go with a man, but with Travis, it wasn't a conscious choice. His hands, his mouth, his very essence all seemed to meld with mine and thinking was not part of the equation.

As he peeled my shirt from my body and removed my bra, I understood that while I'd had sex before, I'd never experienced anything like this.

Chapter Sixteen
Massive, You Say...

TRAVIS

This wasn't the way I'd wanted this to happen.

But don't mistake me. I very much wanted this to happen.

I just hoped to be free from the other entanglements in my life so that this thing between me and CeeCee could develop without any complications. I'd planned to wait until the fake relationship ploy was over, until I'd had a chance to sign my name on the dotted line for Daphne.

But it was too late for that.

CeeCee's beautiful body was pressed to mine, moving beneath me on the bed, her silky skin bared to me as I marveled over and over again at the fact. How had I gotten this lucky? How was it that this perfect woman had ended up here with me? Like this?

They were questions for later.

For now, I had a job to do. I was going to worship the woman before me, make her feel as beautiful and special as I'd always thought she was. Because if I was really honest with myself?

I'd admit that I'd fallen in love with CeeCee a long time ago. Long before she asked me to pretend to be in love with her. Long before I'd gotten to spend every day with her, confirming what I already knew.

That she was the perfect woman.

She was tough and confident, but still delicate, and so painfully beautiful.

I nipped a path down her stomach, letting my tongue trace circles against her skin as my hands filled themselves with her breasts. It was a crazy rush of sensation, and my head spun with the wonder of it all. But when I reached the waistband of her pants, all rational thought slid away.

Slowly, I kissed a path around the top of her hips, teasing her until her hips were pressing up from the mattress, her hands at the sides of my head, guiding me lower. My body was thrumming, demanding release, but I shoved the need away. I was going to ensure that I took care of CeeCee first.

I unfastened the button, lowered the zipper, and hooked my fingers into the waist of her pants, tugging them off. She lifted her hips to help and I stepped away, both to pull the pants from her legs and so that I could take a breath and admire the woman splayed on the bed.

Fucking perfect.

Her skin was creamy and smooth, dotted with freckles that I intended to memorize the way astronomers knew the stars above. The constellations of CeeCee's body were the only navigation tools I'd need. While I was up, I moved to the corner dresser and pulled a condom from the box tucked inside. I'd brought it without really planning to need any. After all, this was not why I'd come to Kasper Ridge.

CeeCee watched me through glassy eyes, her chest rising

and falling rapidly, and her open vulnerability pulling me back to her. I tossed the condom onto the bed and leaned forward, my hands wrapping her slim waist and my forehead pressed to her stomach.

I inhaled. She always smelled faintly of fresh air and sunscreen, and now I caught a scent that was purely CeeCee, something primal and so sexy I could feel my pants growing even tighter around me. But I didn't want to rush things.

Lowering myself to my knees, I tugged CeeCee down the bed so I was positioned between her legs, her hips just at the edge of the bed. I coaxed her legs over my shoulders and inhaled deeply pressing my nose to her center, eliciting a breathy moan from her.

My hands teased over the cotton of her panties, my fingers skating across her most sensitive areas as I let my hot breath wash over her.

"Please," she moaned in a breathy voice that sent spears of need straight to my dick. "Travis."

I rose, pulling the panties from her waist and then pushing off my own pants, freeing the raging erection that had been stiffening since the first touch by the fire outside. And then I knelt between CeeCee's legs again.

My tongue and fingers worked in concert, teasing the delicate bud that made CeeCee squirm and moan, and eventually delving deep into the heat of her body. When I circled my fingers inside her and sucked hard with my mouth, she bucked beneath me, crying out. I was seconds from losing control, but I reined it in, wanting to focus on her, to give her . . . everything.

"Oh god," she moaned, wrapping her legs tight around me and guiding my head with her hands. She was grinding down on my mouth now, my fingers still pressing and gently pumping, filling her while my mouth worked. "Ohhh," she rasped. "Ohhh god . . ." and then she let go.

I could feel her pulse around my hand and beneath my tongue, and it was potentially the sexiest thing I'd ever experienced. This moment would be filed for the remainder of my life. I waited her out, struggling with my own self control.

"Come here," she whispered once the spasms had receded. "Holy fuck," she said, pulling at my hair to move me up the bed. I did as she ordered, tugging her up with me so that we were fully on the bed, and CeeCee's eyes met mine.

Without another word, she reached for me, kissing me in a way that I thought might just be everything I needed for the rest of my life. Her hands traced my skin, moving down my back, pulling me against her body. I slung a leg over her hips and she pulled at me until I was straddling her fully, her lithe body pressed against the length of mine.

"You're perfect, you know that?" I asked her between kisses.

She made a purring sound in her chest and her hands continued to explore, sliding between us and grazing the hot flesh of my erection. I hissed in a breath and CeeCee pressed up against me, rolling me to my side so she had better access.

Her warm hand enveloped me then, stealing my breath and any hopes for rational thought, and she began working me, her tight fist moving up and down in the most erotic rhythm I'd ever imagined.

As pulses of electricity shot through me, I kissed her deeply, feeling more at once than I'd ever felt. It was like everything in the world had stopped so that we could experience one another. Like every sensation that existed in the world was here, was between us, moving back and forth and building toward something I couldn't even imagine.

"I want you," CeeCee growled in my ear, guiding my tip toward that hot perfect place between her legs.

I reached over her head to where I'd tossed the condom and made quick work of rolling it on, and then I rested my weight on my forearms, CeeCee's hand back on my dick, driving me crazy.

She moved slightly as I kissed her, opening herself to me, welcoming me with her body, and I felt the enveloping heat of her against me.

The groan that escaped me was guttural and potentially a little desperate, but it had the effect of making CeeCee groan in response, pressing herself against me, taking me deeper.

I pressed on, centimeter by centimeter, relishing the intense heat of her body and worshipping the softness of her skin. As I pushed inside her, a scattered thought came and went—I was lost. To this. To her. I'd tried to be careful, to do things in the right order, to be honest and good. But now that I was here, I couldn't regret it, and I knew I'd spend every second of my life remembering what it felt like to be this close to her, this bound to her.

CeeCee surrounded me. Her scent filled my senses and her body wrapped mine, her legs around my waist and her tight heat sending sensation shooting up my spine. We moved together, in a slow languid rhythm that I knew I couldn't maintain. The urge was building in me to move, to thrust, to take. But I held back, because CeeCee was guiding this rhythm, and I was going to give her what she needed, even if it killed me.

Her body gripped me, and released, repeating the undulating pressure over and over until I thought I might lose my mind. And then I felt it. Everything in her tightened—her arms around my neck, her legs around my waist, her channel around my desperate dick.

"Oh god," she cried, breathless and high. "Oh, god, I'm . . ." In the next breath the orgasm took her, and I watched, mesmerized, as the woman I loved rode the waves of the ecstasy we'd created. It was by far the sexiest thing I'd ever experienced, her mouth forming a little o as her body rolled and pulsed around me. Her breath caught and whimpers escaped her as the sensation moved through her, and I did my best to keep up the rhythm she'd built as she lost control.

"Holy," she breathed, her eyes slowly opening to meet mine as she came down, her body relaxing around me. "Oh my god."

I smiled, desperation rocketing through me and my balls pulling up so close to my body I thought they might just disappear back inside me. But I wasn't about to move. I wanted to make sure she wrung every ounce of pleasure from her orgasm before I even thought about mine.

As if she understood completely, she began to move again, faster now. Sensation rolled through me, and I took over, careful not to thrust too hard, too far, despite the animal urge driving me forward.

"Harder," she whispered, and I popped my eyes open again to be sure she meant it. She met my gaze with a devious look that made me believe she knew exactly what I needed, and her hands on my ass were coaxing me forward. "Harder," she said again.

I complied, and the tingling started at the base of my spine, and the flames licking through me began to overtake rational thought. Sensation flooded my body and a moment later I was exploding, every cell in my body focused on CeeCee, on this second, on this connection between us—our bodies and something so much deeper. I came hard, blackness sweeping my vision until pinpricks of light blasted through the dark, and finally I collapsed, careful not to crush the gorgeous woman beneath me.

"Holy fuck," I managed, echoing CeeCee's pithy statement from before.

"Yeah," she agreed.

We lay together for a while, until our breathing aligned and calmed, and then CeeCee chuckled.

"You're laughing?" I asked, unable to lift my head to look at her. "What's funny?"

"You're smothering me."

I rolled to the side, realizing I'd let myself relax too much. "Sorry. You okay?"

"Yeah, you're just . . . you're not a small guy, Travis."

"I know."

"In any way."

I opened one eye and looked at her, loving the flush of her cheeks, the messy halo of her strawberry blond hair. "Are making reference to my dick, ma'am?"

She giggled. "I might be."

"I'll allow it."

"Oh, you'll allow it? You'll allow me to compliment your massive dick?"

"Massive now, you say."

She burst into another fit of giggles, and a second later I was on her again, half tickling her as I kissed her silly. We both ended up breathless, and once again I was splayed on top of her.

"You're smashing me again."

"Maybe you deserve it," I suggested.

She laughed and I rolled off of her. "I'm gonna clean up a bit." I stood, and headed for the bathroom. When I stepped back out into the bedroom, CeeCee was sitting on the edge of the bed, fully clothed, and tugging her boots on.

"You're leaving?" I asked. I didn't want to acknowledge the disappointment sweeping through me, the sudden loneliness threatening to overtake the happiness I'd been feeling a moment before.

She stopped what she was doing and looked up. "I just figured . . ."

"I don't want you to leave." The words were out before I considered how they might sound.

CeeCee hesitated, watching me carefully. Then she seemed to decide something, removing her boots again and sliding her phone out of her pocket and walking to the nightstand to deposit it. "Okay."

The smile that crossed my lips didn't begin to signal the happiness I felt. "Okay?"

"I'm sleepy anyway. I'll stay. But I have to text my mom so she won't worry and I'll probably need to head out really early so I can get back for our full day hike tomorrow."

My heart lifted as CeeCee went into the bathroom and then returned a few minutes later, pulled her clothes back off, and slipped beneath the covers of the big bed.

"Want a T-shirt or anything?" I asked her.

She smiled and shook her head against the pillow. "You'd only end up taking it off of me."

"Probably true." That was definitely the plan.

I switched off the light and climbed in beside her, warmth suffusing every cell of my body as she nestled herself at my side, fitting me perfectly. I held her, expecting to remain awake as I enjoyed the sensation of listening to CeeCee dream.

But that wasn't what happened. Instead, I drifted to sleep, only to find my nightmare lying in wait, ready to erase every ounce of calm happiness I'd found in CeeCee's arms.

As the dust swirled around me, the loud chop of the helicopter providing an overwhelming and unyielding soundtrack, the woman with the blue scarf appeared in front of me again. She thrust the bundle into my arms over and over, and explosions pierced the chaos of the night.

"I can't take him," I explained, wanting to reach for the baby but finding my arms anchored to my sides. "I can't—"

"Travis!"

My eyes flew open, and where I expected to find dust and destruction, there was only CeeCee. Her eyes were wide and worried in the low light from the window, and her hands were on my shoulders. We were both sitting up, and the sheets were a tangle around my sweaty torso. I tried to catch my breath, to reorient myself. I was here. CeeCee was here. It was okay.

"Sorry," I muttered, the fog of the dream still lingering in my mind. "I just—I . . . sometimes I don't sleep well."

I could hear Roscoe whining from outside the closed bedroom door.

CeeCee glanced at the door, but then leaned closer, wrapping her arms around me and pressing herself to me. "It's okay," she whispered, as if I was a child in need of soothing.

For a moment, I stayed stiff, adrenaline and fear still holding me captive. But as CeeCee rubbed my back and crooned reassurance in a soft voice, I let myself relax into her comforting embrace.

"It's okay," she said again, and as we both lay back down, our arms wrapped around each other, I thought maybe it could be.

Chapter Seventeen
Elevator of Shame

CEECEE

It had been a long time since I'd slept anywhere but my childhood bedroom and it was disorienting for a moment waking to my alarm in the shelter of Travis's arms, the sun just beginning to light the tops of the trees out his window.

I rolled to face him, and for a few moments I just looked into his face. Sleep made him look softer, younger than he was. His jaw was relaxed, as was his forehead, and the tension I often saw in his expression was gone. None of the terror I'd found in his gaze after his nightmare remained, and I found myself even more invested in this complicated man.

He was handsome, without a doubt. But there was something more. When I looked up into the face I'd grown to love as a friend before I'd ever considered climbing into bed with him, my heart swelled inside me and a word formed in my mind. Mine.

For long quiet seconds, I watched him breathe, and let my hand trace the soft lines of his quiet face.

His eyes popped open, and the full lips that had driven me to helplessness the night before spread into a lazy smile.

"Good morning," I whispered.

"Hi beautiful."

"I should head out so I can get ready for today."

His arms tightened around me in response. I nestled tighter into his embrace and felt the hard evidence of his arousal against my thigh.

I rubbed against it, pressing myself closer.

"Don't start something you don't have time to finish," he warned.

But I couldn't help it. I wanted him.

"We have to be quick," I said, and Travis responded by rolling to his back, pulling me with him. I found myself straddling his massive body.

"Yes," he said, his voice still thick with sleep. "You should be quick. I'll just lay here."

"You want me to do all the work?" I laughed, already rubbing myself up and down against his solid length, sending sparks of desire through my stomach.

In truth, I didn't mind at all. And when I sank down onto him, filling myself with him once I'd rolled a condom down his length, it didn't take long before I felt my body coiling with the need for release.

I moved over him, relishing the sensation of being filled, being sated, having this gentle giant to myself, and I came to the words repeating over and over in my head.

This could be real. This could be real.

When he came, I watched him, still feeling as if my life had been transformed suddenly in some kind of crazy kaleidoscope, fractured and reassembled into a form I didn't completely recognize.

But the truth was, it felt like Travis fit. And I wanted this, to see where it might lead.

"I have to go," I whispered to him as he held me tightly against his chest. "But I'll see you in like an hour at the shop."

"Yes," he agreed, and I had a sneaky suspicion he planned to go back to sleep.

"You're getting up, right?"

"Getting up now," he agreed, still not opening his eyes.

"I'll see you in an hour."

"See you in an hour," he repeated.

"Travis." I leaned up and whacked him on the chest.

His eyes sprung open in surprise. "Ow."

"Wake up. We can't be late."

"I'm up. Seriously." He smiled, and he did look pretty awake. "I was just enjoying having you here. But don't worry. I'll see you in an hour."

"Okay." I kissed him lightly and slid off of him, heading for the bathroom and then moving for the door a second later. Travis was sitting on the edge of the bed rubbing his face as I departed.

"See you soon," I called from the front room. Roscoe was curled in a bed in the corner, and he lifted his head at my voice. "See you later, boy," I told him. He dropped his head back down to his paws.

Everyone wanted to sleep in today.

* * *

I tried not to feel any shame as I rode the elevator downstairs and stepped into the lobby, but this particular exit wasn't one I made often. Still, despite the current optics, I had no regrets about what had happened.

Those moments in the dark of night replayed in my mind—the moments when Travis had cried out, had looked around like he wasn't sure where he was. It made me happy to have been there for him, and my heart broke a little thinking about him having horrible dreams and being there all alone to deal with them.

The door slid open. There were a surprising number of people up and about the lobby, but I reminded myself that I, of all people, should know that those heading out for a day's exploration got an early start. I wasn't the only adventure outfit nearby, and it was possible folks were heading off to rock climb, hike, or raft with other guides today.

There was one group at the front desk that caught my attention, however, mostly because there were two men in the group who would give Travis a run for his money in a sheer size competition. I couldn't help giving them a closer look as I passed by, noticing the slight twang of a Texas accent and marveling at how much like Travis the younger man looked.

Aubrey was typing something into the computer system as they stood before her, and I took a moment to pause and retie my boot, something about the group making me want to linger and learn more.

There were two men and two women—the older couple of the group appeared to be together, and the younger ones . . . it was harder to tell.

I didn't have time to waste, so I secured my boot and headed out, pushing aside the odd recognition I thought I'd felt upon seeing the guests. I had a hike to prepare for, and that meant a quick shower and a race to the shop to get it opened and set up for the day before we headed back over to pick up our guests.

* * *

Travis strode into the shop at exactly the appointed time, Roscoe at his side. He shot me a smile that was potentially cocky, and I narrowed my eyes at him teasingly.

"Morning beautiful," he called, potentially for the benefit of the camera trained on him from the side of the shop.

Pleasure rolled through me. "Morning sleepyhead," I called back.

Travis stepped behind the counter and wrapped me in a hug, which I lingered inside of for a long moment.

"You two are adorable," Adelaide said, stepping out of the back. She was going to take the morning shift at the shop today while we led the hike. I tried not be annoyed with her, knowing she was the reason I'd had to come clean to my family. They would have found out some other way, if not from her.

I smiled at her. "Thanks." Travis had just arrived, but it was time for us to head to the resort and pick up the hiking group. "We'll be back in about half an hour to outfit everyone for the hike."

Adelaide nodded.

"They get Kasper Guides water bottles and fanny packs as part of the package," I reminded her. "So if it's quiet, you could get those set up. First aid kits, sunscreen, lip balm, and a snack bar inside please."

She nodded and moved to the end of the counter where there was a box that held all our branded gear.

"You ready?" I asked Travis and Ned, who was going to accompany us in the van to pick up the guests.

"Let's go."

Back in the lobby at the resort, we had to wait a bit for a few of the guests to appear. In the meantime, I found myself glancing around for the group I'd seen earlier, but they were no longer at the desk.

Aubrey was still there though, and as she spotted us, she glanced around herself as if to be sure no one needed her immediately, and then walked toward us, an odd look on her face.

"Hey guys," she said, glancing toward the ever-present camera.

"Hey Aubrey," I said.

Travis grinned at her.

"Um, Sass? You have a second?" I wasn't used to hearing Aubrey sound uncertain, and it caught my attention.

"Yeah, just getting ready to head out."

I sensed that Aubrey had meant for Travis to step away a bit with her, but he didn't move and she came close again. "It's just, uh . . ." she glanced at me and moved even closer to Travis. "It's just . . . well, your mom and dad checked in this morning."

Surprise flickered through me, but then it made sense. The Texans. I didn't know why they were here, but I wanted to meet them.

A grin spread across Travis's face. "They did?" He looked around wildly as if they might be standing in the lobby.

"Yeah, kind of. I mean, they didn't have a reservation and the resort is booked for the week with that wedding coming up next weekend. I talked to Ghost and we gave them rooms on your floor."

I thought about the men I'd seen earlier. The older one must have been Travis's dad.

"Rooms?" Travis asked. "They're not sharing a room?" He looked worried.

"No, uh, that's the thing." Aubrey looked like she was about to reveal something else, but then her eyes snagged on Ned, who was filming, a happy look on his face. She cleared her throat and her face morphed into a strange false smile. "Um, that's the thing. Your brother is here too," she said. "With his wife, Daphne." She nodded a few times and I wondered if something was wrong that she wasn't mentioning.

Then I remembered Travis's phone call with someone named Daphne. It had to be the same person, but I wasn't sure what might be going on. Was Travis involved with his brother's wife? No, that didn't make sense. I stared at the huge man at my side, trying to make sense of this.

"Oh." Travis's voice lost any hint of excitement it had held when he'd heard his parents were here.

Despite Travis's reaction, a strange little excitement bubbled up inside me at the idea of meeting his family.

"Yeah," Aubrey said, shooting me a smile that looked a lot like an apology. "So I wanted you to know. I guess you'll see them when you guys get back here this afternoon."

"Yeah," Travis repeated as Aubrey glanced at Ned again and then headed back to the front desk.

"That's exciting," I said, leaning into Travis and looking up into his face. "Right? Seeing your family? Did you know they were coming?"

"I mean . . ." he lifted a hand to grip the back of his neck. He did not look especially happy. I wondered if it was me—did he not want to introduce me? Maybe he felt like it was just too early? "We talked about maybe having them visit, but . . . no, this is . . . It's a surprise."

"And your brother!" I grinned. "I actually saw them this morning when I left the hotel, I think. Two men who looked a lot like you, mostly because they were huge. But the younger one, your brother I guess, his face looked like yours too."

Travis didn't seem to be listening, his eyes had caught on something in the distance, and he was frowning.

"Hey," I said, wrapping my arms around his waist and looking up at him. "You okay?"

It appeared to take a lot of effort, but he shook his head slightly, and cleared his throat, his arms finally going around my waist and holding me there. "Yeah. Yeah, I'm good."

It was clear there was something more to this situation, but I chose to let it go for now. I was too happy, and we had guests ready to head out. "Ready to hike?"

"Let's do it." He dropped a kiss on top of my head, and we turned to face the gathered group.

"Hi guys!" I called to get their attention. "Ready for a breathtaking hike?"

The group cheered, and I felt a surge of overwhelming joy work through me. This job, this life . . . and now, this man at my side. It all felt so right. I hadn't known things could be so perfect. Not for me, at least. Maybe what I'd said to Lucy before had been wrong. Maybe I would get to have the life—the man, the family. I was getting ahead of myself, but it all felt so possible suddenly.

I glanced at Ned, giving him a happy smile. Something inside me told me it was a sure thing, that we'd win this contest easily. Because that was what my life had become suddenly. A happy, lucky certainty.

"I'm CeeCee and this is Travis and our hiking dog Roscoe. We're from Kasper Guides and Gear, and we're going to lead the hike today after we get you some complimentary gear from the shop that you'll get to keep.

"This hike is incredible, and through Kasper Gulch, you'll get to see a lake, a waterfall, and some ridiculous views of the peaks of the Rockies. We've got a gourmet boxed lunch for you, and the weather looks absolutely perfect. You really couldn't ask for a more perfect day." I grinned at them and then winked up at Travis, whose arm was still around my waist. He still looked tense, but he gave me a quick nod.

"Let's go!" I cried, and we all headed out for the day.

Chapter Eighteen
All Good Things Must End

TRAVIS

Daphne was here.

And I hadn't gotten a chance to talk to her. Or to CeeCee. I hadn't explained any of what was going on, and now my wife was here, in the same place where the woman I loved was. And I was . . . a disaster.

"Travis, you okay?" I'd taken up the back of the hike again, but as I wandered after the group along the dusty trail that led between towering pines, past scenic vistas, and finally to a lake nestled high in the mountains, I wasn't seeing any of it. I was seeing the mess I'd made of everything, and as I glanced up, I saw Ned, his camera trained on me.

"Yeah, babe." I answered CeeCee, trying for a casual nonchalance. "All good back here." I'd let myself fall behind again, and CeeCee and the others had paused, waiting for me to catch back up. "Sorry, just tired today, I guess."

CeeCee grinned at me, knowing exactly what would have

resulted in me being sleepy today, and I wished I could return the sweet, happy smile she gave me. But my heart was twisted into a painful knot, knowing the depth of the mess I'd created. The cameras were still on, and I couldn't ruin this for CeeCee. We just had to get through this hike, and they'd be gone.

We'd stop playing pretend, and go back to our regular lives.

The problem was that I wasn't sure what my regular life would be at this point. Go back to being married to someone who didn't love me and whom I didn't love? Continue whatever this was with CeeCee? Would CeeCee even be interested in continuing things once she found out I was married the whole time we'd been pretending to be engaged?

I thought of my wife, her long blond ponytail hanging over one shoulder and her dazzling smile. But every time I pictured her as she was today, the image got smudged and smeared, replaced with a much older picture—one of a tiny light-haired girl who lived down the road from my family's ranch. A girl who was too small, too dirty, whose parents never seemed to notice that she stayed out way past dark and was never around during the day.

Because as a kid, Daphne pretty much lived at our house. She was scrawny and small, underfed and neglected, and my parents probably fed her twice as many meals as she got at her own house. My mom had gone over there once, when Daphne first started wandering over to our place. She'd had it in her head to give Daphne's mom a talking to, or at least to see if maybe they were struggling, if they needed some help. Mom had been shouted off the property, Daphne's father drunk and belligerent, and her mom evidently passed out or asleep on the couch in the cluttered living room where every surface was covered with cans and bottles.

"I'm not sure those folks even know they have a daughter," I'd heard Mom whispering to Dad one night.

So Daphne was like a little sister to me.

And when I'd gotten the orders to Afghanistan and she'd just ended another relationship, finding herself looking at moving back home after the latest in a string of boyfriends booted her out, we'd come up with the idea of getting married because I couldn't imagine her going back to that house. And if I married her, she could move into my apartment while I was gone, and she'd have health benefits and my salary to take care of her until she figured things out. I wasn't using them, and I didn't expect to return home. I thought going to Afghanistan would be the last thing I did.

"Seriously, man, you're gonna get hurt." Ned interrupted my dark train of thought as he grabbed my elbow, helping me regain my balance after I'd stumbled over a fallen tree across the trail. "You're out of it today, huh?"

I glanced at the photographer. I couldn't trust him. In this scenario, he was the enemy.

"Yeah, a little," I agreed. "Thanks."

"Need to talk?" he asked, his perceptive eyes scanning my face as we paused for a moment behind the others.

"Thanks," I said again, pulling my water bottle out and taking a swig. "I'm okay. Appreciate it, though."

He nodded and we proceeded, eventually coming to find the rest of the group scattered in the shade of a grove of pine trees, seated on flat rocks and clearings on the ground. Just up a little rise was an overlook, and I stood close to the edge, letting my eyes take in the incredible view of the majestic landscape around us.

"Beautiful, huh?" CeeCee was at my side, leaning against my shoulder in such a familiar and intimate way it nearly broke me.

"Yeah," I whispered, looking down at her. She was so beautiful my body ached to look at her.

"What's going on with you today?" she asked quietly. "You seem really out of it. Just tired from all the . . . things?" She met my eyes as she asked this last part, giving me a wicked smile that sent still-frame images of the night before spilling across the landscape of my mind.

"Yeah," I began, testing out various words in my mind. Could I tell her now? With the cameras still around and the mics on? I hadn't intended to, but as soon as we got back to the resort, there was a chance it would be too late. Just knowing Daphne was there meant my time had run out. I should've handled this long ago. I should never have let it happen in the first place.

But if I told her now, with the odds that the crew would hear us, even if we switched off the mics . . . I didn't want to ruin everything for her. "Yeah, I'm tired," I said instead. I tried for a meaningful smile to return hers, but probably just looked weirder than normal.

"CeeCee?" One of the guests called from behind us, and CeeCee gave my arm a squeeze and then headed off to answer questions or help, to be the guide she was.

I shook my head, trying to clear it. One thing was certain, I needed to talk to CeeCee before we got back to the resort. I'd find a way to make it happen. Somehow.

The return hike was quicker and quieter. I couldn't escape my thoughts, but at least I didn't manage to wander off a cliff or anything, and at one point I even helped a guest who'd had a run-in with a tree branch manage a Band-Aid application. That was the extent of my guiding contribution for the day. I hoped the camera crew had at least gotten some good shots of the scenery, since I knew I didn't give them anything to work with.

As we drove everyone back to the resort in the Kasper Guides van, my anxiety increased. The guests piled out at the curb, and CeeCee and I got out to say goodbye. Ned and his crew filmed all of this out on the wide sidewalk in front of the resort and then in the front of the lobby, where guests began to head back to their rooms.

Anxiety ricocheted around inside me as I scanned the lobby, wishing Ned would wrap up and that I could pull CeeCee off somewhere and explain everything before it was too late. But Ned and the crew seemed intent on dragging this out, keeping the cameras trained on us as we said goodbye to the last straggling hikers.

I relaxed a bit, seeing no familiar blondes in the lobby, but just as the last of our hikers headed toward the elevator, it dinged and the doors slid open. And even before I saw them, I heard the voices that had populated my childhood. Mom, Dad, Tony, and Daphne. Dread swept through my gut as they spilled from the elevator. I turned and considered running away, but one second later, they'd spotted me.

"Travis! There you are!" My mother wasn't a small woman, and she'd never been quiet, either. She was tall and broad, and every bit the proud southern mama one might expect you'd have to be to manage raising four boys and handling a cattle ranch and everything that came with it.

Dad smiled at her side, taking his hat off as he took in the woman at my left arm, and Tony was giving me a dubious look. The last face, the one I was almost afraid to look at, was Daphne. And she just looked sad. Maybe a little disappointed.

God, I hated disappointed.

"Your family!" CeeCee said. Oh god, this couldn't possibly be worse. My mind scrambled for some kind of hail Mary move that would save me from the mess I was about to create, but nothing came.

Roscoe pressed himself against my leg, sensing my worry.

"Hi Mom," I said. No matter the situation, there was never

an excuse not to greet your mother properly. I pulled her close and kissed her cheek.

"Sir," I said, shaking my father's hand.

"Turdwaffle," I offered Tony. Old habits died hard.

"Nice," he said, pulling me into a brief hug.

"Hi Daphne," I said, uncertain how to greet my wife.

She returned a quiet hello, but her eyes were on CeeCee.

I glanced past CeeCee to where Ned stood, filming all of this. Nausea joined the anxious dread I felt. This was going to ruin CeeCee's chances at winning this thing. And it would be my fault. And one more failure to add to a very long list.

"You gonna introduce us, son?" My mother asked, clearly disappointed with my failing manners.

"Um, yeah. Sorry. Of course. Everyone, this is CeeCee. She runs the adventure guide shop up here, and I've been, uh . . . helping her out." This last part ended almost like a question, and my brain stuttered, trying to figure out how to align what Ned thought he knew of us with what my family definitely did not know. "And this is Roscoe," I said, indicating my dog, who'd sat practically on my right foot.

After proper hellos were said, Daphne stepped just a bit closer. "So," she said, in a voice that had me wishing she was one of those quiet-talking types. "This is the girl you've been making out with all over Instagram." Why couldn't Daphne be as social-media dense as I was? Of course she'd seen everything. Why hadn't it occurred to me that my family would see the publicity around the contest? That was the whole point, right?

I could practically feel Ned's interest perk as he captured this all on film. Over Daphne's shoulder, I spotted Paul, the other cameraman on Ned's team capturing another angle of what was certain to become a disaster any second.

"Um . . . right." CeeCee glanced up at me for guidance. But how the hell could I explain any of this?

Mom's mouth dropped open and she looked between Daphne and CeeCee. This revelation was going to be hardest for her—she'd loved the idea of Daphne and I married. She was the reason we'd had a real ceremony with cake and everything. Mom needed to believe this was real. She believed we were in love.

"Travis, aren't you going to introduce your wife to your, uh . . ." Mom trailed off.

"Wait, what are you guys doing here?" It wasn't the right thing to ask, but the question had popped from my lips because it was the one thing I just didn't understand. All four of them arriving here was so unexpected my mind still hadn't come to terms with it. As I looked between them, I heard CeeCee repeat softly, "your wife?"

"Son, when you're kissing women who aren't your wife all over social media, we figure there's gotta be something wrong. We came to see if you need some help up here." Dad looked vaguely amused by all this.

My stomach roiled. Dad had just announced the bulk of the issue to Ned and the camera crew, not to mention dropping everything in front of CeeCee.

"You could have called," I suggested in a weak voice. CeeCee had stiffened at my side, and Daphne's face was redder than I'd seen it.

My mother looked between Daphne, CeeCee, and me. Then she stepped forward. "Since you all seem a little confused about things here, let me just clear it right up. This here she said to CeeCee"—she pulled Daphne forward a step—"Is Travis's wife. Daphne."

And there it was. The bomb exploded there in the lobby of the Kasper Ridge Resort, taking the life I'd constructed here with it, and lodging shrapnel into the lives of everyone I cared about. I'd known I was a walking disaster, though things had definitely gotten better since coming to Colorado. But there was no fixing this now.

Everything was ruined.

Roscoe whined and pressed his head into my thigh.

CeeCee took a sharp breath, and then collected herself faster than I ever would have imagined was possible. "It's nice to meet you, Daphne." She glanced up at me quickly, but the glance was enough for me to see the pain and disappointment there, and then she turned back to my family. "If you'll excuse me, I need to get back to the shop."

Without another word to me, CeeCee turned and left, taking the shattered remains of my heart with her.

I watched Ned signal to Paul to stay with me, while he darted outside after CeeCee. Everything inside me wanted to run after them, do something, anything to make this right. But there was no making it right. Not for CeeCee, not between us . . .

I'd ruined everything for both of us.

My family stood staring at me, waiting for me to behave normally, like the brother and son they'd known. I cleared my throat, doing my best to shove down the impulse to chase CeeCee. "Should we, uh, maybe go sit down?" I asked, gesturing toward the bar. Maybe now was a good time to become a devotee of Wiley Blanchard's famed Half Cat whiskey.

"You've definitely got some explaining to do here, son," Dad said, putting his hat back on.

Tony was staring at me hard, maybe trying to shoot lasers from his eyes or something, and I did my best to ignore him. I fell back on old habits instead, taking Daphne's arm as we walked into the bar, and settling her and my mother at one of the tables in the back. When I'd helped them into their chairs, I took their orders and headed over to talk to Wiley, my brother glued to my side.

"Fucked this one up good, little brother," he said as we rested our elbows on the bar side by side.

"Yeah."

"Mom's pissed."

"Yeah."

"Your wife wants to kill you. Embarrassed them both back in town."

I sighed. It hadn't even crossed my mind that Mom and Dad would be embarrassed, that they would even know what was going on. But just because I lived in a bubble didn't mean everyone in my family did. Of course they'd seen the promo. And of course they'd been ashamed of me. I cringed, feeling the same kind of irrevocable shame wash over me that I remembered from when I was a kid. "We should never have gotten married in the first place."

Tony nodded, saying nothing for a moment. "But then you did."

I let out a sigh, my heart like a singed and painful wound in my chest. "She called this week. Asked for a divorce."

"Something you should have worked out as soon as you got back."

"I know." I'd never wished more to rewind time and make different choices. "I was trying to do the right thing. She's like our sister," I said. Tony's face darkened and I couldn't figure out what caused him to drop my gaze. "I just wanted her to be taken care of."

Wiley moved over to help us, a towel slung over his shoulder and the easy grin I associated with him firmly in place.

"Holy shit, there's two of you, Sasquatch."

"Wiley Blanchard, this is my brother, Tony."

Tony stuck out a hand. "Nice to meet you, man."

"You too," Wiley said, the smile firmly in place as he looked between us. "What can I get you?"

I ordered for my family. "And a couple fingers of your whiskey, please. Maybe a little extra just in case."

Wiley lifted an eyebrow, pouring a healthy amount of whiskey into a rocks glass.

"I'll try some too," Tony said, indicating the bottle.

Soon—too soon—we were all settled at the table in the back of the bar. I'd downed at least half the whiskey already, but didn't feel any braver as a result.

"Okay, son. Let's get this all figured out, should we?" Mom sipped her beer, never taking her eyes from my face. She had her no-nonsense look on, the one she'd always worn to mediate fights between me and my brothers when we were kids.

"I can't believe y'all came all the way up here because of some social media posts," I said, part of me hoping to distract them from what I knew they wanted to say.

"Not the point," Tony reminded me.

"Yeah." I knew he was right.

"Does the dog go everywhere with you?" Daphne asked, looking down at where Roscoe lay at my feet.

"Yeah, pretty much," I told her, happy to be talking about anything besides the disaster that was my life. "He's a great dog."

"Get to it," Dad said sternly.

"Start with kissing the guide girl," Daphne said. "While you're still married to me."

I glanced past her to where Ned had positioned himself, capturing everything on his camera. "One sec," I said, rising and moving to where he sat.

"Any chance I could just talk to my family? Like, off camera?"

Ned gave me a look that told me he understood why I'd ask for that. "I wish I could man, but this is kind of why I'm here."

"To ruin my life and any chance CeeCee has of winning this thing?"

"You mean any chance you have, right? The two of you?" he asked.

"Yeah." I wrapped a hand around the back of my neck, rubbing the tension forming there. This was getting worse. There was no way to fix things. "Look, man. I love her, okay?"

"Which one are we talking about?" Ned asked. He actually sounded protective of CeeCee, and my respect for him grew even though I was frustrated that he wouldn't leave.

"CeeCee," I snapped. "I know this is all a mess, but I need you to know that. What you saw between us, that was real."

"And this? Your, uh . . . your wife?"

That damned camera was still aimed at my face. "I love her too, but not in the same way. Things there are complicated."

Ned nodded as if he understood, but he couldn't possibly.

"Son?" My father was getting impatient. I gave Ned one last pleading look and returned to the table.

"The papers are signed," I told Daphne, thinking about the envelope that had arrived via FedEx after I'd left the message. "They're up in my room."

She stared at me, and then dropped her eyes and said quietly, "Thank you, Travis." She reached her hand out sideways, to Tony. I watched him take her hand and gaze at her lovingly as understanding began to flicker to life.

"Doesn't really help matters now, son. Everyone back home is talking about this." Mom cared a lot what everyone back home thought about everything.

"Yeah," I said, understanding. "I messed up. I'm sorry. I just . . . I didn't want to let you down," I looked at Daphne, wishing everything was different. "Or you," I added, looking at my mother.

"So you cheated on your wife instead." Mom sounded tired.

I sighed. "That's the thing, Mom. It was just never like that with us. We got married so I could take care of Daph. So she'd never have to go back to that house." We'd been a couple in name only.

Mom looked surprised at first, her head swiveling between me and Daphne, but then her eyes snagged where Tony and Daphne held hands below the table, and she nodded slowly. "I see. So you've all been lying to us all along."

She might as well have stabbed me and poured whiskey in the gash. I couldn't bring myself to look at her. "Yes ma'am."

"I'm sorry," Daphne said, her voice small. I hated that she got hurt in all this. The whole point had been to protect her, take care of her. Daphne was like a sister to me.

I sighed. "So what now?"

"You can show us around," Tony said. "And then you can get those papers for Daph."

Chapter Nineteen
The One Where I'll Be Fine

CEECEE

Driving back to the shop, I felt like I was holding my breath the whole way. If I didn't let myself breathe— if I somehow kept myself from actually living, processing, thinking, then I didn't have to try to understand what had just happened.

I parked the van and registered vaguely that Paul, one of the camera guys, had followed me here and was now getting out of his car and heading into the shop with me.

"I'm, uh . . . I'm going to be closing up in a few minutes here," I told him. It was nearly five o'clock, and luckily today wasn't one of the days I stayed open in the evening. Cole had seen me pulling up and had gleefully headed out as soon as I'd come in, wishing me a good night. Clearly, he had some place to be, and I was glad for it.

"Okay, yeah," the guy said, something sympathetic in his

voice making me feel very small and vulnerable. "Just . . . do you want to talk?"

The camera he held reminded me that Paul was not my friend.

"Thanks, no, I just . . ." All the things I'd forced myself not to think about yet were pushing against my consciousness, demanding to be considered. I couldn't ignore them forever, and I didn't want to have to deal with all of that with Paul here.

I cleared my throat and lifted my chin. "I'm good. It's all good. Did you enjoy the hike today?" The note of brightness in my own voice turned my stomach.

Paul dropped the camera to one side. "Hey," he said softly. "What happened back there was a lot to process. It's okay to be upset."

I sniffed, willing myself not to cry, the waves of emotion threatening to unleash themselves at any second. "I'd rather not do that on camera," I said finally.

He dropped my gaze, staring for a moment at the camera in his hand. "I get that."

"So maybe you could just go? You guys got everything you needed, right?"

"I mean—"

"Thanks for everything." I held the front door of the shop open for Paul, and it didn't take him long to take the hint and head through it.

"Good luck, CeeCee."

I nodded to him, the emotion in my throat making words impossible. When he'd stepped through the door, I pulled it shut, locking it behind me and staring blankly into the place that had felt like home to me for so long. My store. My life.

Now?

Everything about this place was touched by the week I'd just spent, the falsehood I'd pushed Travis to participate in, and the way it had all fallen apart. And for what? The whole thing had been caught on camera, and now not only my heart was pulverized, but my dreams of winning the show were too.

I let myself lean against the glass of the door, staring sightlessly at the world I'd built, all the emotion and processing I'd managed to hold off for the drive back and the conversation with Paul finally rushing over me in a deluge.

Tears pricked at the backs of my eyes and a sob choked its way from my throat. And a moment later, I'd slid to the floor, heaving sobs wrenching themselves from my body.

I wanted to be crying for the dream, for the loss of the contest I'd worked so hard to win, for the life that winning it might have made possible. But that wasn't what was tearing me apart inside.

It was him. Travis was married.

He was married, and he hadn't thought to mention it. Not when we first met. Not when we'd become friends and I'd learned about his family back home, about his life in the military. And not when I'd asked if he would pretend to be my boyfriend for this ridiculous charade. At any point there, he could have told me.

But he didn't.

And I didn't understand why.

I buried my face in my hands, my knees pulled up to my chest, and let myself cry, the confusion and humiliation alternately spearing me inside, making me feel small and stupid, and so, so weak.

I'd felt things when Travis looked at me, when he touched me. And I thought—no, I knew—he felt them too. He'd told me so.

So why had he lied to me? Why had he gone along with the pretense if he wasn't free to do it?

After a while, I scraped myself up off the floor and headed

to the back, where I could cry piteously somewhere there wasn't a plate glass window behind me. I doubted anyone was out there, but since the front of the shop was all glass and I'd collapsed in a puddle of tears before I'd managed to switch off the overhead lights, I was pretty much wallowing inside a fish-bowl. A vague thought crossed my mind that Paul might have recorded it—me devastated and crying—and I found I didn't even care. The contest was over anyway, and it was clearly lost.

Back in the office, I stared at my desk, the tears slowing to a miserable drip and sniffle combination, with the occasional gasp mixed in when a particularly horrible thought pulsed through me.

This. This was why I didn't bother with men.

I'd never left a relationship unscathed, and in every instance, men had callously broken my heart and walked away, leaving me slightly less confident and complete than I'd been before.

And this time?

I wasn't sure how much of me was going to survive this one. I didn't want to admit it, but I'd let myself fall in love with Travis. I'd thought there was something vulnerable and sweet in him, despite the enormous outer packaging (which I didn't mind in the least . . .)I'd thought we had a real connection, and that he appreciated it too. I couldn't have imagined all of it, could I?

But even if he'd felt something, it didn't matter. He wasn't free to feel anything for anyone besides Daphne. I should have known at the beginning. When I heard him on the phone. I shouldn't have trusted so easily that Daphne wasn't a threat.

The woman with the gorgeous long blond hair and the bright blue eyes.

His wife.

His fucking wife.

I dropped my head into my arms on my desk and stayed that

way, wishing I'd never met him. Wishing I'd never suggested we pretend to be dating. Wishing I had a way to leave this place, to escape the humiliation and pain that I knew every day ahead of me would hold since my humiliation was about to broadcast for the whole world to see.

My phone buzzed in my pocket, and I lifted my head, pulling it out with some ridiculous hope that it might be him.

But it wasn't. It was Douggie.

I'd have to talk to him eventually. I was already miserable—might as well get it over with.

"Hello?" I thought I managed to sound put together.

"Oh, honey."

Evidently I didn't sound quite as good as I'd hoped.

"Hi."

"Ned called me. Are you okay?" Douggie sounded concerned, and having someone care, even a little, made everything hurt more.

"No." I sniffed, grabbing a Kleenex from the end of my desk. "No. I think this broke me."

"Oh sweets, I know it feels that way right now." He was quiet a moment. "I can't believe he agreed to pretend to be with you when he was married. He knew this was going to be aired publicly, right? That it was for a national television show?"

I swallowed. Douggie knew we'd pretended to be dating. He didn't know I'd fallen in love with Travis. "I think he knew."

"So he's gorgeous but maybe not all that smart. Unless his wife lives under a boulder, of course she'd see this..."

"That's not the worst part."

He was silent a moment, and I could almost feel it over the phone when understanding clicked in on his end. "Oh girl. You didn't."

"We did."

"So these tears," he said slowly. "This isn't about the show?"

"I mean, yeah. It is. But it's so much worse than that." I swallowed hard. "I think I love him." Saying it out loud made it feel even worse, made me realize exactly how much I'd lost today.

"Shit, CeeCee."

"Yeah."

"Ned says there was a ton of great stuff before the blond Texas demon arrived at the resort."

The moment replayed in my mind—Daphne being introduced to me. As Travis's wife. "I don't think she's a demon."

"For right now, she is. Tell me everything. Start at the beginning."

I leaned back in my chair, staring sightlessly at the familiar space of my little office, and told him everything. I told Douggie how Travis had immediately accelerated our fake relationship past dating and straight into an engagement. I told him how he looked out for me, made me feel taken care of. I told him how good he was with the kids on our adventures, how good he was with people in general—caring, genuine.

None of it made sense, but I told him everything anyway. How he'd touched me so gently. Kissed me like his next breath depended on it. Taken me in his bed in ways that had made me understand that the other men I'd been with had no real idea what they were doing.

And how he'd lied so convincingly that my heart had gotten wrapped up in it all.

I told Douggie how I'd fallen for him.

And when I was done, I felt the tiniest bit better. But poor Douggie was in tears at the other end of the line.

"You okay?" I asked him.

He sniffed loudly and in a broken voice, said, "in any other situation, I'd tell you to go fight for your man. But the sacred vow of marriage is a whole other thing."

"Right." Desolation and hopelessness swept through me.

"Okay," Douggie said, clearly trying to pull himself together. "Okay. Well, that's it then. You'll pick yourself up and move on."

"Sure."

"Listen, CeeCee, you haven't lost a damned thing."

"Um. The contest? My heart? My self-respect?"

"The contest isn't over," he said, though I could hear the doubt in his voice. "And you decide what happens to your heart and your self-respect. Don't let him take those from you."

He was right, but I wasn't quite ready to put on a brave face just yet. "Yeah."

"You gonna be okay?"

"Eventually," I said, though I wasn't sure I believed it at the time. "What choice do I have?" I had a shop to run, clients who would be counting on me.

"Okay," he said, sniffing again. "Call me tomorrow?"

"Sure," I said. "Thanks for everything, Douggie."

Douggie was still trying to pull himself together as we hung up, and it was almost as if I'd transferred a bit of my sorrow to him because I felt just a bit stronger as I stood and prepared to go home for the night.

I could handle this. I could move on from here.

I would be fine.

The tears that streaked my face as I drove home tried to convince me otherwise.

But no, I reassured myself. I'd be fine. I always was.

And as I pulled into the driveway at my childhood home, staring up at the familiar roofline, seeing the exact same view I'd seen since the day I was old enough to acknowledge it, I knew it was time to move on.

In every way imaginable.

Chapter Twenty
Roscoe Offers Advice

TRAVIS

I loved my family. I loved Daphne too, in a way. She was essentially family, after all, which explained the whole marriage situation. Sort of. Even though I loved them, I hated the idea of spending the rest of the evening showing them around the resort when all I really wanted to do was get in my car and find CeeCee, see if I could explain in any way that made a lick of sense.

I must've pulled my phone from my pocket thirty times, but even Roscoe seemed to think texting some kind of apology was a bad idea. When I held the phone too long, staring at it as if the words would appear without me having to figure out what they should be, he groaned loudly.

"You're right, boy. I need to find her and talk to her in person."

Roscoe stared up at me, his big amber eyes telegraphing something.

"I wish I could speak dog," I told him, dropping to a squat and sinking my hands into the fur around his neck and shoulders, rubbing him hard and taking what comfort I could from his constant presence.

"You're pretty into your dog, huh?" Daphne asked, emerging from the lobby bathroom. Dad, Mom, and Tony had stepped out onto the back patio to look around while we waited. With just the two of us here, it was hard to be angry at Daphne. In reality, she had done nothing wrong in all this.

"He's basically a service dog," I told her. "Except that I would've had to wait years to get an actual service dog so I trained him myself."

Daphne frowned at me. "I don't think that's how it works."

I shrugged. "Kinda seems like most things in life work how you make them work." I'd never understood the idea of following rules just because they were rules. But it also explained why marrying Daphne hadn't seemed like a terrible idea, and why I'd been willing to help CeeCee.

Of course there were some other reasons for that too.

"Dad and Tony are out back," I told her, and we turned, heading out the big glass doors to meet them.

Tony was already in conversation with Ghost, who no doubt identified him from the few times I'd had family visit back in the squadron days. Or maybe because Tony looked a lot like me.

"He's been a big help up here," Ghost was saying to my father as we walked up. "Hey Sass. So cool to have your family here."

"Yeah," I said, trying to sound like I actually agreed. "Archie, I'd like to introduce my mother."

"Nice to meet you, ma'am."

"And this is, ah . . ." I hesitated, looking at my wife. "This is an old family friend, Daphne."

"Hello Daphne."

Daphne greeted Ghost graciously and did not make a point of announcing herself as my wife, for which I was grateful.

"And you've already met my dad and my brother, Tony."

"I recognized Tony from the couple times he met up with us in Corpus Christi when we were training."

"I'm giving them a little tour, and then I'll probably turn in for the night. I'm, uh . . . I'm done over at the guide shop, so I'll be in the kitchen early getting prepared for the big wedding this weekend." I hoped I could ditch my family early enough that going to CeeCee's might still be possible. I could at least try to call her in the quiet of my room.

"You getting married again, Travis?" Tony asked under his breath.

Ghost shot him a curious look but didn't ask any questions. "Sounds good," he said. "Nice to have you all here," he told my family.

I led an awkward tour around the property, showing my family the yurts, the ski setup, and taking them inside through the shop, the lounge, the movie theater and bowling alley, and winding things up back in the lobby, feeling nearly desperate to get away from them. "That's about it," I told them.

"And Archie and his sister did all this work themselves?" Mom asked, looking around at the gleaming lobby, which had been musty and dark when I'd first arrived.

"We all helped, and of course there was a local construction crew doing a lot of the renovation."

"Our rooms have not been renovated," Daphne sniffed, crossing her arms.

"No, not yet," I agreed. "The Kaspers have to do things in phases. Money is a little tight."

Dad looked around at the people milling through the space, filling the bar and lounge. "Not for long, I'd say."

"Hope not. Ghost deserves a win up here."

Tony caught my eye and leaned in as we turned to the eleva-tors. "So do you, bro."

"Thanks." I raised an eyebrow at my brother. He'd been quick to give me a hard time earlier, but having him say some-thing supportive was a relief. Tony had always been the closest of my three brothers to me, probably because we were closest in age.

We headed up to the staff wing, where my family had three rooms down the hall from mine.

"Why don't you get those papers," Daphne suggested. "And bring them to my room. I'm two doors down from you," she said when I stopped at my own room. She pointed to her door.

"Yeah, okay." I would do that, and then I'd go look for CeeCee.

"And I think we'll get cleaned up and then go down and see about some dinner," Mom said. "Join us?"

I needed some time alone, time to fix things if I could, time to think. My chest felt empty and hollow, like everything had been violently ripped out of it this afternoon. I wanted to wallow a bit, to decide if there was any fixing any of this. But first, I needed to get those divorce papers for Daphne.

"I think I'll turn in early," I said. "I have to be up at four to bake."

Tony frowned at me. "To bake?"

I pulled my shoulders back. "I pitch in where I'm needed around here. Lately, I'm baking."

He nodded. "Okay."

Mom and Dad exchanged a look, and I wondered what they said about me when I wasn't around. I could guess—the mild worry on their faces said most of what I needed to know. That I would never settle down. That I'd never find one thing and stick with it. That I was rootless, drifting, destined for loneliness. My mother had pretty much said those exact words to me when I'd told her I was coming to Colorado in the first place after I'd spent a year living in Florida after getting out of the Navy.

"Papers," Daphne said, pushing me into my room and stepping in after me. "I'll help."

The door swung shut, and for the first time in years, I found myself alone with my wife. And Roscoe, of course.

Roscoe trotted off to the corner after giving Daphne a quick sniff and determining that she was neither a threat nor a potential playmate. He curled up on his bed and watched us with his big expressive eyes.

"They're right here," I said, crossing to the little desk where the divorce papers sat beneath my laptop. I pulled them out and carried them to the counter, where I set them on the peeling laminate.

"Travis," Daphne said, her voice suddenly much less forceful than it had been all day. "What's really going on?"

The question took me by surprise. "What do you mean?" I pointed to the spots where convenient tape flags had been placed to help me dissolve my marriage without having to think too much about it. I'd spent enough time thinking about it anyway. I hadn't wanted to sign—because I'd been worried that doing so would be letting Daphne down, failing at yet another thing... but now it didn't really feel that way. Now it felt like it was exactly what Daphne wanted. And what I wanted too. I was closing the door on one part of my life so that there might be a flimsy possibility of having something more.

I held out the papers to Daphne, who took them slowly, gingerly, as if she wasn't sure what to do with them.

"I mean, why are you up here? What's going on with you?" she asked.

"I don't even know how to answer that question." I tried for a smile, but my head was spinning and my heart hurt. So much.

She stared at me for a long beat, and then seemed to decide

something, her face clearing. "I want to put these into my bag so there's no chance I lose them or forget them," she said. "And then we should talk. Bring that." She pointed to the bottle of Half Cat whiskey that had been sitting on the counter in the kitchenette since I'd arrived. I wasn't much for drinking alone, so I hadn't opened it. But now did seem like a valid occasion. Plus, I wasn't alone.

"Sure," I sighed, realizing it would probably be a while before I'd get to figure anything out with CeeCee tonight. Family was a closer alligator to the boat and I'd need to handle it first. And even though we'd complicated things a bit, Daphne was family first.

I followed her down the hall two doors to her room, and she opened the door with a big metal key like the one I had for my room. "This is sort of quaint," she said, holding up the key.

"It is."

She pushed the door open to reveal a room a lot like mine, similarly out of date and a little dusty, and I reminded myself to thank Ghost later for scrambling to get my family situated today while I'd been away. They were lucky to have rooms at all, even if these were a little worse for wear.

Daphne put the papers on the end of the counter against the wall and pulled two glasses from the tray that sat next to the sink.

"Want me to find some ice?"

She looked up at me, the fierce determination in her eyes reminding me of the fiery little girl she'd once been. "I think I can handle it neat."

I shrugged and poured, and then we moved to the couch and sat.

"I'm sorry, Daphne. I should've just signed the damned things when you first asked me."

"We never should've gotten married in the first place," she said. "But I've been meaning to thank you for it."

I was glad the anger seemed to have faded from her, and I caught her eye now, the whiskey burning a path down my throat as I did. "It wasn't a big deal."

She frowned. "Yes it was. Don't do that."

I gulped more whiskey, wishing for a tiny bit of oblivion maybe, wishing I could undo things somehow. "Do what?"

"The thing you always do. Discount yourself. Act like nothing you do matters, like you're just this bumbling joker, stumbling through your life."

"Honey, you pretty much just described me."

She finished her whiskey and put the glass down on the low table, hard. "You forget that I've known you my whole life, Travis."

I didn't respond. What did you say to that?

"And that I've seen you for years. Really seen you. I know the way you looked out for your mama when you were in high school and your daddy was sick. I know how you admired and idolized your big brothers when you were little. I know how you made sure no one messed with me when kids at school figured out my parents barely knew I existed.

"Your family—but especially you—you saved my life. Without you, I would've turned out just like my mama. Or worse."

I hated thinking about that neglected little girl, stumbling into our yard, hungry and alone. Even at six years old, I'd known our lives at home were very different. "It was nothing. You were a kid, Mama already had four, feeding one more didn't make a difference."

"You know it was more than that. And it didn't stop with the food. Your family raised me. And you looked out for me when I should've been old enough to do it myself." These last words were delivered quietly, her eyes on her hands.

I shook my head, remembering Daphne in high school, dating anyone who showed the slightest interest. I picked up the pieces after many of those flings went south. "I don't know what to say, Daph. You're family. We take care of each other."

She dropped my gaze then. "I've thought a lot about it. And I think I was working so hard to find someone so that your family could finally be done with me."

"Done with you?"

"Done having to take care of me. Worrying about me. None of you needed that."

"We never thought twice about any of it."

"And then you had to go and suggest we get married." Tears stood in her bright eyes now, and what was left of my heart twisted in my chest. "Why did you do that, Travis?"

I finished my whiskey, poured us both some more. "You know why. You had nowhere to go. I thought I had a death sentence, basically, and I knew if I didn't come home, you'd be taken care of for life."

My benefits would have ensured Daphne wouldn't have to worry about the future, and knowing she'd have them had made me feel like at least I'd done one good thing in my life.

"I never really understood it," she said. "And it just made everything harder."

That surprised me. I put my glass down. "Harder? How?"

Daphne dropped my gaze and sniffed. "You freed me in a way, but you also helped me step inside a cage. What we did put us both in one."

I didn't know what to say to that, so I sipped my whiskey. If I agreed with her, she'd feel guilty. If I denied it, it would be one more lie.

"You're in love with her."

That got my attention. "What?"

"The woman in the photos. The one we met in the lobby today. You love her, don't you?" Her voice was soft, not accusing me of anything wrong. Just asking. And it made my heart wince inside me.

"Yeah, I do."

"And I screwed it up for you?" She lifted her head now, her lower lip trembling, but her chin high.

"No, Daphne. I did that all on my own. That's my signature move, after all."

"No." She stood. "This ends here. No more discounting yourself or making jokes about your abilities or your intelligence."

I stared at the little girl I'd grown up with, suddenly a determined and somewhat intimidating woman glaring down at me. I'd looked out for her. I wasn't sure what to do now that she seemed to be protective of me. "Um . . ."

"I'm tired of it. I've watched you do it my whole life. You're the best man I know. You're kind and thoughtful and so smart, and always looking to help people. And yet, you tell me over and over what a failure you are, how you can't seem to stick to anything, how you ruin things. And you've got it all wrong! Travis, life is in how you look at things. You're smart and curious, you like to experience new things, try things. Sometimes they don't go as well as they could, but you're never afraid to try.

"God, I respect that. And I wish you could see yourself the way other people do. You're handsome, and huge, and so, so kind . . ." she trailed off, tears dripping down her face.

"Don't cry, Daphne." I stood to face her, my heart protesting as I demanded yet more emotion from it today. I was exhausted, but seeing Daphne cry made me feel like fighting whoever had caused it. It was habit and instinct. But in this case, the guy I'd have to fight was me.

"I'll stop if you'll agree to fix things with her."

Surprise joined the sympathy and sadness inside me.

"I don't know if I can."

"You," she said, stepping close and poking me in the chest. "Can do anything. You've already proven it so many times. Why don't you see it?"

I couldn't think about this now, this habit she was illuminating in my character. Was she right? It didn't feel wrong, but it didn't matter. I needed to get to CeeCee. At least I could agree with Daphne about that.

I rubbed my neck, exhaustion sweeping over me. "Put those papers in your bag, Daph. After all you went through to get them, you don't want to forget them here."

She nodded and turned, breaking the tension that had grown between us, and swiped the papers from the counter, carrying them into the bedroom. There was some shuffling, and then a crash, and Daphne cried out, "Dammit!"

I rushed in to see what had happened, and found Daphne staring at a toppled luggage rack and a hole punched through the wallpaper on the wall.

"What happened?"

"I bumped the suitcase, and the rack tipped, and my bag slid right through the wall!" She put out a hand and pushed aside the hanging paper. "I actually don't think there was a wall here at all."

I moved closer as she picked up the luggage rack and moved it aside. We held back the dangling wallpaper to reveal hole cut between the studs. She was right, the hole had simply been papered over. And when I pulled her suitcase from the wall, surprise sent my limbs tingling.

There, stacked neatly between the studs inside the wall, was a mountain of typed pages.

"What is all this?" Daphne asked, picking up a bound stack

of typewriter paper. There were two lines of text typed across the front.

Carefree in Chicago
Screenplay by Marvin Kasper

"Holy shit, you found them!" I turned to Daphne, probably grinning like an idiot. "We have to find Ghost!"

"Found what? A stack of old papers?"

"Yes!" I grabbed the script from her. "That's exactly what this is!"

"Oh joy," she said, sarcasm lacing her words. "Where are we going?" She trailed me from her room and down the stairs to the hallway where Ghost's room was.

I pounded on his door, the excitement of something good having come out of today making my knock more forceful than it strictly needed to be.

"What?" Ghost asked, pulling the door open, looking exasperated. "Sass, for fuck's sake, you're gonna knock the door in. You don't know your own strength." He glanced to my side. "Hello Daphne."

"Hi," she said. "Travis said you needed to see this." She pointed at the script in my hand, and I pushed past Ghost to drop it on the long dining table in his suite.

"Is that . . ." He began, coming to lean over the script. "Is this what I think it is?"

"Proof!" I shouted.

Ghost flipped a few pages and then turned to me with an enormous grin. "Yes!" He shouted, and then, without either of us planning it, we executed a perfect leaping chest bump, both of us hollering at the same time.

"What in the world?" Daphne asked herself, looking on with wide eyes.

"Sit down," I suggested. "We'll explain everything."

Chapter Twenty-One
Dudes and Booty

CEECEE

The day I left Travis in the lobby with his wife had felt in so many ways like the end of everything. The end of whatever had been between us, clearly, but also so much more. My hopes for winning the competition, my dreams of being awarded some grand adventure that would take me far away from Kasper Ridge to see the world, and the opportunity to become something more than just the small town in which I was raised.

Now I just wanted to start over somewhere else, to become something more than just Cecelia Ann Moore, that girl from a tiny mountain town—the one who runs that adventure shop and is so strong and independent, she doesn't need a man.

But this day, three whole days later, I had a bit more perspective. Or at least I felt like I did. Travis had called, texted, and even stopped by the shop and the house. But as if fate was telling me that avoidance was the best policy, I'd managed to be out guiding whenever he dropped through the shop, and had spent the night at Bennie's the first night after we broke up. So he'd had an interesting conversation with Mama, who told me he looked terrible but that she hadn't thought I should marry him in the first place. As if that had ever been a possibility.

So when Lucy and Bennie suggested we meet up for dinner the third day after we'd broken up, I agreed, even though part of me still felt like the best thing to do would be to wallow and mope. That part was clearly wrong. My head knew the only solution was action. And it didn't hurt that avoiding the shop and my house meant avoiding more potential drop ins by a certain huge handsome man I was trying to convince myself I could just never see again.

"So you're leaving?" Bennie sat across from me at the corner booth at the Toothy Moose, her eyes big and round.

Lucy was watching me carefully, listening intently as I explained the small parts of the plan I'd figured out quickly these last few days. I shrank down slightly in the corner, hoping to avoid any interested eyes around the restaurant. I wasn't sure what parts of the show had been aired on social media, but I knew it was only a matter of time before everyone in town knew exactly what had happened.

"And the shop can run without you?" Lucy asked now.

"I'll have to hire a manager," I explained. "But I think so, yeah. I'd just have to contract the guiding out to another outfit." I'd lose market share, but maybe it didn't matter.

Bennie was shaking her head, still looking distraught. She corkscrewed a finger into her mass of amber curls—something she'd done as long as I'd known her, whenever she was nervous or upset.

"I get it Ceese," Lucy said, dropping her chin into her hand. "It's just hard to hear, you know? The three of us have been together since kindergarten. It won't be the same here without you around."

"I know," I said, looking back and forth between my friends. "But I won't be gone forever. The shop and my family are still here—" But for a while, I was going to be gone. I was going to go see something else, someplace else, even if it was only a few hundred miles away instead of a whole continent.

"And us," Bennie said. "We're here."

"Of course," I told her, squeezing her hand. "But I can't stay here for you."

"Would you stay for Travis?" Lucy asked. My stomach sank and I dropped her gaze. I knew I needed to close that door, let him say what he wanted to say and then tell him goodbye. But I hadn't been able to do it yet. It was like my heart was still hanging on to some tiny shred of hope.

I had already told them everything that had happened after Travis had agreed to pretend to be my boyfriend for the show. They were appropriately angry on my behalf, but their indignant fury didn't make me feel better.

"I will take this opportunity to remind you of one crucial point," I said, trying to keep my voice light. "Travis. Is. Married."

"Will says he signed the divorce papers and that his . . ." Lucy struggled with the word. "His wife . . . was that in name only. They weren't romantically involved."

Bennie, who was the most strait-laced among us, looked between us. "Does that really matter? The guy's married and he lied about it."

"I mean," I jumped to his defense and then wondered why I was doing it. "He didn't lie. He just . . . didn't mention it."

"A lie of omission," Bennie pointed out.

I nodded.

Lucy took a sip of her wine and straightened up in her chair, fixing me with the steady gaze I'd seen her use when she was working, ordering around crews of huge rough men for her construction company. "Listen, CeeCee. It's your life, and you clearly should do what you need to do. But it won't serve you to make decisions without having all the facts in hand first."

"I think I have all the facts," I told her. I'd rehashed everything so many times in my mind. "And there are at least three guide spots open in Aspen, but they're hiring right now and I need to be there in person for the interview."

"A few facts you might have missed, I mean. One," she said, holding up a finger. "Will says Travis is miserable without you, and that even his dog looks awful."

I didn't like thinking of Travis being miserable, but part of me was glad to hear it. I was miserable too.

"Two," she went on. "You haven't even given him a chance to explain. You need closure, if nothing else."

"I guess, but I don't think I do—"

"You do," Bennie interjected, jamming her finger into the tabletop. "Ow."

"You okay?" Lucy asked her.

"Yeah." Bennie was holding her finger, rubbing it gently. "But this is how much I don't want you to go, Ceese."

"Please don't hurt yourself over it."

She smiled sadly. "Has he called you or anything?"

I lifted a shoulder. I'd ignored the calls Travis had tried to make, and told myself not to read his texts, even though I had. How could I help it?

"Yeah. But it doesn't really matter. This isn't some little misunderstanding or a bout of misplaced jealousy, guys. This is a legal, binding oath he made to another woman. It's kind of a big deal."

"It is," Lucy agreed. "But even the most complicated situations have two sides. Should you let him explain his?"

I dropped my head to my chest, the familiar sadness and exhaustion sweeping through me again. "Maybe."

* * *

I went to bed that night doing my best to maintain my resolve. Travis was married. He let me believe otherwise. That was wrong. It wasn't a thing easily looked past, or gotten over. He'd made me an unwitting adulterer. He'd made me the other woman. And that felt dirty and shameful.

But as problematic as that all was, the real problem I was dealing with was that I had actual feelings for him. And while we'd been apart, he was almost all I thought about, a shadow lingering there behind anything I was doing, any other thoughts I was focused on. He was there, and so was the deep aching sadness I felt when I considered that whatever brief thing we'd shared was over, just as surely as my chances to win the competition were.

I was puttering around in the shop the morning after seeing the girls when Douggie called.

"Hey you," he purred, making me laugh as I greeted him.

"Hey."

"The drama, oh my lord," he said. "Ned says you guys are off the charts. He sent me a few little segments."

"Yeah, but they were there when I found out about Travis's wife. They know we lied."

"Do they?" Douggie asked.

I frowned, sinking onto the stool behind the long glass counter at the back of the shop. "What do you mean?"

"They know *he* lied."

"Same thing."

"No," Douggie said. "The way it looks on the show is that you guys were totally into each other, and that your hot big boyfriend is just this sympathetic tortured hero type who got into things with you before he even had a chance to come clean."

"He lied."

"Maybe, but I don't think that's what the network is seeing. Or if they do, they really don't care."

I blew out a frustrated breath. I was moving on. What difference did the details make now?

"Drama makes good television," Douggie said. "The network loves you. Plus," he went on, "if you win, that's one ticket on some ridiculous world-traveling vacation instead of two. You'd be saving them money."

"There's no way I win after all that." I paused, the wheels in my head spinning. Was that even possible? "I'm not winning, right? That's not what you're saying."

"I don't know," Douggie said. "I'm just telling you, don't pack away your passport just yet."

Inside all the misery filling my soul, a tiny flicker of hope glowed just a bit stronger at his words.

"Okay," I said, contemplating how they could still be considering me, after everything. "Thanks, Douggie."

"You doing okay otherwise?"

"Not really. But I'll survive."

"Of course you will. You're fierce and strong. And you don't need no man." He asserted this in a hilarious little twang that I was not expecting.

"Right," I laughed.

"Course," he added. "That doesn't mean you don't want one . . ."

"Douggie."

"And," he went on, interrupting me, "it doesn't mean he doesn't want you. Or that you shouldn't let him apologize and explain and then take you immediately back to bed."

"That's not happening." I couldn't even think about being in bed with Travis, those memories had been shuttered away, locked and sealed.

"You're no fun."

"Goodbye, Douggie," I said, as a group of young women walked in, moving toward the kayaks on the far wall.

"Bye Cee."

I helped the girls, doing the best I could to be present and enthusiastic, but half my mind was firmly absent, exploring the possibility of the contest deciding to award me the prize, and it felt like the other half was busy wondering if I should forgive Travis or if it really was time to move on.

Chapter Twenty-Two
Brothers Are Sneaky

TRAVIS

G host was rejuvenated with the discovery of his uncle's scripts, and he'd put in a call to a friend of ours from the squadron who'd gotten out and gone to law school a few years back. Aiden "Swiper" Swanson had assured Ghost there was something there, and promised to get back to him with some more information.

"What do you envision happening?" I asked him Wednesday night as we sat out by the yurts after midnight. My family had joined us each day, pitching in where they were needed and blending surprisingly into the fabric of the resort's daily operations. Since the place was becoming busier by the day as the wedding of the century geared up, it was actually pretty helpful.

I'd slipped away multiple times a day to try to find CeeCee. That had resulted only in a couple uncomfortable chats with her brother and her mom, a scolding from Adelaide at the shop, and Cole pretending not to see me as he helped other customers and told them loudly that CeeCee was the best lady he'd ever met and that if they ever wanted to go on an adventure she would look out for them and would never, ever lie. I was pretty sure that little gem was aimed at me.

CeeCee didn't return my calls or my texts, and I hadn't seen her at the resort. In the darker hours of the night, I had begun to feel like I'd imagined the whole thing, like I'd invented her in some kind of sleep-deprived fantasy.

Ghost was petting Roscoe, who sat between our chairs, his mouth open and his eyes shut as the firelight danced on his sleek dark fur.

"I'm hoping Swiper says there's a case there."

"So you're going to sue Mountaintop?" I asked. Will had gone to Los Angeles the previous year to try to confront Rudy Fusterburg, Marvin's old friend and the head of the studio, but Rudy had passed away. It was his daughter that Will had found in the fancy house up in the hills.

Ghost lifted a shoulder. "Maybe? We have proof that Marvin wrote movies he was never compensated for. I think that's what he was trying to tell us."

"Why didn't he just tell you that? Why the treasure hunt?"

"Uncle Marvin was an odd duck." Ghost grinned.

Roscoe plopped into a pile between our chairs, groaning as he settled.

"It's just a little convoluted," I told my friend, my mind running through the very complex trail his uncle had left for us. "And it wasn't like we had a clue where to look for those scripts. Finding them was a complete fluke. Daphne only found them because she was pissed at me."

Ghost stared into the fire. "Yeah. I know. I don't have all the answers." He was quiet a moment, and then spoke again in a low voice. "How's all that going, by the way?"

"All that," I repeated. "As in the marriage that should never have happened, the one we're now ending?"

"Yeah, that."

"It's fine. We're friends. That's all we've ever been, really." Now that it was done, it felt like a weight had been lifted from my shoulders.

"She's pretty cute."

"Ghost, man. She's like my sister." A protective flare went off inside me, but I tamped it down. Daphne was not actually my sister, and she'd be lucky if a guy like Ghost decided she was the one he wanted.

"Just sayin'. Besides, I think she's spoken for."

I frowned at him. "That's over. I signed the papers."

He cocked his head at me. "You're so busy wallowing around in your own crap that you haven't noticed what's going on with her and your brother?"

"Tony?" I thought about how he'd taken her hand in the bar. I'd figured it could be just reassurance at the time, but I had a feeling it had been more.

"Do you have other brothers here right now?"

"There's something going on with Tony and Daphne." I said it, testing the idea out. I looked around as if proof would present itself on the other side of the fire, but I only found Aubrey and Wiley, sitting together on a chair, their faces close. A twist of envy and sadness stabbed at my heart and I looked away.

Roscoe stood and came to press his head into my lap. I let my hands sink into his fur, allowing his presence to soothe the hurt inside me.

"Huh." I managed. Tony was older than me. He hadn't grown up with Daphne as a playmate, exactly. Maybe that allowed him to see her a bit differently.

"I'm gonna head in," I told my friend, standing to head back

194

to my room. "I've gotta practice the cake tonight, and there's a bunch of dough to get ready for Saturday."

"Okay," Ghost said. "Have fun with your dough. See you tomorrow."

I headed back along the little trail through the trees and into the resort, my mind struggling the whole time with thoughts of CeeCee. I missed her, but she hadn't responded to my texts. I was going to have to find a way to talk to her. This wasn't over until she at least got the whole story. She'd probably heard most of it from other people by now, but she needed to get it from me. And then we'd see.

Chapter Twenty-Three
Action Movies Rock

CEECEE

"This is the part where . . . yes!" Jensen was overexcited about the amount of explosions in the action film he'd convinced Mama and me to watch, but I was thankful for the noise and distraction. They kept Mama from voicing whatever it was that had her giving me side-eye from her recliner.

We hadn't talked about everything, not outright at least. She'd told me that Travis had stopped by a few times. I'd told her that the engagement was off and that I was sorry for all the drama. She'd asked if I wanted to talk about it. I'd said no. That was pretty much it. For me, at least. But she'd been watching me lately whenever I was home, giving me that knowing Mama look that made me feel at once guilty and worried. And a little bit touched that she was still trying to look out for me.

"Why did the tall guy kill the guy in the boat?" I asked the room. The movie's plot was probably not worth trying to figure out, but it wasn't as distracting if I didn't at least try to follow it. If I just sat there, staring at the television, my mind and heart joined forces and tried to lure me into memories and wishes that included a hulking, smiling, former fighter pilot instead. And I didn't want to go there.

"I'll get it!" Jensen yelled this and sprang up from his chair in one motion, and it took a moment for me to realize there had been a knock at the door, that it wasn't just part of the movie.

A moment later, Jensen came back, looking at me with a wary expression. "Should I tell him you're out?"

Travis.

He'd finally caught me at home.

"He can see my car," I reminded my brother, rising from the couch as if my bones were made of lead. I couldn't put this off forever.

As I followed Jensen back to the door, my heart and mind were at war inside me. My heart wanted to melt, to flitter and leap at the thought of seeing Travis again. But my mind was telling me there was no real explanation that would make everything okay. He'd lied to me. And I wasn't sure I could get past it. I couldn't fathom any good reason why he'd done it.

"Do you want me to stay?" Jensen asked, pulling the door farther open to reveal the man who'd populated every single one of my dreams for weeks now standing there looking sheepish.

I looked at my brother, who was trying to be protective, though he seemed so small next to Travis. "Thanks," I told him. "It's okay."

Jensen moved back to the living room, and I faced Travis, my heart still hopeful even though I told myself it wouldn't matter what he said.

"Hi," I managed, stepping out the screen door to the front step where he waited. "Want to sit?" I motioned to the two folding chairs on the front porch, and lowered myself into one of them.

"It's so good to see you," Travis said, his voice scratchy.

We stared ahead, not looking at one another, and I tried to imagine myself flying away, up into the dark indigo stretch of sky overhead. Away from pain and confusion. Away from Kasper Ridge.

"Listen," he said, and I felt him turn to face me but couldn't bring myself to look at him. I worried I'd give in, that I'd tell him it was all okay, that my heart would win over what my mind knew I needed.

I nodded, still not looking at him. "I'll listen, Travis," I said, working to hold my voice steady. "But you lied to me. And that's one thing I'm not sure I can ever get past."

He was silent, seeming to absorb that for a moment. "Maybe not," he said. "But you deserve the truth, even if it's coming too late."

"Go ahead."

Travis cleared his throat and began to talk. "Daphne and I grew up together."

Wonderful. A childhood sweetheart.

"She was basically my sister." As I listened, Travis went on to tell me about Daphne's childhood, about her neglectful parents, and about how his own family had adopted her in every way that mattered.

"We fought like badgers as kids," he said. "And in high school I pretty much just served as a bodyguard. She dated losers. One guy always worse than the last.

"When I came home from flying, I did it to say goodbye basically. I knew what was waiting in Afghanistan, and I didn't really expect to make it back. It wasn't that I had a death wish or anything . . . but it felt like I still hadn't found a way to make my parents proud, to make myself proud. I'd moved from one thing to the next, and it felt like a string of failures."

I wanted to interrupt, wanted to ask questions, but held myself firm instead, waiting for the answers to my questions.

"Daphne had just ended a relationship. A bad one. He'd stolen from her, gotten her fired from her job. She'd almost married the guy, and one night when we hung out together during that time, she told me she just needed some kind of security, some way to set herself right so she could make something of her life. And she could absolutely not go live with her parents again."

I nodded. That all made sense.

"I offered her my apartment while I was gone, told her I'd pay the rent. But then I had a better idea. My military benefits were good. Healthcare, life insurance. I figured if we got married, she'd have all my benefits and my apartment and even my salary. I didn't need any of it overseas. And since I didn't expect I'd survive, I figured she'd get the payout when I was killed, and then she'd be taken care of."

"You were planning to die?" I finally turned my gaze to him, unable to imagine him wanting to be killed.

"I didn't want to. I just thought the odds were pretty good."

"Oh my god."

"We had to pretend a bit for my mom. She wanted so badly for it to be real, so we did the cake and the party, said we'd finally figured out that we'd always been in love."

"But you weren't?"

"Not even a little bit," he said. "But that didn't mean I didn't want to see her taken care of."

"Right."

"We just didn't think far enough ahead. We didn't talk about what would happen if I did come back."

"And you did."

"Yeah."

I took a deep breath and looked up into those soulful brown eyes. "I'm glad."

Travis gave me a sad smile that turned my heart inside out. "Thanks."

"Why didn't you end it when you got back?"

"Because it didn't seem fair to Daphne. She'd lose all those benefits—or most of them. And I didn't expect to meet anyone, not really. Mom and Dad thought we'd had some problems, so they didn't ask questions when I didn't move back in. Guess they thought we'd work it out."

"But Daphne wanted out?"

He nodded, staring at his open hands in his lap, thoughtful. "Yeah. I kind of thought she was just trying to be nice or something, so I didn't give her what she wanted at first. I thought she felt beholden to me or something dumb, and I still didn't see how the marriage harmed anyone. I didn't know she'd met someone else."

"She did?" I watched him, but he didn't show any sign of sadness about this part of the story. I believed him when he said there was nothing romantic between them.

"Yeah. Tony. My brother."

"Wow."

"Yeah."

"So it's over now?"

"Takes a while for the legal dissolution, but yeah." He turned to me then, his eyes shining in the moonlight. "Ceese, can you forgive me?"

I took a deep breath, trying to sort through the feelings warring for prominence in my heart and mind. "I understand why you did what you did. And I don't blame you. I forgive you . . ."

A smile tugged at one side of his mouth. "What does that mean for us?"

I shook my head. "I don't know. Maybe nothing. I need some time." I dropped his eyes and stared at the warped wood at the edge of the deck. "I'm actually planning to leave."

"Leave Kasper Ridge?"

"Yes."

"When?"

"Soon as I can." Even as I spoke the words, sadness filled me from the tip of my toes to the top of my head, threatening to spill out in big, salty tears.

Travis sighed and shook his head. "Please don't go."

I stood up, fighting the urge to lean into him, to take comfort in his size, his strength. "I need to think."

He stood and watched me for a long moment, then said, "yeah. Okay."

As Travis descended the steps of my front porch and climbed into his SUV, I let the tears fall. I didn't know what I was going to do, but I knew that acting on emotions and whims was the wrong answer.

Chapter Twenty-Four
Even Sasquatch Needs Mom Now and Then

TRAVIS

I'd felt hollowed out after talking to CeeCee, but at least I'd finally gotten to explain. The thing was, it didn't seem to be enough. I understood. She'd trusted me. I had broken that trust.

But she still loved me. I was sure of it.

I climbed into bed, but it still smelled like her, coconut and sunshine . . . and sleep was a far-off mirage.

The kitchen's silence was welcome after the few hours I'd spent in my room. CeeCee was on my mind, as were Tony and Daphne. I was happy for them, if what Ghost said was true, but somehow the idea of their happiness made me feel even more alone.

I switched on the ovens and pulled the big cake rounds I'd already baked from the freezer to thaw. I'd handle all the resort's daily needs, and then they'd be soft enough to frost and assemble. I had to make sure I could do what I'd said I could. Annalee was confident about the decorating—she'd decided to do it herself, and had been practicing all week, leaving roses and swirls in frosting on sheets of parchment paper all over the kitchen counters. Now I just needed to ensure the cake was perfect. Once I got this one assembled, she'd practice decorating it, and we'd eat it after dinner. The real cake making would start tomorrow.

I was just turning the cinnamon roll dough into a huge metal bowl to rise, when the door the kitchen swung open, surprising me.

"Hello, Travis!" Mom chirped, going to the sink to wash her hands. "I was up early, and figured you might be able to use some help down here."

"Sure," I said, watching my mother tie on an apron and turn to me with a bright smile. She was fully made up, as always, despite the fact it was barely four in the morning. There were lines around her mouth that I didn't remember, and some crinkles at the corners of her eyes, but for the most part, the woman before me was exactly the way she'd always been. Bright, optimistic, and full of life. I realized how much I'd missed her as I stared at her getting herself ready to help.

"I'm glad you're here, Mom," I told her.

She pressed her lips together for a brief second, and then crossed to pull me into a hug, ignoring my floury hands and the dramatic height difference between us. "I felt like you might need me, honey."

If I'd been the crying type, that might've done it right there. "I think I did," I told her.

She released me, and brushed the flour from her apron. "All right then, what are we making?"

I pointed her to the recipes lined up along the counter for muffins and coffee cake, and she got to work, humming familiar tunes from my childhood as she did.

Hours later, when there were trays of finished muffins covering the long countertops and I'd successfully crumb coated and assembled a four-tier cake, she caught my eyes and then dropped my gaze, looking uncertain. It was a look I recognized. She wanted to say something.

"Out with it," I suggested, handing her a big cup of coffee.

"It's not my business, honey . . ." Despite the sentiment, it was clear she was going to say whatever it was anyway, so I waited. "But I'm sorry about this thing with Daphne."

Mom had always had a soft spot for Daphne, which explained how she'd ended up at our house so often.

"It was never real, Mom," I began explaining again.

She lifted a hand and my mouth snapped shut.

"Travis, you interrupted me."

"Sorry, Mom."

"What I was going to say was that I am sorry for any part I played in encouraging you kids to get married. I liked the idea of it, but I think even back then, I knew it wasn't the right thing."

I waited, feeling pretty sure she wasn't done, and not wanting to be at the brunt of Mom's fiery reprimand again.

"Besides," she said, sipping her coffee and then putting the mug on the counter and leaning a hip against it as her hands smoothed her hair. "I had my eye on the wrong son where that one was concerned."

So it was true. Tony and Daphne. Now that initial shock at the idea had passed, I liked it. It made sense.

She went on. "But this other woman," she said, pointing a finger at me. "The woman we met that first day. What about her?"

My heart pulsed at the thought of CeeCee.

"That's over," I said miserably. "I didn't tell her I was married, and now she hates me."

"She said that, did she?" Mama's smile told me she knew the answer.

"Not exactly, but I'm pretty sure, because I would hate me. And I don't know if she's speaking to me."

Mom picked up her cup and stared into it for a long minute before looking back up at me. "I love you son, but I'm ready to see you step up in your own life."

That hurt, and I felt myself absorb the hit. "I mean . . ."

"Sure, you've done amazing things. You flew that plane, got that Purple Heart, saved people. You befriended Antonio after you had to share the news about his brother. You're a hero for everyone but yourself."

"Mom, I—"

"Do not interrupt me again Travis, my patience is wearing thin. I didn't haul myself outta bed at three in the morning so you could decide not to listen to what I needed to tell you down here."

I knew she didn't just happen to be up this early. I sighed and settled against the counter, waiting for her to make her point.

"I think you had something special with that girl. I saw the pictures on social media, remember? I think you might even have fallen in love with her, and now . . ." she shook her head in disgust. "You're going to take no for an answer just like that. You're going to sacrifice yourself—again—because you think that's what someone else wants."

I wasn't sure how to answer.

She was still shaking her head at me. "What about what you want, son?"

I wanted CeeCee with all my heart. More than I knew I was capable of wanting.

I shrugged. It was too late for what I wanted.

"It's time you actually try, Travis. Might she tell you to go jump off a rock? Yes. That could happen. But what if she doesn't? What if there is actually a chance for you to get the thing you want? The love you deserve? The family you long for?"

I didn't like this conversation one little bit, but my mama was literally the only person in the world who could say these things to me and keep me standing here in front of her to listen.

"It's hard for you to hear because it's true," she told me.

I sighed, pain radiating through me. It was true. I wanted all those things, but I'd resigned myself to the belief that they were not going to be. Not for me. Especially not now.

"If you don't at least try," she whispered, "you'll never forgive yourself."

"And you'll never forgive me?" I asked her, hating the tears standing in her eyes.

She blew out a breath and a shaky laugh. "Honey, I'll forgive you just about anything. You're my baby. But I don't know if I can forgive you for making that same baby so miserable and keeping him from ever having a chance at happiness. That might be hard for me."

She stepped close again and pulled me into her arms, and for a long moment, I let myself be small, be the little boy I was once, rocked in Mom's arms.

And then, I stood up and let her words sink in. She was right. I needed to try. For once in my life, I needed to go after what I wanted, even if it meant certain failure.

"Okay, Mom. I'll try."

Chapter Twenty-Five
Bridezilla and the Board

CEECEE

Things at the shop were getting busy with the influx of guests arriving for the big wedding taking place over at the resort. Instead of bachelor and bachelorette parties, the bride and groom had decided on a day of hiking and stand-up paddle boarding.

To meet their (very specific) demands, I'd set up two group hikes to converge at the lake, where I'd already have the equipment for the paddle boarding staged, thanks to an access road on the other side of the lake. Cole was leading the hike for the men, and I was taking the bride and her bridesmaids, something I regretted almost as soon as we set off from the trailhead.

"He was trying to tell me that the crystal flutes were ridiculous and too expensive," the bride said loudly, continuing a detailed explanation of her registry as her bridesmaids listened in apparently rapt attention. "He looked at the list and tried to remove like half of the things I'd put on there, which was so ridiculous because for god's sake, when has Brian ever planned a proper dinner or hosted a party, right?"

"Totally." A tall, rail-thin woman with lanky dark hair had been glued to the bride's side since I picked them up at the resort. Maid of honor, I figured.

The bride was a petite woman with perfectly sculpted curves that seemed potentially augmented to me. Who had a butt that round? She showed up in the lobby for our hike with perfectly glossed lips, fake eyelashes, and a tank top so tight I was a little worried about her ability to get it off. For the most part, the entire group had ignored me after we'd said hello, giving me the impression that I had been relegated immediately to my role as hired help.

"I know what you mean," one of the bridesmaids said, scurrying up to the front of our little group as we hiked up a wide trail that sloped gently upward, pine trees towering on either side and a blazing blue sky above. "Joe and I got in a huge fight because he thought I spent too much on redoing the living room before we had that big holiday party."

There were chuckles that sounded like agreement from the other women.

"I mean," the dark-haired woman went on, "those couches we had? They were like four years old. They had butt indentations in them!"

The group laughed, and I thought about the comfortable living room where I'd spent most of the evenings of my life, with my parents in their matching recliners, and my brother and I sprawled on a floral fabric couch atop a light green shag carpet. If four years was old for a couch, ours was ancient.

The closer we got to the lake, the more annoyed and disgusted I was becoming, with the bride especially. Here was a woman who clearly had more than she appreciated, and she talked about it all like it was her due in life. Something she was owed for what? For being born wealthy? Or pretty?

"I made her do them over again," she was saying now, holding out her manicure for the other girls to see. "She acted like it was such an inconvenience, talking about her next appointment and whatever. And then she tried to charge me for two manicures!"

"Seriously," the rail-thin woman said, rolling her eyes.

"Welp," I interrupted as we arrived at the lake. "We're here."

Normally, when I brought a group over the last rise in the trail to get their first view of the sprawling indigo blue water of the lake surrounded by mountain peaks and graceful pines, there was an audible gasp of appreciation.

Not with this group.

"It's smaller than I thought it would be."

"Is the water very dirty? It looks . . . dark."

I tried to force a smile that probably looked like indigestion, and turned to spot Cole and his group approaching from the other trailhead a few yards away. "And there's the rest of your group," I added.

The bride turned to watch the men approach, and then turned back to the ladies. "Oh my god. I told Brian to throw that shirt away. Don't judge me based on his total lack of fashion sense, okay?" She laughed as if saying something crappy about the man she was about to marry to all her friends was just cute and adorable, and I had to stifle the sound of annoyance that ejected itself from my lips.

"Hey there," I said, greeting the other group in as enthusiastic a voice as I could manage.

"Hi," one of the men said, stepping forward and extending a hand. "I'm Brian. Thanks so much for organizing all this today. We really appreciate it."

"No problem," I said, gazing up into the groom's friendly face. He wore a baseball cap and a T-shirt that had a ball poised on top of a ramp, and the words: I Have Potential. "I like your shirt," I added loudly. I could appreciate a good physics joke as much as the next girl. (The next girl was clearly not the bride in this case.)

"You don't have to bend over backwards thanking her, honey. We already paid her a fortune to take us on this silly walk." The bride glued herself to the man's side and I watched in fascination as he draped an arm around her and chuckled apologetically.

The groups mingled a bit on the waterfront as Cole and I moved to ready the boards. Some boards stayed there permanently and were shared between the outfits, but I'd ported up ten of my own, knowing this party might be a bit pickier about their equipment.

As we pulled life vests and paddles from the shed, Cole asked, "How was the hike?"

"Don't ask," I said. "The actual hike was fine. The company was a little painful."

"Same," he muttered. "These guys are all, like, stockbrokers or something from New York. I've never heard so much bragging in such a short time before."

"Ditto," I said, turning away from him and back to the group.

"Okay," I called out, hoping to pull their attention from the conversations they'd all fallen into as they waited. "Hopefully you all remembered your bathing suits. We'll just go through some basic instructions here, but the key things are these: One, everyone wears a life vest all the time. Even if you're a great swimmer, the lake is cold, and it can sap your energy pretty fast if you spend too much time in it."

The ladies gave each other wide-eyed looks at this.

"Second, if this is your first time, and you're worried about falling in, you can kneel instead of standing. If you want to stand, just remember to do it slowly. I'll demonstrate as we get in the water here."

I moved my board to the water after demonstrating how we'd hold the paddles and pointing out the landmark rock that marked the farthest point we'd be paddling to.

"If you get into trouble, you have a whistle on your vest. Cole or I will come help." I kind of hoped the bride did go for a swim, but tried not to let my feelings show.

The ladies began stripping off their clothes, revealing a collection of the smallest bikinis I'd ever seen up close. Most people chose to wear shorts and sports bras, which was what I'd suggested ahead of time to this group.

We moved into the water amid plenty of shrieks and cries about the water temperature. Since it was snowpack runoff, it was very cold, but the sun overhead and the dry air provided a comfortable contrast, and ensured that anyone who went in would dry quickly.

After a bit of uncoordinated paddling around, most of the group was proficient, and we all moved a bit farther out into the water. I wasn't leading any kind of focused tour of the lake, so once I was out close to the turnaround point, I sat on my board and just did my best to keep an eye on the group and enjoy the day. Cole was helping some of the women, and I suspected he was only in it for the flesh, but I couldn't really blame him. He was a red-blooded twenty-something-year-old guy, and these ladies appeared to like the attention, the bride especially.

She was making a show of not understanding how to balance, asking Cole plenty of questions about how to hold her body and her arms. At one point, when Cole had moved some distance away and was helping someone else, her fiancé paddled close.

He leaned toward her a bit, whispering something in her ear and playfully swatting her half-exposed rear end.

"Brian!" she shouted, sounding not at all pleased, and then she leaned away from him and toppled into the lake, coming up shrieking. Her fiancé knelt on his own board, then moved to sit with his legs on either side, and reached to try to help her out of the water.

If it had been me, I might not have rushed to help her, but since I was being paid, I started in their direction trying not to enjoy the fact that her hair and makeup had been ruined.

"Get away from me!" she screamed at Brian as he tried to help. "You're making everything worse!" She finally managed to haul herself back onto her board, and then gave his board a mighty shove, sending him floating in the opposite direction.

Brian shook his head and shrugged as he paddled back toward the guys, but the expression on his face suggested his feelings might be a little hurt. I felt sorry for him.

When the boarders had paddled around for just over an hour, we gathered everyone up and headed back down the trail as a group. I did my best to ignore every word out of the bride's mouth.

She treated her fiancé like just another thing she'd bought with her money, like his presence and attention was her right somehow, and it turned my stomach.

The groom, though arrogant and too loud for my taste, didn't seem like a bad guy, and I actually felt sorry for him. Especially when the bride loudly related a story about a gift he'd gotten her that she hadn't appreciated.

"He made it himself, if you can believe that!" she laughed, finishing the story as I watched Brian's shoulders slump a little lower.

By the time we were loading up the vans, I was in a dark mood.

How was it that a horrific and insensitive shrew like this—Jessica was her name—deserved a guy like Brian? How was it that she'd ended up adored by someone she treated horribly, in the most beautiful location in the world, about to have the wedding of the year, and she didn't appreciate any of it?

My mind went back repeatedly to Travis, to the way he'd checked in with me and looked out for me when we'd hiked together. Even back at the shop, he'd made a point of making sure I was good, seeing if I needed a cup of coffee or a break.

Had I appreciated it?

I thought I had, but it was hard to separate the sweet and caring Travis from the man who lied to me about being married.

Except, he hadn't really lied. He just hadn't said anything about it. And if what he'd explained was true, it kind of made sense.

And really, he didn't owe me anything, did he? We'd been pretending. It wasn't as if he was really asking me to marry him that day in the shop when he'd announced that we were engaged. It was all just for show.

Nothing in my line of thinking made any of it any better. I couldn't fix what had already been broken.

Why did my bedroom feel emptier and lonelier now than it ever had before? Something about today had shaken me up, couldn't figure out what it was.

I just knew that I didn't want a relationship like that one. If I ever decided to trust anyone with my heart again, I'd want a man like Travis.

Chapter Twenty-Six
The More Flowers the Better

TRAVIS

Roscoe and I went for an early morning walk the day of the rehearsal dinner. I'd finished the cake the previous night, and now it was in Annalee's hands. The woman, who we called Monroe back in our squadron days, could apparently do anything.

I wondered what that would be like. Where it felt like everything I touched turned to shit, it seemed like everything Annalee touched turned to gold.

Even as I had this thought, the words of the women who'd known me my whole life came back to me and circled over and over through my mind.

I was glad CeeCee had accepted my apology, though it didn't really change much. I strolled among the soaring trees, letting the dry warm air of Colorado's summer settle my soul a little bit. CeeCee's response wasn't exactly exuberant. But it wasn't awful, either. It was something, at least, after days of nothing. And my heart wasn't ready to give up. She hadn't said no. Only that she needed time to think.

"Maybe it's time to do things differently," I told my dog, who had trotted up ahead, but turned to look back at me now, his bright curious eyes seeming to agree with me. "Maybe I do need to step up in my own life," I said.

Roscoe appeared unconcerned about my situation, turning back to lower his nose to the trail and trot ahead happily, soaking in the wilderness.

As we walked that day, I thought about what kinds of things I might say to CeeCee, how I might set up some kind of situation where I'd even have the opportunity. She'd been scarce at the resort since Ned and the crew left, and even when I did spot her gathering a group in the lobby, she was busy or gone so fast I didn't get a chance to talk to her again.

We turned back toward the resort and I realized that Daphne and my mom were both right in a way. My natural inclination was to discount myself, to stop pressing before I had a chance to fail at things, and to roll with the punches in life. I'd always thought I was just easygoing. But maybe it was something else. I was pretty sure now that it was fear.

And I didn't want fear to ruin the one thing I'd found that made me feel the opposite of afraid. When I was with CeeCee, I'd found a part of myself that I liked, a part of me that could put my past aside and face the world with wonder and hope because that's how CeeCee saw it. I missed her fiercely—not just the precious moments I'd gotten with her in my room, though that played pretty much on repeat in my head—but the simple companionship we'd shared, the partnership.

I wasn't going to let fear stop me from trying with her for real, if she'd let me. I just had to figure out how to ask.

Roscoe and I returned to the resort in the early afternoon, and the place was buzzing with a tension I'd never felt there before. The rehearsal dinner was being set up on the big back patio outside the restaurant, extra heaters being positioned around the space and flowers appearing literally everywhere.

One side of the huge outdoor patio at the base of the mountain had been cleared of the chairs and low tables that usually populated it, ready to hold rows of white chairs and the most insane arch of flowers I'd ever seen, which was being built when I'd set off this morning with Roscoe.

"A lot of flowers," Brainiac commented when I found him standing near the entrance doors, staring around at the changed environment.

"I guess flowers are important to a wedding," I said.

"For certain people I guess," he said. "Penny and I didn't need them when we got married." He frowned. "I don't think we did."

I shook my head. He and Penny had fallen in love fast and then gone through all kinds of complications to be together. They were one of those couples who just felt meant to be. "You didn't need 'em," I assured him.

The resort didn't have a proper ballroom, but the lobby had sweeping high ceilings hung with glittery chandeliers, a smooth polished marble floor, and plenty of open space. The couple getting married had bought out the place for the weekend to ensure the only guests in residence would be theirs, and they'd still managed to fill the hotel. Front desk services had been moved to a back office for the couple days the lobby was in use, and the enormous wooden reception desk had been shifted into a secondary bar to supplement the actual bar at the front of the space.

The cake, which was still in the kitchen, would stand on a side table, towering over a space strewn with yet more flowers. Annalee had done an incredible job so far, creating realistic-looking flowers draping all down one side, exactly matching the photo the bride had sent us weeks ago.

"Saw the cake in the kitchen. Looks good," he said.

"High praise from you," I said. "But you're wrong. The cake doesn't look good. It looks fucking awesome."

"Agreed," he said, and a tiny surge of pride rushed through me.

People were moving around pretty much everywhere, setting up chairs, spreading table cloths and doing all the other work that an event of this size commanded. Ghost had made it clear that a wedding like this could make or break the resort, since these were people with power and influence, who had a network that would certainly be paying attention.

I didn't care about any of that though, as I spotted CeeCee walking through the big space with Lucy, heading out the front doors. She looked gorgeous and perfect, her back straight and her hair piled in a knot on top of her head. She didn't look at me, didn't see me, and I was glad because I was pretty sure I was gaping after her like a lovesick cartoon puppy.

"Dude," Brainiac said at my side. "Just talk to her." At this point everyone seemed to know exactly what had happened between CeeCee and me, and they seemed equally certain about my feelings.

"Yeah. I will."

"What the hell is that?" A screeching voice came from the direction of the elevators, and I turned to see the bride storming toward me, her hands in fists as her skinny arms swung at her sides in her march across the lobby. Evidently, she was talking to us.

"Sorry?" I said, looking around.

She pointed at Roscoe, who sat obediently at my feet. "What. Is. That?"

Most people knew what dogs were, so I assumed her question was somewhat rhetorical. "This is Roscoe. Support dog."

Her nose wrinkled, making her face look distorted and cruel. "Get it out of here." She planted her hands on her hips, and I felt a surge of irritation at the way she was acting as if the resort was her private mansion.

"He's got permission to be here. Resort owner." I didn't feel like her attitude deserved full sentences.

"If you had any idea what we are paying the resort owner to use this place this weekend . . ." she shook her head and looked around like she expected the fancy people police to arrive to help her say nasty things about my dog any second. "I didn't realize I needed to be specific about the required absence of mangy animals."

"He's a service dog," I told her. "And he's not mangy."

She stared up at me, her face reddening, and then shrieked. "I don't give a flying fuck! Get this animal out of here!"

Brainiac stood at my side, completely silent, but I could feel his amusement without even looking at him. I knew I should respond appropriately and apologize or just turn and take Roscoe upstairs, but I found this irate and ridiculous woman very interesting—people like this really thought they ran the world. It was fascinating.

"Well?" she screeched.

I was about to find some appropriate words when a man appeared from the bar—the groom, I thought. I braced for more maligning of poor Roscoe, and waited.

"Honey," he said, crossing the space quickly on long legs. "Jess, honey, what's going on?"

She threw her arms to her sides and turned to him. "There's a dog in here," she whined. "First there's that awful room, and now the place is turning into a fucking petting zoo." Her voice was high pitched and cloying, and my stomach turned.

"You don't like your room?" Brainiac asked her, sounding concerned.

"The room is a complete disaster," she said, "But the issue right now is this fucking dog, getting his disgusting fur and dog slobber everywhere in here where my guests are supposed to be able to enjoy an incredible and beautiful party without getting covered in dog hair."

"Our guests," the groom said, under his breath.

She shot him a look that made me just a tiny bit sorry for the guy.

"Roscoe and I were just heading upstairs," I said, realizing there was really nothing else to say. "I'll make sure to keep him on the back stairs until after the wedding when we come down."

"Ugh." She let out a noise of annoyance, and the groom put an arm around her shoulders, shooting me a half-smile.

"You're just stressed, Jess. Everything is great. You'll see. The wedding will be perfect."

"You smell like alcohol!" she said, turning her irritation to her groom. "Have you been drinking?"

"The guys and I are—"

"No," I heard her saying as Roscoe, Brainiac, and I headed for the back stairs. "If you are drunk for dinner..."

The heavy steel door on the stairwell cut off the rest of her rant.

"Well that marriage seems destined for joy," Brainiac said.

"Eternal bliss, definitely," I agreed. "Poor guy." I looked down at my dog. "It's okay, boy. You aren't disgusting. She is." We climbed the stairs, and I worried about the cake I'd spent weeks planning. How much pull did this woman actually have? If she hated her cake, could she actually hurt Ghost? "I hope she likes the cake."

Brainiac grunted. "She's not going to be happy with anything. Wouldn't worry about it."

The familiar acceptance of another failure loomed inside me, except I was one hundred percent sure that cake was not a failure. I wasn't a baker by trade, but I'd made sure that wedding cake was exactly what she'd asked for, and the decoration was flawless.

"The cake is perfect," I said, assuring both myself and Brainiac.

* * *

That evening, Roscoe stayed in the room, but we'd all been asked to help out downstairs to make sure dinner was served on time and that drinks flowed all night. I was helping in the kitchen, moving finished plates to the serving station for the waitstaff to pick up.

As I slid two more beef wellingtons onto the counter, I looked up to see CeeCee coming in the double doors, dressed like a server. She wore black pants and a long-sleeved buttoned up white shirt, and she looked beautiful, her hair in a neat bun on the top of her head, a few tendrils escaping to frame her pretty face.

"Hey," I said, my heart suddenly in my mouth.

"Hey," she said, meeting and then quickly dropping my gaze.

"You're, uh . . ." Words did not seem to be my friends. I hadn't expected to see her tonight, since she didn't technically work at the resort.

"Lucy said they were short a couple servers so I'm helping out." She picked up the plates and disappeared out the doors.

For the rest of the service, it felt like I lived only for the glimpses of her in and out of those doors.

It was torture, but it also made the entire evening fly by, spending each moment on the edge of anticipation, feeling like every second I could be close to her was stolen and undeserved.

As the dessert plates began coming back in, I took a deep breath and called to her before she could step out again. "CeeCee."

She looked up at me as if I'd caught her by surprise. "Yeah?"

"Do you think maybe we can talk? Later tonight when this is done?"

CeeCee glanced around the kitchen, like maybe she was looking for a reason not to talk to me. My heart fell a bit. But still, I had to try. I had to at least tell her how I felt. "Yeah," she said finally. "Okay." She bit her lip as she looked back up at me with those big blue eyes and I had to fight off the urge to lift a finger to it, feel the plump softness of her mouth.

"Okay," I said, unsure what came next. I'd figure it out. Until then, I had to work on keeping my feet on the floor and my head on the dinner I was working—a crazy lightness had filled me when she'd said yes and I wanted to sprint a victory lap around the kitchen.

She turned and headed back out the doors to the party.

Soon, the guests had begun to filter upstairs to their rooms, out back to the fire, or through the lobby to the bar. When the kitchen was gleaming and the staff was busily prepping for the wedding dinner the following day, I hung up my apron and stepped out into the lobby.

CeeCee had agreed to talk to me, but we hadn't made a plan for where or when. I hadn't seen her in a while, and now I was worried maybe she'd left.

There were people milling about in the lobby, and I searched everywhere for that familiar strawberry blond head, listening for the laughter that made everything feel lighter, better. Finally, I found her coming around the back of the patio out back.

"There you are," she said.

She was looking for me too? I imagined us running laps, looking for each other but neither of us catching up to the other. "Here I am. Should we find somewhere to sit down?"

"I want to, Travis," she said, her eyes shining and wide. The tone of her voice told me this wasn't going to be a good time, however. "But I've got to get home."

"Oh." I managed not to sound like my heart was breaking all over again. "Okay."

"Jensen's car is acting up again and he's got a couple late night rides to do. I told him he could have my car."

"Right," I said, "Okay."

"We can talk tomorrow?"

I nodded as disappointment made my limbs heavy.

I watched her head back inside, and then went that way myself, going upstairs and knocking on the suite door where my family had agreed to hang out while the wedding festivities were going on.

"You're visiting us in our banishment?" My brother asked, opening the door. "How generous!"

There were plates scattered over the table and a couple bottles of Half Cat on the sideboard. Ghost had felt awful about asking them to stay out of sight during the rehearsal dinner.

"I see you had some food up here," I said, looking around.

Mom and Dad were side by side on the couch, and Daphne was curled up in an armchair. They all had a glass in hand, and seemed in good spirits.

"Your friend Archie brought it up himself on a cart," Mom said. "Apologized profusely for hiding us away and gave us the same dinner the bride and groom were having downstairs, I guess. Very kind of him."

"It was," I agreed, moving to pour myself a whiskey as Tony motioned to an empty glass.

"What have you been up to?" Daphne asked. "Did you have to work for the bridezilla and company?" By now most of the staff and evidently my whole family had picked up on the fact that our bride was somewhat hard to please.

"I did," I said, settling into an empty chair. "But I got to stay in the kitchen, so I was out of harm's way."

"That's good," Dad said.

We chatted and laughed, and I did my best to just enjoy some time with my family. Dad talked about the ranch and my brothers Evan and Cory and their families. They saw each other all the time—I was the only one who'd never migrated back to Texas—and I was a little homesick by the time I went back to my own room that night.

I'd seen pictures of my nieces and nephews, and had a front row seat to the romance blooming between Tony and Daphne. I was happy for them all.

And that much more determined to talk to CeeCee, to win her back.

Chapter Twenty-Seven
Escape from Kasper Ridge

CEECEE

I knew I couldn't avoid talking to Travis forever, though I hadn't been too upset about Jensen's emergency since it gave me more time. The delay didn't change things, though. I'd told him I was looking to leave Kasper Ridge, and now it was happening.

I'd accepted a position on a ranch up in Wyoming, river guiding and organizing adventures at a place that operated just over the Colorado border near the park. I'd considered some of the ritzier locations in Colorado, but my close-up experience with the bridezilla of Kasper Ridge cemented my suspicions that I didn't want to spend my days around overprivileged rich people. Maybe that's what we'd get at the ranch, but at least those people knew they were coming for a week to work and rough it. It was more my speed. This position paid well, and while it might not be quite the same as an all-expenses-paid trip to Africa, if I worked there a year, I'd be able to finance a little smaller trip myself.

As I went to bed that night, I did my best not to think about the light I'd seen in Travis's eyes, or the desire that his plea had sparked low inside me. I did want to talk to him. I wanted so much more than that.

And it wasn't that I was holding a grudge about his dishonesty. It was more that I was holding on to the reminder that relationships were complicated and messy—for me they had been, at least. And the life I really wanted was simple. I wanted to explore and experience, and if I did it alone, that was actually okay with me.

It was only in these late dark moments when I had flashes of what it had been like to lay in Travis's arms, or know that he was right behind me as we headed up a trail, that I let myself imagine what it would be like to have a real partner.

I could give it another chance if I was staying, but the timing just hadn't been right for us. It was another relationship disappointment I'd get used to living with.

The next day, I arrived at the resort at noon to help set up all the last minute details for the wedding itself. Initially, the bride from hell was nowhere to be seen, and I imagined that a woman like that would take at least seventeen hours to prepare for something as important as her own wedding. But to my dismay, I heard her screechy voice out in the lobby just a couple hours before the ceremony was supposed to begin.

"This won't work!" she was practically screaming.

I stepped out of the lounge set to one side of the lobby to see her standing with Archie and Aubrey in front of the table where the gorgeous four-tier cake stood, covered with perfect frosting flowers and surrounded by real flowers. The entire arrangement looked like something out of *Town & Country Magazine*.

"It looks almost exactly like the photograph you sent," Aubrey said as I stepped closer. I knew the time and effort Travis had put into that cake, and I felt an unexpected wave of protectiveness surge through me.

"It looks like some kind of amateur bake-off failure," the bride moaned. "And I tasted the sample the baker sent to our room. It's dry and claggy."

"Claggy?" Archie repeated, sounding confused.

"Yes!" The woman cried, waving an arm at the cake again. "Claggy and horrible. It tasted horrible." She emphasized this last word as she pointed a finger into Archie's face.

"I'm sorry," Archie said, stepping back. "I just don't think there's much that can be done about it at this point." I hated hearing him apologize to this ridiculous shrew.

"That's enough!" The words were out before I realized I had decided to speak them. I marched across the lobby, ignoring the shocked looks on the faces of my friends and the bride.

I stepped close to her. "I have listened to you complain about literally everything since the moment you arrived here. The hike, the water, the resort, the cake . . ." I shook my head and took a breath. "There is absolutely nothing wrong with this cake. Any bride would be lucky to have a cake that someone put as much effort and care into as this one, and it looks fucking incredible," I told her, my voice going low and menacing. "This cake is exactly what you said you wanted, and if you've changed your spoiled little mind now, it's too damned late!"

The bride's jaw dropped open, along with Aubrey's, but I couldn't stop.

"Everyone here is bending over backwards to make you happy," I told her. "Including your poor groom. And if you can't manage to be even the tiniest bit grateful for all the work they're putting in, the least you could do is be quiet!"

The bride looked stunned, and she recoiled as if I'd slapped her.

I was a little out of breath after my rant, and as I came back to rationality, it occurred to me that screaming at the most important guest Archie and Aubrey had was probably not the right move. But the cake was something Travis had worked hard on, and worried about, and it really was absolutely phenomenal.

"You'll be hearing about this," the bride whispered to Archie and Aubrey, but the steam seemed to have left her. She walked toward the elevators and disappeared.

I'd let things get out of hand, and regret and shame were rising inside me. Had I ruined everything? Just was I was about to apologize to the resort owners, a big hand landed on my shoulder and I turned to see Travis towering over me, grinning. "That was awesome," he said.

"I mean," Archie added, rubbing a hand through his dark red hair. "It was probably not the right move . . ."

"She deserved it," Aubrey told him. "Someone needed to put her in her place."

"Just maybe, like . . . after the wedding," Archie said.

I shook my head and dropped my gaze to the floor, feeling miserable and confused at the crazed feelings shooting around inside me. "I'm sorry, you guys, I just . . ." I looked up at Travis, who was still smiling at me, and I had the urge to throw myself into his arms. "I didn't like what she said about your cake."

Aubrey and Archie headed away, probably to apologize to the bride and see what they could do to offset the fact she'd just been yelled at by a perfect stranger in the lobby.

"I'm sorry," I muttered again, even though they were gone.

"Hey," Travis said, touching my chin with one warm finger and tilting my head back up to meet his gaze. "Thank you."

I stared into his warm eyes, the confusing hurricane of feelings intensifying inside me. I wanted to stay there, staring into his eyes, forever, if possible. But it was definitely not possible. "You're welcome," I managed.

"I don't think anyone's ever defended me like that before," he said, dropping his hand and then wrapping it around the back of his neck, shaking his head gently.

"That's because you're like eight feet tall and huge, and you don't really look like you need defending," I told him, finally managing to recover a bit.

"That's just the packaging," he said. We were walking side by side toward the lounge, where rocking chairs and couches sprawled in front of an enormous fireplace on one side of the room and a wall of windows made up the other. Without any explicit agreement to do so, we sat in the far corner of the room, facing one another.

"I'm sorry we didn't talk last night," I told him.

"It's okay," he said, and he took one of my hands in his, the warmth of his big fingers enveloping mine. "We're here now."

"Travis," I said, a rush of emotion racing through me as I looked into his face. I wanted to stay here forever, with Travis holding my hand and making me feel like I had a partner in this world. But plans had already been made that would make that impossible. "I got a job."

"You have a job," he said. "I don't think you have time for another one."

I shook my head, knowing he was kidding. "In Wyoming."

"Rough commute," he quipped. His voice was light, but there was a depth of sorrow in his eyes that told me he wished things were different too.

"It just . . ." I started, trailing off. "I think I've had enough of people like her." I nodded toward the cake.

"I think we all have," he agreed.

"I love guiding," I said. "And now that the contest is over . . ."

"Did you hear anything? Is it really over? Who won?" He tilted his head to one side.

"I don't think they've decided yet. The news isn't supposed to come out for another week, but after everything they saw here . . ." I pushed aside the disappointment I felt at that missed opportunity.

Travis smiled, knowing what I was referring to. It wasn't a happy smile.

"I am sorry about all that."

"Ned told me they actually really liked the drama back at the network."

He shrugged, "good?"

"But I think they'll choose a couple that's staying together for the grand prize."

He nodded. "Makes sense." His thumb rubbed over the tops of my fingers, sending chills through me. I wanted to kiss him, and found myself staring at the full lips I still dreamed about. But that would only make everything harder.

"Thank you for all the help," I said. "And for being willing to pretend."

"It never felt like pretending."

We stared at each other for a long moment, my hand in his, and it felt like goodbye. My heart cracked inside me and I experienced a pulse of sadness I'd never known.

"Sass!" A voice came from the doorway, and Travis dropped my hand, turning to look at Antonio standing in the entrance. "Sorry to interrupt. Can you help with this flower arch thing? Sucker's heavy."

"Be right there." Travis turned back to me, his eyes mirroring the sorrow inside me. "I hope you find everything you want, CeeCee."

I dropped his gaze, worried he would see how close I was to tears. "You too," I whispered. We stood and he pulled me into his arms, and the tears broke free. I sniffled and turned my head, probably leaving a little wet spot on his shirt. And then he let go and headed out the door to help Antonio with the arch. And even though I didn't ever hope to retrieve it, I knew he took part of my heart with him.

Chapter Twenty-Eight
Single. But Not for Long.

TRAVIS

I helped Antonio with the enormous arch, flowers falling off all around us as we tried to move the thing. I hated walking away from CeeCee, but I also knew that as much as that moment seemed final, I wasn't going to go down without a fight.

"This is ridiculous," Antonio said, a lily draped over the top of his head as he hauled one side of the floral arch across the lobby.

"This is an important lesson to us both," I told him.

"Don't bother with enormous flower arrangements when we get married?"

"No, brother. Build the flower arch in the spot where you intend to use it," I said, struggling to move the thing without crushing the roses that covered the leg I was moving. "And maybe also, don't build the internal structure out of concrete."

"Seriously," he huffed as we made it to the patio. "I guess they wanted to be sure this wouldn't tip over in a breeze."

"I guess," I said, finally getting the thing in place.

We took a few steps back and stared at it.

"Shit," Antonio breathed, and just as we both stepped close to try to rearrange the flowers that had gotten crushed or were missing, the voice I was coming to dread sounded behind us. Way, way above us.

"Do you morons know what those flowers cost?" The voice shrieked from a window somewhere overhead.

Antonio and I exchanged a look, and decided that fleeing would be the best option. I dropped the lone rose I held and headed back inside.

"She'll never get down here in time to yell at us properly if we hide," I told him.

"Good plan." We headed in different directions, and I tucked myself into a far corner in the bar, sitting down at a table that was blocked from sight from the doorway by the structure of the bar itself.

"Ready for all this?" Wiley asked, gesturing to the lobby, decked out for the wedding.

"I am, but I'm less sure about the bride and groom."

"How are things in the marital realm for you?" he asked.

"Single again," I told him. "But I've got a plan for that." A giddy excitement bubbled in my chest.

A slow smile lifted one side of his mouth. "That right?"

I picked up my phone. There were a few calls I needed to make.

Chapter Twenty-Nine
Ned from the Network

CEECEE

I went to Lucy and Will's house to get dressed for the wedding. It was closer than my house, and Lucy had suggested it when the resort staff had been informed that they'd be expected to help the hired wedding staff. I'd volunteered to help out, though at this point all I really wanted was to go home, close myself in my room, and sleep until it was time to pack up for Wyoming.

"You look miserable," Lucy told me when I emerged from her guest room in the black pants and white top we'd been told to wear. I knew my face was puffy from crying and my skin was sallow from lack of sleep.

Lucy, on the other hand, looked gorgeous, her own black pants and white blouse hugging her curvy figure. She held Teague in her arms, and the baby stared up at his beautiful mother with wide dark eyes, cooing and reaching a chubby fist up to grasp her long dark hair.

"That's not a nice thing to say," I told her, stepping close to look at the baby. "He's so cute," I said. Babies had never been my thing. I didn't plan on them any more than I'd ever figured I'd be the marrying kind, but looking at Teague was doing strange things to my heart.

"Where's my great-grandson?" Lucy's grandfather emerged from a back doorway and he came in reaching for the baby. "Don't you all have to go help bridezilla or something?"

"We were just finishing up getting ready," Lucy told him.

I greeted the man I'd known most of my life with a hug, just as my phone began to vibrate in my pocket. "Excuse me," I said, pulling it out and moving toward a window looking out over the front yard.

The screen said the call was from Ned, and I answered it reluctantly, figuring this would be the official news that I hadn't won the competition. No point delaying the inevitable.

"Hello?"

"CeeCee, hi. It's Ned from the network."

"Hi Ned." I tried to coax some cheer into my voice, but that was something I was having trouble finding lately.

"Listen, the crew and I are back in Colorado, up in your neck of the woods, and I realized we didn't get enough exterior shots of the resort."

I had put this fiasco behind me and wasn't eager to open the door again. Plus, I'd watched them filming a ridiculous amount of landscape and building shots, but what did I know? "Oh, okay."

"So we're heading over there now. Would you be able to meet us there?"

"Oh, Ned. There's a wedding there today, I'm not sure it's a good time . . ."

"We'll stay totally out of the way," he promised. "Meet us just outside?"

"Uh, okay," I agreed, imagining Jess the murder-bride's reaction to this unplanned portion of her "special" day.

At the resort, Lucy headed inside, and I waited a moment, then watched as Ned and his team appeared around the corner of the building from the parking lot.

"Guys, this bride is seriously grumpy," I told them. "I'm not sure this is a good idea."

"Hey Ned," Travis's voice came from behind me, stirring up excitement and heartbreak all over again inside my chest. "Right this way."

I turned in confusion, and watched as the crew followed Travis into the lobby.

"Come on, CeeCee," Ned called cheerfully.

It was like there was some plan everyone else was in on, and I was just along for the ride. Had Travis been expecting Ned?

Confusion filled me as I followed them through the lobby-slash-ballroom and out to the back patio opposite the side where the wedding was setting up to begin.

"I thought maybe right here?" Travis said, pointing to the far edge of the space, where one chair sat alone, its back to the green drape of trees beyond the patio.

"That works," Ned said, looking around with an evaluative eye. "Light's perfect too."

Paul and Simone moved to the sides, their cameras trained on the chair, and Travis walked toward me as my heart began to beat faster. What was going on?

"Ceese, could you just sit there?" He took my hand and guided me to the chair.

"What's going on?" I asked him.

Travis turned to Ned. "Ready?"

"Whenever you are."

Travis nodded at me and then took a deep breath as I looked up at him from the chair he'd put me in. Then he dropped to a knee and took my hand, meeting my confusion with dark eyes full of so much certainty that words slipped from my mind entirely.

"CeeCee, there are some things I need to say. And I asked Ned and the crew here to make sure they got them, since the story they captured on film when they were here before wasn't the whole story."

"I-I . . ." I had no actual words, so I snapped my mouth shut again. There were so many potential questions floating around in my mind I didn't know which one I'd ask anyway. My stomach flipped and my heart raced.

"I was married when we met. That much is true."

I nodded.

"But I married Daphne in a kind of misguided attempt to look out for her, since we grew up together." He didn't explain it all again, but Ned and the crew were nodding as if they already knew the story. How long had Travis been planning this . . . this . . . whatever this was?

"I did it because I figured at the time that I'd never find anyone I really wanted to marry. I wasn't sure I'd live that long, first of all. And secondly, failure was kind of my trademark move. So I thought if I went ahead and married Daphne, expecting nothing from the arrangement, then I couldn't fail at it.

"Except I still managed to fail."

"Travis," I whispered, wanting to understand what was happening here, but the look on his face quieted me again, and he took my other hand in his.

There was a sudden commotion behind us, and I looked past Travis and the crew to see a small group of older women gather on the back patio, looking concerned and talking in low voices. I did my best to ignore them, but they were buzzing like a hive of disturbed bees.

Next, the groom appeared, his face a mask of anger. He strode to the edge of the back patio and cupped his hands around his mouth, turning to look up at the back of the resort. "Jess!" He screamed at the building. "Jessica!"

There was no answer from above. There was clearly something very wrong with the wedding, but I was desperate to hear whatever else Travis wanted to tell me.

"I failed at the fake marriage," Travis said, a wry smile taking his lips and turning the corners upward as his eyes met mine again. "Because the only way that could succeed was if I had never met you."

He paused, his warm hands enveloping mine fully as his eyes shone.

"Because when I met you, I realized that marriage without love wasn't marriage at all. It was just a piece of paper—a transaction. By marrying Daphne, I'd cheated the meaning of marriage, if that makes sense. But the bigger problem was that it meant I wasn't free.

"And when I realized how completely and totally I had fallen in love with you . . . that became a real issue."

Travis let those words float between us, and just as I was about to speak, the rail-thin dark haired bridesmaid I recognized from the hike came bolting out the back door. She turned to the group of women, which I now realized included the bride and groom's parents, whom I'd seen the day before.

"The wedding's off!" she cried. Shock hit me first, but then I realized I wasn't surprised. I also wanted them all to be quiet so I could focus on Travis.

"What?" one of the women trilled. "No, of course it's not." She turned to the windows above her and cried out, "Jessy, honey!"

"Everyone can go home!" A voice came from high above us. The groom had sunk into an Adirondack chair near the

enormous flower arch and was drinking a beer, looking unconcerned as guests were arriving and being seated in the white
chairs in front of the arch.

"I'm going up there," one of the older women announced,
and she stormed back to the glass doors.

I turned back to the man kneeling in front of me, who was
still holding my hands. There was so much emotion swelling
inside me that I didn't trust my voice.

"I've never felt this way before, Ceese," he went on. "And I
know you've already got plans to go, and that you're strong and
independent and maybe you don't want to be tied down . . ."

"Harry!" A voice came from above us now, and one of the
older men who'd joined the little group next to the doors looked
up. "Harry! Come up here. She's refusing to come down!"

"Oh for chrissakes!" A grey-haired man exclaimed, turning
on his shiny heel to head inside.

The rest of the little group moved to where the groom was
sitting and pulled him from the chair to move closer to where we
were.

"She just said she changed her mind," the groom said, shrug-
ging. "Something about all the signs and omens, and how she
should have known better because I have a hairy back or something." The groom did not sound especially concerned that his
wedding appeared to be falling apart.

"A hairy back?" One of the older women repeated. "You can
just use Nair or whatever, you know. We should have handled
that."

"Mom," the groom said, sounding tired. "She doesn't want
to marry me because of some hair."

"You just said that."

"So doesn't that tell you anything? Like maybe we never
should have thought about getting married in the first place?

Like maybe this isn't a woman who loves me for me? From the moment we met, she got busy trying to change me. She hates my T-shirts, she doesn't like my cologne. I don't know how we got here in the first place, if you want the truth."

I was eavesdropping, but there was such an overwhelming press of emotion surging through me, the groom's acceptance of his situation was just one more thing adding to the tide welling up within me. She didn't deserve him anyway. I hoped he would find someone who loved him for him, who didn't care about his back hair, or who knew how to apply Nair. Someone who would adore him the way I adored Travis.

Clarity smoothed out all the confusion inside me.

I turned back to the man in front of me, who was staring up into my face with a hopeful expression on his.

"Repeat the last part," I suggested.

He cleared his throat and dropped my gaze. "I know you have things planned. That you're thinking of moving, and maybe you don't want to be tied down . . ."

"I do!" I said, gripping Travis's hands tightly. In that moment, when he'd been talking about how I probably didn't want the commitment, how I probably didn't want to be tied down, a series of images flickered through my mind. Lucy's baby. The flower arch. The beautiful cake. And in all those mental pictures, one thing was always the same. Travis was there.

"I do want to be tied down. I want all of that. But only if it's with you."

"You do?" Travis's eyes widened as if this was not the answer he he'd expected at all.

"I mean," I said, uncertain now. "Yeah, if that's what you want." I swallowed hard. I'd never uttered these words to any man, but I felt them with my entire body. "I love you, Travis."

"Excuse me," one of the guests had wandered over to where the groomsmen and families were still talking nearby. "Is the wedding off, then? Should we, uh . . . should we go?"

"Hold on a minute, sir," Travis called to the man, and then he met my eyes, excitement and love and some kind of question there.

"Wait," I said. Was he suggesting we should get married? Here? Today? "I mean . . ."

Travis squeezed my hands and met my eyes. "CeeCee, we've been engaged once before. Would you be interested in making it real?"

"Are you . . .?" The crowd, including the groom, was drawing closer, listening for my answer.

Travis nodded, hope gleaming in his eyes. "CeeCee, will you marry me? For real?"

"Yes," I whispered, my body buzzing with happiness.

Travis scooped me up, leaping to his feet with me in his arms as the little crowd clapped. I looked up into his handsome face and felt every missing piece click right into place. I tipped my chin up and Travis's lips met mine.

"I love you," he said, breaking the kiss but keeping his forehead pressed to mine as he held me.

"I love you too," I said. Happiness surged through me, drowning out every other thought for a few blessed moments. But then I realized what he might be suggesting. "Wait, do you mean right now? Here?"

He grinned and shook his head. "If that's what you want, yeah."

The groom, standing at our side, shrugged as if to give his permission.

"It won't be real until the divorce is legal," Travis said quietly.

I shook my head. I didn't care about the details, but if I was

going to marry Travis, I wanted to do it right. Enjoy the anticipation. Have a bachelorette party and a shower. "Let's wait," I
said quietly.

Travis kissed me again, and the little crowd began to dissi-
pate, leaving us finally alone, only the camera crew still paying
attention to us. Travis set me down gently.

"Do you think you'll still take the job? Move away?" he
asked.

"I'd rather be with you," I told him, the logistics coming
back into focus now that the shock of Travis's gesture were
settling in.

"You can do both. I'll come with you," he said.

I thought about it, but Kasper Ridge was home, and maybe
I'd already found what I'd been looking for out in the world. I
still wanted to travel, but the drive to escape was gone, replaced
by the warm security of the man at my side. "We'll figure it out,"
I assured him.

There were people milling around looking confused, and
the groom came back out the doors a moment later, approaching
us.

"Reception's already paid for," he said. "Everyone might as
well have dinner and cake." He grinned at us. "Congratulations,
by the way. Mind if I, uh, stick around?"

"Of course," Travis said. "And thank you."

"I'm sorry," I offered, but he shook off my condolences.

"Dodged a bullet," he said. "I knew it wasn't right. And now,
after seeing you guys together? I know it for sure. I'm not going
to settle for anything less than this."

"No wedding folks," Travis called to the wandering crowd.
There was a disappointed murmur. "But if you want to come
inside, we're still going to have an awesome party with one hell
of a kick-ass cake!"

The mood of the gathered guests lifted, and people began

filtering inside as Travis took my hand and shot me a smile that made my heart leap around in joy.

Chapter Thirty
Stealing a Wedding

TRAVIS

That night, we danced and drank with a bunch of strangers, my family, and our best friends in the world. CeeCee's mom and brother joined us for the reception, and her friend Bennie made it over too.

When it came time to cut the cake, I was a little nervous—after all, bridezilla had evidently deemed it horrible and unfit. But once we sliced it and we each had a piece, I knew it was as perfect as the rest of the day had been. CeeCee tasted hers and then smiled that beautiful smile of hers and kissed me, and I tasted lingering chocolate and hazelnut. Everything was delicious.

Ned and the crew left soon after dinner, letting us know it would be a few more days at least before the contest winners were chosen. Though it was a real contest, Ned explained, the show's production would occur during the decision process, and some of the footage would determine the final winner. I hoped we'd given them what they needed to make CeeCee's dreams come true. And if she got the trip of a lifetime, I hoped maybe I'd get to go too.

Toward the end of the night, many of the guests—who we'd gotten to know as the evening wore on—bid us farewell and headed off to their rooms.

"Think we can sneak away soon?" I asked CeeCee as her head rested against my chest and we swayed together under the lights twinkling above the dance floor.

She smiled up at me, a dreamy look on her face. "Let's try."

I slipped her hand into mine, and together we turned and headed for the elevators. I couldn't wait to have her alone again, to have time to reacquaint myself with every perfect curve and freckle on her body.

But the elevator doors slid open to reveal someone waiting inside. Jessica.

"Did you enjoy my wedding?" she asked, sounding only half as angry as she had during all the other encounters I'd had with her.

"It was beautiful," CeeCee said sincerely. "Thank you."

Jess sniffed and looked between us. "You look pretty happy."

"We are," I told her.

Jess's face crumpled for a second, but then she pulled herself tall again. "You going to steal my honeymoon too?"

We stepped into the elevator and she didn't get out, letting the doors close again, trapping the three of us together.

"No," CeeCee said. "Where's it to?"

Jess stared at her for a moment and then dropped her head miserably. "We were going to go to Belize. Luxury on the beach. Cabana boys, et cetera."

"That sounds awesome," I said.

"It would have been," Jess confirmed.

"You should go," CeeCee told her.

Jess lifted her chin to look at CeeCee in confusion. "By myself?"

"Totally," CeeCee said. "Traveling by yourself is really amazing. I mean, I've never been on a trip like that . . ." she trailed off.

"I was supposed to be married. I was supposed to be happy. I had everything planned." For the first time, Jessica sounded like a human being, someone who was disappointed, and had maybe been hurt.

"I know," CeeCee said. "But you figured it out in time. He wasn't the one, was he?"

"No."

"If it was me?" CeeCee said, speaking carefully, like she didn't want to assume too much or invite Jess's angry side back out to play. "I'd go. I'd take the time to enjoy and really get to know myself again. Figure out what I really want."

"Looks to me like you got what you want." She looked between us. "I don't think Brian ever looked at me the way he's looking at you. I hope our rooms don't share a wall."

I chuckled and pulled CeeCee tighter into my side. "He's out there, Jess. Maybe he's in Belize."

She sighed as the doors opened, and we stepped out.

"Good luck," CeeCee told her.

"Congratulations, you two," Jess said, and for once, she sounded sincere.

The doors slid shut again, and I leaned down and swept my almost bride up into my arms. "Let's go," I told her. "I can't wait any more."

CeeCee giggled as I pushed the door open, and Roscoe lifted his head from his bed in the corner to watch us enter and head directly for the bedroom, dropping it again.

I set my fiancée on the bed gingerly and then stepped back

to look at her, hardly able to believe that this was real, that she was mine.

"You're so beautiful," I said, dropping to my knees in front of her.

She smiled at me, practically glowing. "So are you," she said.

I laughed. No one had ever called me beautiful. I was called Sasquatch for a reason, and beauty was not it.

I reached for her then, carefully unbuttoning the delicate buttons that dotted the front of her shirt, and feeling my body coil in anticipation with every additional inch of milky flesh that was exposed.

When the shirt fell from her shoulders, exposing a light pink lacy bra, I inhaled sharply. "So. Beautiful."

CeeCee's hands moved to cup my face, and she leaned forward to kiss me, pulling me closer. I moved up onto the bed, scooting her backward so I could cover her with my body. Our mouths explored as her hands pulled my shirt from my pants, pushing up my back as her smooth hands skated the planes of my back.

I pulled the shirt off and knelt above CeeCee, looking down at her between my legs and feeling a surge of something like pride mixed with joy. She chose me. She was mine.

I leaned down, letting my mouth explore the perfection of her collarbone, moving myself lower and lower as she gasped lightly above me, her hands in my hair. I nipped and licked across the top of each breast, my hand finally moving to palm first one, then the other, as I kissed lower, finally arriving at the button on her black pants.

She reached for me as I unfastened it, and together we pushed them off. I removed mine then too, wanting as little between us as possible.

CeeCee lay there, her chest heaving, in light pink underwear that must have been made just to drive men completely insane. It wasn't too sexy, wasn't too chaste. As much as I admired the garments, I wanted them off immediately. But I also didn't want to rush things.

I rolled my weight to one side of her, leaving my hand and mouth free to worship her body, and I began again with the fascinating pink bra. I slid one strap down her shoulder, then the second, releasing the cups so that I could hold her breast in my palm as my tongue and teeth teased her other nipple. CeeCee wiggled beneath me, unclasping the bra and throwing it to the side.

I nipped and sucked, loving the sounds that she made, and soon, she was reaching for me, palming my length through the boxer briefs I wore and driving me close to desperation.

"Take these off," she murmured, pushing the elastic at my waist down. I wasted no time complying as she slipped out of her own underwear.

She reached for me again, taking me firmly in her hand, and reaching the other to cup my balls, sending a jolt of ecstasy through me.

"Shit, CeeCee," I managed. I moved my body away from her, not wanting to embarrass myself by coming too fast before the main event.

As much as I wanted to drive into her right that second, I forced myself to go slowly, take my time. I kissed her again, deep and slow, letting my hand tease the heat I found at the apex of her legs. She was wet, and the discover had me hardening even further, though I would have said that was impossible if asked.

"Oh," she moaned as I teased the little nub beneath my fingers, rubbing it and then teasing her slick entrance. "Oh god," she breathed as I slid two fingers inside her, letting my thumb continue to rub that bundle of nerves.

She kissed me harder then, pressing herself into my hand, seeking more contact, more stimulation. Her hips were arching and I kept at it, working my thumb and my fingers as CeeCee writhed and devoured my mouth, her hands pulling desperately at my back.

"I'm... oh!" She cried out as she came, and I felt her pulse around my fingers, keeping my hand right where it was as she rode out the waves of her orgasm. "Oh," she breathed, regaining her breath and fluttering her eyes open to look up at me. "Oh," she said again.

"You're at a loss for words," I said, feeling proud of myself.

"My turn," she told me, looking around. "Condom?"

We separated for a brief moment so I could go into the bathroom to get a condom. I returned with it in my hand, bowled over by the beautiful flush covering CeeCee's face and chest when I returned. I'd done that, I thought proudly. I'd put that happy look on her face.

"Travis?" She asked as I moved next to her on the bed again, pulling down the covers this time.

"Yes, fiancée?"

She giggled. "Do we need the condom? I'm on the pill."

I looked at her seriously. I wanted nothing more than to throw the condom to the side and feel every glorious centimeter of her with nothing between us, but I'd never done that before. "I don't know," I said honestly. "If you're asking if I've been with anyone recently, the answer's no. Except you, there's been no one for years."

"Years?" She echoed.

I shrugged.

"Come here," she said, pulling me close and then throwing a leg over my hip, opening herself to me.

As I kissed her, a kind of glorious certainty flowed through me, something I'd never felt before. This—this relationship, this marriage, this whatever it was—it was right. It was meant to be. I knew it as surely as I'd known that flying wasn't for me, that I needed to find something else.

And as she reached for me, guiding my cock to her entrance... As I slid into her, every hot, wet inch welcoming me and holding me tight, I experienced a kind of blissful transcendence I'd never thought was possible.

"God, I love you, CeeCee," I whispered.

"I love you too," she answered.

And then, for the first time in my life, I made love. I worshipped and adored the one person I ever wanted to be with. I did my best to explain through actions that she was all I'd ever need, all I'd ever hoped for or dreamed of. And when we climaxed together, gripping each other tightly, it was if all the burdens I carried unleashed just a little and became lighter.

That night I slept soundly, the woman I loved at my side. That night I didn't dream, except of calm waters and the smile of my favorite person in the world. And Roscoe.

Epilogue 1

CEECEE

"Are you sad about all the dudes you're missing out on up at that dude ranch?" Travis asked me this as I lay in his arms, still regaining my breath, the sun filtering in around the edges of the window shade.

"It was an adventure outfitter, not a dude ranch."

"I like thinking of you in chaps and a cowboy hat though," Travis smiled lazily at me.

There was something lighter about him lately—since we'd worked everything out. He'd always leaned a little toward silly, but now humor was infused in everything he did. The only time I ever saw glimpses of the once prevalent darkness Travis carried inside him was at night when he had the dreams.

"Hey," I said, rolling to face him. "You had that dream again last night, huh?"

His arm tightened around me, pulling me closer. "Yeah."

"Do you want to tell me about it?" All he'd shared was that

it was dark, menacing, shadows of things that had actually happened when he'd served in Afghanistan. It worried me that he still carried so much stress from his time overseas.

His eyes dropped shut and he pressed his forehead to mine, not answering.

"You could talk to someone about it," I suggested, not sure how much to press.

"I'll talk to you," he said, popping one eye open and pulling back to look at me. "It's gotten better," he said. "Since I met you. The dream used to be so vivid it was like I was there again, back in the middle of everything. And there was always this woman," he paused, his voice barely above a whisper, "this woman, handing me this baby."

"A baby?"

"Yeah, but it was also not a baby, if that makes any sense. It was like she was handing me everyone I couldn't save, everyone I could see around me who I knew I just couldn't help."

"That's awful."

"It was." He was quiet a while, and we lay together, our breathing synchronized as the sky brightened in a line above the curtain. "Did I tell you how I met Antonio?"

I'd picked up on a bit, but this was the first time Travis was really talking about any of it. "No."

"His brother was a Marine. We were friends. I saw him die." His voice cracked.

"Oh god."

"He loved his brother, talked about him all the time, about how he was a famous soccer player out in San Diego for some team called the Sharks. So when I got back, I found him. I think I felt like I needed to apologize or something, like if I could get my buddy's brother to forgive me for not saving him, it would be like getting some kind of absolution for it all."

I stayed silent, my hand caressing his back, wishing I could take all the pain from him somehow.

"Antonio kind of gave me that, in a way. We became good friends."

"He's a good guy," I said.

"The best." He pressed his forehead to mine again. "I sleep better now," he added.

"Since you met Antonio?"

He chuckled, and the sound broke some of the tension that had grown around us. "No. Since I met you."

"That makes me happy."

"I used to get up in the middle of the night and roam around the resort. It's why the baking wasn't an issue. I was awake anyway. But now...I've got more reasons to stay in bed, I guess."

"Plus, Ghost hired that baker." A part-time baker handled four days out of the week now, letting Travis stay in bed with me a little longer.

"That too."

I kissed him then, slow and languorous, doing my best to communicate all the happiness I felt, all the love that swelled inside me whenever I looked at him, thought about him. "I love you, Travis," I murmured, looking into the warm brown eyes.

"I love you more," he answered.

* * *

Later that day we headed to the shop to take over for Cole, who opened on Sunday mornings if we didn't have anything scheduled. As the heat of summer began to fade into cooler days of fall, it was normal for things to slow down a bit. People didn't vacation as much as the holidays approached, and the idea of rafting or hiking when there was a real possibility of snow was far less appealing.

I didn't mind. The slower days gave me a chance to organize the shop, bring in new products and prepare for snow season.

Travis had started coming in regularly, helping out for real, and we'd even discussed forming a partnership.

"Babe," he said, coming out of the office with my phone and handing it to me where I stood frowning into a box full of bindings for snowboards that I didn't remember ordering.

"Yeah?" I looked up to see him holding my phone out to me. I must've left it on the desk.

"Answer it." He had a weird lilt to his voice. "It's Ned."

The screen confirmed what Travis said, and my heart picked up a bit. This time I was sure it was the official call letting me know I'd lost, but I'd still been anticipating the call.

The contest results had not been announced on schedule, and we'd been waiting several weeks to hear the decision. They were holding the show until the spring season, so nothing had been given away yet, though their ad campaigns and social media promos had been going strong.

"Hello?"

"Hey CeeCee. How've you been?"

"Good. How are you?"

"Great," he said. "Listen, I've got the final news for you. Are you ready for it?"

"I've been expecting it," I told him, a little frustrated that the tone of his voice didn't offer a clue as to whether the news was good or bad.

"Yeah, it took a while longer than we meant it too. Not everyone over here agreed about who ought to win."

"Oh." I wasn't sure what that meant. Travis was watching me, waiting for me to give away whatever Ned was saying. "But you've decided on a winner now?"

"They have, yeah. So I hope you and Travis have some idea

where you want to go with all that money. Still thinking Africa?"

My grip on the phone tightened, and I sucked in a gasp of surprise. "What?"

"You won, CeeCee! You and Travis. How could anyone compete after that reunion?"

"But . . . oh my god." There were so many thoughts and feelings roaring around inside me I couldn't form words.

Travis was still staring at me but now his mouth was widening into a smile. "We won?"

I nodded, barely able to process the details Ned was giving me about how the money would be delivered and when we'd need to appear in person for the live finale show.

"Holy shit!" Travis yelled, bouncing around the office in a way that had me worried he might break a chair or a bookcase. "Yes!"

Roscoe padded in and stood in the doorway, watching him with a look of concern.

"Still thinking Africa?" Ned asked.

"I don't know," I told him. "That was my plan before, but now . . . since it's our trip, I guess Travis will have to get a say."

"Legoland!" Travis suggested in a shout.

"No."

He frowned at me as Ned laughed on the other end.

"Congratulations, CeeCee. You deserve it. We'll be in touch, okay?"

"Thanks so much," I told him, hanging up and pushing the phone into my pocket with shaking hands. "We won," I said, mostly to hear the words one more time and let them sink in.

"Hell yeah, we did! We're going to Disneyland!" Travis cried.

"It's supposed to be an adventure," I told him, stepping close and wrapping my arms around his waist. "We need to at least leave the country."

He grinned down at me, his big arms pulling me in tight. "CeeCee, I'll go anywhere you want. As long as we're together." Roscoe stepped close and pushed his big head between us. "And maybe somewhere dog friendly?"

I laughed. I wasn't sure Roscoe would be invited, but we had time to figure it out. For now, I let the happiness I felt bloom inside me until there wasn't room for even the tiniest sliver or doubt or worry. I had everything I'd ever wanted, and I hadn't even had to leave Kasper Ridge to find it.

Epilogue 2

TRAVIS

"They're subpar," I told Ghost, pulling apart a cinnamon roll baked by his new part-time baker.

"They're good," Aubrey said from her end of the table. "They just have raisins and yours don't."

"No one likes raisins," I pouted.

"I like raisins," CeeCee said at my side. My opinion of raisins raised slightly. If CeeCee was behind something, I'd give it a chance.

"They call them sultanas in a lot of the world," Brainiac piped up even though absolutely no one cared.

"Can we focus?" Ghost asked, sounding exasperated.

We were having a staff meeting up in his room, everyone around the long dining room table we used as a conference table. It had been a while since we'd all been together, and it felt a little like the first time I'd gotten to see the place, when Kasper Ridge had been a little run down, and the future was pretty uncertain—not just for the resort, but for me too. Except now, CeeCee was at my side. Her shop—our shop—Kasper Guides and Gear had been brought on as the official outfitter for the resort. So now we really did run the place together.

"Swiper called me last night," Ghost went on. "And we definitely have a case. "Every one of those scripts we found was produced by Mountaintop Studios, and not a single one of the movies lists Uncle Marvin anywhere. I've plowed through Uncle Marvin's financial records, and don't see any deposits from the years around each production that might have been payment for writing."

I felt a little glow of pride that my discovery had turned into something real.

"Is it really worth pursuing?" Monroe asked, her hands folded in front of her on the table. "How much would you possibly get?"

"It could be a lot," Ghost told her. "The question is more complicated than that, though. Rudy Fusterburg is gone. Uncle Marvin is gone. Though some cash would be nice, the resort isn't running totally in the red anymore, and I'm not worried about our ability to stay open. So should we—me and Aubrey—pursue some old vendetta that Uncle Marvin had against his nemesis if it's really just going to make things tough for Rudy's family?"

"Rudy's family is living in a pretty pimp house up in the hills over Sunset," Fake Tom pointed out. "And your uncle lived in a run-down resort he couldn't afford to fix up."

"But he never seemed bitter about money," Aubrey pointed out. "Are we sure this is what he intended? For us to lawyer up and sue Rudy?"

Ghost shrugged. "Who knows what he intended? The guy left us a frickin' treasure map. I mean, you could argue that we already found the treasure . . ."

"We did find a chest with jewels in it," Fake Tom agreed.

"Booty," I said, unable to help myself.

Ghost shot me a look.

"And the list of movies," Aubrey reminded us.

Brainiac pressed his palms flat onto the table top. "You have a couple options," he said, sounding all annoying and professory. I rolled my eyes. "You can pursue this, possibly spending as much in legal fees as you'll be able to claim from Rudy's estate. Or we could consider that there may be some other intention here, something we're missing."

Penny blew out a frustrated sigh next to him. "Or," she added. "We could just let the whole thing go?"

Aubrey nodded. "Yeah. Maybe we should."

"He wanted us to figure something out," Ghost said, sounding a little bit distressed.

"Did he?" Aubrey asked him gently. "Or did he think we needed something to do, to keep our minds occupied?"

Ghost snapped his mouth shut and dropped his eyes for a moment, then inhaled and looked around the table. "If this was all Uncle Marvin's way of babysitting me," he said sadly, "and I've spent the last two years dragging you all along with me on some childish search for nothing..."

I wanted to leap across the table and give Ghost a hug. But that would have been weird. I grabbed CeeCee's hand and squeezed it instead, and she leaned her head into my shoulder. I knew she knew exactly how I felt. She was good at that.

"Dude," Fake Tom said, throwing a pen at him. "Don't do that. This has been the most fun I've ever had."

"Yeah," I added. "How many grownups get to go on a real-life treasure hunt?"

"With booty," Monroe supplied, chuckling.

"With booty!" I agreed.

"You consider yourself a grownup?" Brainiac asked me.

I wasn't going to bite. I'd just short sheet his bed or give him a quick upper decker later on. I crossed my arms and lifted my chin.

"Should we maybe talk about business stuff?" Aubrey asked, looking at the clock.

"Yes," Ghost confirmed. "Enough of dragging you all down this path with me. From now on, we focus on resort operations. No more crazy treasure talk."

I didn't like the defeat I heard in his voice.

"The next big thing on the calendar is the conference I told you guys about in November. They've booked most of the hotel." He began laying out the schedule for the conference we'd all be helping to ensure went smoothly, but my mind wasn't on work.

CeeCee and I were leaving in a week for Africa, and I was giddy with the anticipation of traveling on my own agenda instead of the Navy's.

"Sasquatch, are you even listening?" Ghost asked me suddenly, interrupting my daydreams of a safari with CeeCee at my side.

"No, not really." I shrugged.

He looked angry for a second, but then the lines around his eyes relaxed a bit, and he smiled. "Thinking about the trip?"

"Can you blame me?"

"Not even a little bit."

"Tell us the plan," Monroe suggested.

And I spent the next half hour with CeeCee and I taking turns talking, telling everyone the details of our itinerary. She sounded so bright and enthusiastic, I had to resist the urge to pick her up and kiss her.

CeeCee was the sunshine and light in my life, and now that I had her, I wasn't sure how I'd ever survived without her. The idea of spending my whole life appreciating her, making her happy and loving her was like a dream. The kind of dream I never thought I'd get to have.

"You deserve it," Monroe told me as we all cleared out of Ghost's room to get back to work.

I thanked her and smiled, happiness flooding me like sunshine. Maybe I didn't deserve it, but I'd sure as hell take it.

Also by Delancey Stewart

Want more? Get early releases, sneak peeks and freebies! Join my mailing list here or scan the QR code and get a free story!

The Kasper Ridge Series:

Only a Summer

Only a Fling

Only a Crush

Only a Secret

Only a Touch

The Singletree Series:

Happily Ever His

Happily Ever Hers

Shaking the Sleigh

Ingram Content Group UK Ltd.
Milton Keynes UK
UKHW021823170323
418736UK00015B/790